NOT WITHOUT RISK

SARAH GRIMM

CHAPTER ONE

Justin didn't recognize the uniformed officer guarding the hotel room door and identified himself. "Sergeant Harrison, Homicide." He pulled a pair of latex gloves from his back pocket, silently sympathizing with the man's poor hue and pinched expression. "Were you first on the scene?"

"Yes, sir," the man choked out. He swallowed hard.

"Don't worry, it gets easier." The officer was young and as green as his complexion, but he wouldn't remain that way for long. Not with another San Diego summer right around the corner. In the heat of summer the homicide rate always went up.

Snapping the gloves into place, Justin moved slowly into the room. He cringed inwardly as all eyes turned toward him.

Damn, he hated this. His arrival delayed by his morning appointment, the number of fellow officers in attendance was down. Those left on scene were the men he didn't see on a daily basis. The men he saw only at times such as this, when murder brought them together.

1

Although he didn't doubt the sincerity of the greetings that filled the air, he knew he was a subject of curiosity. He hadn't worked with these men in months—it was only natural that he would have to prove himself.

That didn't make him feel any less like a lab specimen under a microscope, as he withstood their examination with more than a little effort.

Unaffected by his sense of dread, the surge of anticipation as he crossed the threshold and stepped into the crime scene was strong. Adrenaline pulsed through him. The thrill of being back doing the one thing at which he excelled.

With no wish to interrupt, he stepped to the side, stood back and absorbed the activity about him. Besides the man at the door, three others occupied the room: two men from the forensics team and his partner, Allan Simmons. Allan moved about freely, which indicated they were all but finished. It would be up to Justin to play catch-up, to assess the scene.

He straightened, ignored the twinge of pain that radiated down his arm, and turned toward his partner. "What have we got?"

Even as he asked, he began to move. As if on automatic pilot, he wandered slowly, allowing his gaze to drift. Yesterday's newspaper lay atop the desk, a dirty water glass at its upper right corner. Alongside the desk sat an empty wastebasket. A suitcase occupied the chair in the corner, its contents piled haphazardly. What might have been the clothing the victim removed before slipping into bed lay on the floor at the chair's feet.

Justin visually checked the corners of the room and the bathroom. He scanned every surface, looking past the dusting of powder the forensics team used while checking for prints. Then, only when he'd seen everything else, he turned his attention to the bed.

The deceased lay atop industrial white sheets—face down, arms stretched out to the sides, the orange-and-red bedspread tangled around his legs. His upper body remained exposed, the sandy-blond hair at the base of his skull matted with blood. The pillow beneath his face was also soaked with blood.

"Glad you could join us."

Justin turned at Allan's words, accepting the quick flash of concern that crossed his partner's face. He waited, silent, as Allan's gaze swept over him before rising once more.

"You're late."

"I had an appointment," Justin responded dryly. He tried not to shift uncomfortably as Allan continued to openly study him. He knew—ten years of working side by side brought a bond stronger than friendship—Allan was sizing him up, silently pondering Justin's physical condition.

"Therapy?"

Justin nodded as he waited for more to be said. He wondered, hoped his easy reading of Allan's thoughts didn't go both ways. If so, Allan would see the pain that kept Justin up most of the night, prowling the house. A clawing pain that remained, exacerbated by his morning workout, and left him questioning the intelligence behind his return to active duty. "So, what have we got?"

He breathed a sigh of relief when Allan moved on to the business at hand.

"Victim's been identified as one Leroy St. John, age thirty-three. Death appears to be from a single shot to the back of the head. The Medical Examiner said it looks like a small caliber. Probably a .22 or .25."

"A throw away."

"Yes."

Justin turned to the forensics men standing with them, McClemmens and Toombs. "Are you done?"

"Yes," McClemmens replied as Toombs packed up their kit.

"Did you find anything interesting?"

"If you find a room all but wiped clean interesting."

"Nothing? No prints at all?" He wanted a smoke. Justin caught himself before fishing for a pack of cigarettes that he no longer carried. He'd quit months ago, but on rare occasions such as this, the urge for nicotine was strong.

"We got a full palm print off the bedside table."

"I doubt if our shooter missed a spot," Allan piped in.

McClemmens shook his head. "I don't think so, either. My guess is it doesn't belong to our shooter."

"Are there any cameras in the lobby?" Justin asked.

"No," his partner replied. "And the desk clerk doesn't remember anyone inquiring about this room number."

"Who found the body?"

Allan pulled his notebook from his front jacket pocket. "A friend of the deceased. A woman by the name of Paige Conroy. She's waiting in the manager's office for us."

Justin looked around the room once again. His eyes stopped on the newspaper. "I don't suppose we're lucky enough to have any witnesses," he commented dryly as he flipped open the paper. "Someone who heard anything?"

"We should be so lucky."

Justin picked up the snapshot as it slipped from the newspaper. The poor-quality picture showed a man standing behind a woman, his arms about her waist. The man, clean-cut and blond, wore a self-satisfied smile just above his dimpled chin. He questioned, his gaze shifting between the two, whether the man in the picture was the same man that lay on the bed. Then, Justin focused on the woman.

Something jumped in his gut, tightened, and for a moment, all he saw was her. The room, its occupants and the noise about him faded away.

Her eyes—he couldn't make out their color—sparkled with joy...a happiness barely held in check. Her cheeks were sculpted, angled in just a way that drew his attention to her plump, full lips. Staggering came to mind as he studied the photograph. She was stunning, with a cascade of rich, reddish-brown hair that hung in loose curls to her shoulders.

"What is that?"

Allan's voice brought him back to the job at hand. He passed the photo over hurriedly, eager to break the strange spell he'd fallen under. Shaken by the thought that his concentration could be broken so quickly by a mere photograph of a woman he'd never before met, he turned to the bed and replaced the image of the woman with the reality of the man.

"You think that could be our victim?" Justin asked.

"That's hard to say."

Justin circled the bed as best he could in the limited space. His concentration returned. His mind clicked into motion. At the head of the bed, he squatted and attempted to get a better look at the victim's face.

"It looks to me like he's pushed pretty far into the pillow. My guess is he was rolled, held down and then shot." The longer he studied the form on the bed, the more he felt his thinking correct. "So our shooter's strong. You've got to have upper body strength to move a man this size, especially if he's struggling against you."

He straightened. "The room's been searched. Is anything missing?"

"Five hundred in cash is still in the wallet along with three credit cards."

"So it's not a robbery. Our shooter's looking for something in particular. He's smart, making certain to wipe everything clean and leave nothing behind. But he missed something, he missed the photograph."

"Maybe he left the photo for a reason," McClemmens piped up. "It might not have interested him."

"Or he planted it, left it for us to find. Our man's cocky, he didn't even attempt to make this look like a robbery."

Wasn't that a disturbing thought? It hinted at something far greater than a simple murder. In Justin's experience, most murders played out in a moment of passion or anger, which left most killers not thinking enough to get away without making a mistake or two. But a killer who meticulously wiped everything down, who had gotten away with walking into a fairly busy hotel and shooting a man in cold

7

blood was another story. Especially when he showed enough foresight to take away everything that could implicate him.

And leave behind a photographic clue.

As if reading his mind, Toombs spoke up. "That's not the worst part."

Based on his tone, Justin wasn't going to like what the man had to say. "What is?"

He caught the evidence bag Toombs tossed him and then flipped it over to get a better look at the contents. Bile rose up the back of his throat. His muscles bunched and tightened, sending new waves of pain radiating down his arm and side.

"Shit." His curse echoed back at him in the now-silent room.

This was not good. Definitely not the kind of case he wanted to face now. Not after just returning from medical leave. This would be nothing but trouble both emotionally and physically, for this meant long, exhausting hours on the job, and stress levels well beyond the norm. Levels high enough that his body would be a mass of tension until they cleared the case. Which, without much evidence, wasn't likely to be soon.

Already, as Justin met his partner's knowing gaze, the ache in his side grew and spread. For in his hand, sealed in the clear bag they used for gathering and storing evidence, sat a gold shield.

"Our vic's a cop."

* * *

Paige paced the floor of the manager's office, her long strides making short work of the distance between the walls. Pulse pounding, body trembling, she worked to push the image of Leroy from her mind. With great concentration, she managed to walk the length of the room without stumbling. Placing one foot carefully in front of the other, she reached the wall in no time and turned.

Paige struggled to breathe. She was on edge, torn up and confused by the happenings of her morning. With perfect clarity, she could see the inside of the hotel room, even though she had not spent that much time in it. She'd walked in, found Lee and left again to call in the police. Yet she could still envision the diamond pattern of the bedspread tangled around his lower extremities. With every deep breath, she continued to smell the room, the sweet scent that hung in the air mixed with a much stronger odor she would forever equate with death.

She stumbled, twisting her ankle as she overcorrected, and kept moving. She worked harder to pull her mind back to the act of movement. In the state she was in, it wouldn't do to let the memories flood in, for if she did, she would either fall flat on her face, or curl tightly into a ball and begin to cry. She would, perhaps, do both.

And wouldn't that be a sight? The detectives she waited for would come into the room to find a mass of female emotion curled into a corner. Frozen, sobbing, unable to give them any insight into what had transpired. That wouldn't do at all.

Squaring her shoulders, Paige continued to pace. She questioned, not for the first time, exactly what had happened in that room on the third floor. Unfortunately for both the investigating officers and for Lee, she had no idea. Sometime late last night, her phone rang. What she'd heard on the other end had been enough to leave her restless and unable to sleep. A voice from her past greeted her, a voice that at one time she knew well. But last night, instead of the friendly voice she remembered, she'd found anxiety in short succinct phrases.

He'd come all the way from Boston to see her. They couldn't speak on the phone. She must meet him first thing in the morning. It was urgent.

Paige stopped abruptly, pushing her fingers against her closed eyelids and breathing deeply. With the past they shared, just the idea of talking with Leroy after two years put her on edge. The tone of his voice and mystery surrounding his words caused what felt suspiciously like fear to settle in her stomach.

Moving her hand from her face, she pressed it against her stomach. She forced her fingers to uncurl, laying them flat against the buttons of her suit jacket. When she opened her eyes, certain to be once again in control, she discovered two men standing just inside the door of the Manager's office. Her gaze flitted between the gold badges each wore clipped to his belt.

"Paige Conroy?"

"Yes."

"Ms. Conroy, I'm Sergeant Harrison. This is my partner, Sergeant Simmons. We'd like to ask you a few questions about your activities this morning."

Sergeant Harrison's hair was a deep brown and cut short, his eyes the color of dark chocolate. Eyes that remained cool—very cool— as they skimmed down her body.

She trembled. Whether from the circumstances, or the unwanted shock of awareness that arrowed through her, she wasn't certain. "I'm afraid there's not much I can tell you."

"I understand you found the body," he prompted.

"I..." A wave of nausea tightened her stomach.

"Ms. Conroy?"

"Yes, I found him. Have you verified... Is it Leroy?"

"It looks that way."

"I wanted to be wrong. Wrong room,

11

wrong something. I was supposed to meet him this morning. He called me last night."

"What did he say to you?"

She tipped her head, hearing again Leroy's voice in her ear. "He said he needed to see me. He sounded anxious, agitated. That wasn't like him. Nothing ever ruffled Lee."

"Did he tell you what had him so upset?"

"No."

"Did he explain why he needed to see you?"

"No. He mentioned he didn't feel safe speaking with me on the telephone, so we made arrangements to meet here."

Sergeant Harrison raised a dark brow. His partner stopped scribbling in his notepad long enough to look up. "It wasn't safe?"

"He didn't explain and I never got the chance to ask. By the time I got to his room—" She swallowed around the lump in her throat. "The door was unlocked, propped partially open when I arrived. Leroy lay on the bed. His hair…there was so much blood."

Her vision blurred and the walls tilted. Reaching out blindly, Paige struggled to keep the room from tilting. A second wave of nausea coursed through her as her vision grayed.

A hand grabbed her upper arm and pushed her into a chair. Another urged her head toward her knees.

"Ms. Conroy?" A voice drifted to her

through the fog. "Ms. Conroy, are you all right?"

As her vision began to cleared, she lifted her head. The light-haired one, Sergeant Simmons, stood to her left. Dressed in a gray suit and loafers, he wore his gun on his belt. A wedding ring, a simple gold band, adorned the hand that held a notebook. His pen stilled as he focused on a spot to her right. Paige followed his gaze and turned her head.

Surprise jolted through her and all she could do was stare. The man who'd asked all the questions, squatted next to her. She blinked, unable to think past the strength in the hand still holding her arm, and the unexplainable comfort his touch brought her.

The spicy scent of his cologne curled around her, sending her senses humming faster. Attraction—something she hadn't felt in years—quickened her pulse and, for a moment, she forgot everything but him. The straight, square cut of his shoulders, the broad expanse of his chest. She let her gaze rise and studied his high-boned face, the cheeks covered in five o'clock shadow, his dark eyes lined with fatigue.

"Ms. Conroy?"

His voice was deep, rich and thick with concern. Paige drew in a shaky breath and fought against the irrational urge to lean into him, to draw from him both the gentleness and strength she sensed in him. To forget the ache that settled just below her heart.

The room snapped back into focus and with it, the reason for her being there. Paige jerked away from his touch and reeled her strayed thoughts back under control. "I'm sorry."

Sergeant Harrison released her and straightened. He moved a step away and watched her, his handsome face expressionless. "What did you do when you found the body?"

"I checked for a pulse. Then I left the room to call nine-one-one."

"You touched the body?"

The sergeant's continual reference to Leroy as *the body* was unsettling. "Yes. Leroy's wrist. I would have checked his carotid artery but..."

"I understand. You say you left the room to call? You didn't use the phone by the bed or touch anything else?"

"No. I know better than to touch anything."

Sergeant Harrison cocked his head. "Are you sure? You were understandably upset by what you found in that room. You panicked and reached for the telephone next to the bed."

"No I..." Paige drew a deep breath. She willed her mind to focus as she placed herself back in the room, standing beside the bed and staring down at Leroy. "I touched the nightstand, but not the telephone."

"Okay."

"I was startled, sickened by what I saw. I moved too quickly and bumped into the nightstand. I put my hand down to catch my balance."

"Was there anyone with you in the elevator?" Sergeant Simmons asked.

"No."

"Did you see anyone in the hallway outside the room?"

"No, just two people in the lobby as I entered. They appeared to be checking out. I saw no one else."

As Sergeant Harrison spoke again, she returned her attention to him. "Where did you go to make the call for help?"

"I stepped back into the hallway and used my cell phone."

He eyed her speculatively, his brows drawn together to form a frown. "You seem to know a lot about not disturbing a crime scene."

What did he mean by that? She'd just admitted to disturbing the scene when she put her hand on the nightstand.

"Do you know if Mr. St. John had any enemies?"

"He was a cop."

Sergeant Harrison shifted as if suddenly uncomfortable and narrowed his eyes. "Meaning what?"

Paige willed her knees not to shake as she stood and took a step in his direction. "I don't know. I would think the possibilities are endless with a cop."

Something flashed in his eyes. His hand lifted to settle on his ribs. "Do you have a problem with people in law enforcement, Ms. Conroy?"

"Of course not." The pressure of his hand against his ribs increased. Paige stepped closer. A quick, surprising surge of concern filled her and she reached for him. "Sergeant, are you all right?"

He twisted away so quickly that she snatched her hand back. His face as expressionless as granite, he shifted his hand from his ribs to within inches of the grip of his pistol.

She moved just as quickly, stepping back with her palms raised in front of her chest. Suddenly craving distance, she continued to walk backwards, stopping only when the manager's desk pressed against the back of her thighs.

Paige regretted her show of concern immediately. Before her eyes, Sergeant Harrison underwent a transformation. Not only did his stance change, his spine go rigid and unyielding, but gone was the man she'd caught such a brief glimpse of. His eyes went flat, his mouth thinned, and he became all cop.

She studied the line of his body, from the polished shine of the black Western boots on his

16

feet, up the long length of denim covered legs. Past trim hips, the open front of his leather jacket, only to stop on the hand still positioned near the rich, black handle of his pistol.

Glock, her mind catalogued the gun instinctively. All of her froze.

What in the world was she doing?

A nervous laugh escaped. "I'm afraid you have the wrong idea about me." Her hands shook. Unease clawed at her. Not from the man's instinctive reaction, but from the memories that very reaction brought back to her. "I wouldn't have any idea whether Leroy had enemies or not. We didn't...I haven't seen him in over two years."

"But you talked with him. On the telephone, or through letters."

"Yes, no." Paige shook her head to clear it. She wasn't communicating well at a time when she desperately needed to. He stood before her, his hand now in his front pocket. Doubt colored his features as his piercing gaze sized her up. For what, she didn't know, but it left her with the knowledge that she needed them to better understand. "Leroy and I barely had contact anymore. When we did, we used e-mail."

"So until the telephone call early this morning, St. John gave no indication that anything was wrong?"

"That's correct."

"You say you rarely had contact with him

17

anymore," Sergeant Simmons stated. "You're implying that you used to talk quite frequently?"

"We were friends years ago." It seemed like a lifetime ago. Long enough ago that she had thought that part of her life far behind her.

The urge to escape flared. Near to breaking, she wanted to run from the room. To give in and allow grief to swallow her whole. She wanted to shout. She wanted to cry. But she didn't cry in front of people, and she sure as hell wasn't going to cry in front of these men. It took all her control to stand her ground.

She had no idea who murdered Leroy and no amount of digging into her memories was going to help. She did know she had to keep it together long enough to finish answering the detective's questions. Once she completed that task, she would relinquish the tight hold she held on her emotions. Then, and only then, she would allow herself to feel what at this moment she fought desperately not to.

"Ms. Conroy." Sergeant Harrison held what appeared to be a photograph, sealed in plastic, before him. "Can you identify the man in this picture?"

A gasp broke loose as she caught sight of the man he spoke of. She shifted her right hand to her throat, concentrating on curling her left hand around the edge of the photograph and taking it from him.

It was more than she could handle. The endless hours of restless sleep followed by the shock of finding Lee dead. Yet nothing compared to what he handed her.

Tears stung her eyes. She swallowed once, twice, wishing against hope that she could hold back the memories longer. She'd built a wall around them, around the pain they brought. A wall she feared was about to crumble. "Yes. I can identify that man."

"Is he Leroy St. John?"

"Where did you find this? Did Leroy have it?"

"Is Leroy St. John the man in that photograph?"

They had to know it wasn't. They would have Leroy's I.D., his driver's license or something. Wouldn't they?

The photograph trembled along with her hands as she offered it back to Sergeant Harrison. She waited, silently pleading with him to take it from her. She needed it gone, needed to pull herself back under control.

But even as he removed the photo from her sight, her shaking continued. Suddenly struck by a frightening realization, something she knew the detectives would soon discover, her tremors increased.

"Ms. Conroy, who is the man in the picture?" Sergeant Simmons asked. "Why would this picture be of importance to Detective St.

19

John?"

Sergeant Harrison jumped in. "That is you, is it not?"

Her throat went dry, leaving her unable to form the words. She wished for a glass of water to wet her mouth. She wished for this to be over, for none of it to have happened at all. But even as she wished, she understood just how impossible that would be. Now, the past she worked so hard to forget came crashing back. And no matter the pain, the mind-numbing ache it caused her, it was about to be picked apart and dissected. "Yes, that's me in the photograph."

"And who is the man with his arms around you?" Sergeant Harrison asked.

"Rick Preston. He was Leroy's partner, as well as my fiancé."

"Was?"

Her voice carefully controlled, Paige answered. "He's dead, Sergeant. Rick Preston was murdered."

CHAPTER TWO

Murdered.

Justin's day slipped from bad to worse. "When?"

"Three years ago. Rick and I had gone out to dinner, a late dinner after his shift." She spoke in a near monotone, as if the strain of the day had finally broken her down. Glassy eyed, she stared off at a place near the far corner of the room.

"We came out of the restaurant. I waited while Rick went for the car. A man, I could see them from where I stood, he approached Rick and they spoke. Then, he pulled a gun and shot Rick once, in the face."

"Ms. Conroy."

She jerked as if slapped and then continued, running her words together as if she would choke on them should she not get them all out at once. "I ran to him, I didn't know what to do. His eyes, I'll never forget..." Her eyes slid closed, then opened with a snap. "The people from the restaurant began filing out. The ambulance arrived, along with an incredible number of police. One of them, a uniformed

21

officer, finally called Leroy. He took me to the hospital, stayed with me that first night. He helped me through the line-up, the funeral, and the eventual acceptance that the man who killed Rick would never go to trial."

Two men. Two partners. Now, two murders.

The connection stood before him wearing a tailor-made suit, the skirt short enough to show off an endless expanse of leg. He didn't accept what he saw and heard as mere coincidence. It couldn't be. She'd been present at both murders. No way could he swallow that as accidental. But what was her connection?

She could be the killer.

He glanced from the photograph in his hand to the woman standing before him. He'd made the connection the moment he stepped into the room. *The woman from the picture.* His eyes narrowed as he took in the familiar chiseled cheekbones, her unpainted lips. The muted-red color of her suit brought out the chestnut highlights in her otherwise brown hair, the vibrant green of her eyes, hidden before by the poor quality of the snapshot. It didn't please him to recall that upon first seeing her in the flesh, his heart began to gallop and sharp arousal shot through him like gunfire. No more than it pleased him to think she could be a killer. Yet, with nearly thirteen years on the force, nothing would surprise him anymore. It would have to be considered, looked into.

Were she not the killer, as instinct told him, then a game was afoot. A deadly game. The picture found hidden in the newspaper told him that much. Sure, Leroy St. John may have brought the photograph in order to help him remember what Paige Conroy looked like. But who could forget a face like hers? Justin knew he wouldn't.

It was more likely that the picture was a plant. Which led to why someone would plant it. What could it possibly mean? Left in a dead man's room, one of the subjects the victim of a three-year-old murder, the other the only witness to both deaths. Two conclusions could be drawn from that, two possible messages someone meant to send. Either Paige Conroy was responsible for the murders...

Or the next victim.

Unease settled between Justin's shoulders at the thought. He shook it loose, tucking the photograph into his inner-jacket pocket. He straightened and listened with keen interest as Allan began asking questions.

"You said Preston's killer would never go to trial. What did you mean by that? Is the case still open?"

"No. They caught the man, but he hung himself in his cell. No one ever discovered why he shot Rick."

"Why do you think he shot him?"

Her gaze slid from Allan to him and back again. A ripple of confusion flashed through her eyes. "I have no idea."

"No idea?" Disbelief colored Allan's words. "What did Preston work on before his death? Anything that had him worried? Did he say anything to you about being concerned that something was about to happen? Any cryptic messages like the one St. John delivered over the telephone?"

"No. Rick never shared... He didn't say anything to me."

"You had dinner that night. He didn't seem upset, preoccupied?"

The shaky laugh that slipped from Ms. Conroy surprised them all. Justin noted her unnaturally pale face as she closed her eyes and pinched the bridge of her nose. "He seemed fine."

She was holding something back. What, he didn't know, but she no longer looked at him or Allan. Instead, her attention focused just to the right of where he stood. As he studied her—so cool and collected, except for the slight trembling of her body—she pulled her full bottom lip into her mouth and bit down.

Awareness surged, surprising in its intensity. Justin slid his hands into his front pockets and set his jaw against the unwelcome reaction. "Ms. Conroy—"

"What do you want me to say?" she asked

24

with impatience. "That night Rick Preston was attentive and caring. I thought things would turn out differently, but they didn't."

"Because someone shot and killed him," he countered.

"Yes."

"And then hung himself in his cell before he could stand trial."

"*Yes.* Look, I fail to see what any of this has to do with Lee's murder. It's been three years since Rick was shot." Her bright green eyes took on a sudden awareness. "You think that Lee's death is related to Rick's."

"No one is saying that, Ms. Conroy," Allan said simply.

"Of course you aren't, but you're thinking it. Otherwise Rick's death wouldn't interest you so much."

When neither answered, she looked back at him. Her face was set, tension radiated from her like a physical force. Clearly, she wanted this interview over, didn't appreciate the intrusion into her past. Or the painful memories his questions must have brought her. The misery in her eyes disturbed him more than it should have. He needed to keep things professional, remain objective. The fact that he found it difficult to do was worrisome.

Justin rolled his shoulders in a vain attempt to loosen the muscles that knotted there. The small clench of empathy nagging at him grew as her eyes welled up with tears.

"Are we done? It's been a rough morning and I'd really like to go home."

"Almost," Allan replied. "You're not planning any trips are you?"

"I'm..." She cleared her throat, dragged the heel of her palm across her forehead. "No, I'm not planning any trips. If you need anything more from me, you can find me at my studio."

"Your studio?"

"I gave all this information to the uniformed officer who left me in this office."

"I understand," Allan assured her. "But we'll need the information as well."

Paige Conroy opened the purse sitting next to her on the desk and retrieved a business card from its depths. She turned, holding the card in Justin's general direction.

He took the card she offered, his fingers grazing hers. A frown formed between her eyebrows at the brief contact. She took a quick step back, then another.

"Conroy Photography," Justin read aloud.

"I have my own studio."

"And when you're not in your studio?"

"When I'm not in my studio, I'm still at that address. I live above it. Are we done? Can I go now?"

"I think that will be all for now. If we need anything further, we'll be in touch."

She pulled a set of car keys from the

pocket of her suit jacket and was out of the office like a shot, the echo of her heels trailing behind her.

Justin watched her go, all but running from the room in an attempt to put distance between them. He pushed her business card into the same inner pocket as the picture.

"Well," Allan began, "she was a surprise. Very astute."

Justin's gaze remained on Paige's retreating form. "Yes."

"She's figured out she's a suspect. But she's tough, she held it together."

"She told us all she knew."

"It seemed that way. A cop killing. Shit. Not exactly the type of case you want to come back to, is it, partner?"

"Two cops are dead. Paige Conroy was right about one thing, I believe the two deaths are connected. It's more than just their partnership, I can feel it."

"Yes, but can you prove it?" When he didn't respond, Allan spoke up again. "Justin?"

"Yeah?"

"Would you prefer I leave you alone with your thoughts?"

He turned at Allan's smart remark and quirked his eyebrow. "Meaning what?"

"You seem distracted." Allan gazed pointedly in the direction Paige Conroy had disappeared. "You've changed, Justin."

"No, I haven't." But he *was* distracted. Distracted by the leggy brunette who'd just left, and the thought that she might be caught up in something beyond her control. Although she'd projected an aura of calm, he wasn't fooled by her casual exterior. He'd seen the truth in her eyes, the fear she tried to disguise.

He turned back toward the door, only to find her gone.

Allan laughed knowingly. "You're like a brother to me, Justin. I think I know what I'm talking about."

"What are you talking about, Allan?"

"She's a beautiful woman."

"Yes, she is." Confused, Justin faced his partner. "What does that have to do with me?"

"Paige Conroy is a beautiful woman. I would expect you to notice. But you have many beautiful women in your life, and I've never met one who could distract you from the job. Not until now."

"Since when do you doubt my ability to do the job?"

"I don't doubt your ability, Justin. I'm just voicing an observation."

"That Paige Conroy distracts me."

"That you should be careful. You said it yourself, two cops are dead. Paige Conroy could very well be the killer."

"She didn't kill St. John. She doesn't have the upper body strength."

Allan's eyebrow arched.

"Damn it." By defending her, he cemented Allan's opinion. Justin scrubbed a hand across his face. His eyes felt gritty. Pins and needles raced up and down his side. "I'll do the job, Allan."

"And if it includes arresting the woman that just walked from the room?"

He lifted his chin. Paige Conroy attracted him in a way no woman had done before. She drew him, ignited a fire within him the moment he saw her picture. It burned in his gut still, stronger now that he'd met her.

Silently, Justin acknowledged that his attraction to her was a complication he didn't need. He was conducting an investigation. Paige Conroy was a suspect—their only suspect—and that meant *hands off*. He'd worked hard to get put back on active duty and nothing he felt, no matter its unusual intensity, would affect his job. He was a cop, first and last.

With renewed fervor, he assured Allan, "Even if it means arresting her."

* * *

Paige stood beneath the shower's pelting rays, her hands against the wall before her. Her head pounded, her body ached with fatigue. A single tear slipped from the corner of her eye.

She swallowed hard, accepting the act as stress and too little sleep. Under normal circumstances, crying was a weakness she wouldn't allow herself. But nothing about her day could be labeled normal. From the late-night telephone call, to becoming the number-one suspect in a murder investigation.

Swallowing back the sob that clawed at her throat, Paige closed her eyes, pushed her head beneath the spray of the water and wet her long mass of hair. She felt dirty, soiled by the brutality of murder. Her hands shook as she worked the shampoo into lather. Guilt filled her.

Lee deserved better. He deserved remorse, regret for a life cut short. But to allow herself to grieve for him would be opening herself up to pain and sorrow of memories best forgotten. Rick and Leroy were too closely tied together, in life and now in death. She couldn't recall one without the other. So she kept it all buried inside. She pushed away thoughts of the quiet, sensitive man so brutally murdered that morning, and stowed away the grief. No matter the cost to her sanity.

Paige turned the water off with a quick twist of her wrist. She stepped from the shower, squeezing some of the wet from her hair before wrapping it in a towel. With swift, brisk movements, she dried herself and pulled a pale blue T-shirt over her head. Her legs she shoved into her favorite jeans, a well-worn pair that offered comfort, both physical and emotional.

She didn't bother to take the dryer to her

hair, for it just made more of a mess of her curls. Instead, she ran a quick comb through it and left it hanging down her back.

She left the bath behind, moving on silent feet through the upper floor of her converted warehouse. She needed to rest, she thought, as she shifted the pile of clean towels waiting to be folded to the other end of the couch. She needed to clear her mind. She flopped down and pulled her legs up and under her. She closed her eyes and tipped her head back to lie against the couch. Slowly, her tension eased, her mind cleared. A deep inhale and exhale helped. Tense muscles relaxed.

With brutal swiftness, the image of Lee's blood-covered body atop the tangled sheets assaulted her mind. Paige fought back, willed it to recede, but her mind wouldn't let go. As if turning the lens of her camera, the image shifted into focus until she stood in that third-floor hotel room once more. Silence settled around her, the acrid scent of death filled her.

Her stomach turned abruptly. Her eyes popped open. Grief, a throbbing ache, settled just beneath her heart, making it difficult to draw a deep breath. She jerked her legs out from under her and shoved her head between her knees. She willed the room to stop spinning.

A groan slipped from between closed lips. She tightened her jaw in acknowledgment that she wasn't going to relax anytime soon or get

31

the rest her body cried out for. Her mind wouldn't shut off.

Praying with everything inside her that the room would continue to hold still, she placed trembling hands upon the floor and slowly shifted her gaze from her feet to the wall. When the room stayed in focus and she was fairly confident she could move without her world turning, she stood, heading for the stairs and the studio in the lower level of her home.

Paige knew now what she had to do. She had to work. Through work, she would find relief, no matter how momentary. And were she to work long and hard enough, she just might be able to fall into exhausted sleep. The kind of dreamless sleep where pain could no longer reach her. Then, perhaps, she could let death go.

* * *

He shouldn't have come by.

Not for the first time that night, Justin repeated his litany. He stood next to the steel outer door, eyes scanning the deserted street behind him, and cursed under his breath. The neighborhood wasn't a neighborhood at all, but a nine-to-five business district, already empty now that the sun hung low over the Pacific. The only light for blocks, that didn't come from the street lamps, spilled from the front window of the two-story converted warehouse before him. Every other building was dark.

What sort of person chose to live like this?

The image of the cool, professional woman he'd met that morning settled in. While shaken and upset, she'd still managed to portray elegance and success. From the severe twist in her hair, right down to her reptile-skin heels.

Justin focused on the purse he held in his grasp. Though not as large as some women carried, it was crafted from the same material as those fancy shoes she wore. He'd bet his next paycheck the color was a perfect match to her suit and that the whole ensemble cost more than all the clothes in his closet put together. He wouldn't have pegged Paige Conroy as the type to live like this. He'd figured her too patrician.

Justin skimmed his hand across the knotted muscles in his neck. He should have called and told her where she could pick up the purse, instead of showing up on her doorstep. He didn't normally go for women like her— uptight and out of his league. She probably didn't even know how to relax, how to let her hair down and have a little fun.

The thought turned his frustrated breath to a curse. He hadn't come to get to know her better, or to see if those striking green eyes of hers had lost their haunted look. He was here to work an investigation, to ask questions and get answers. Not to see if her trembling had finally eased. His *job* brought him to her door, he reminded himself.

He only wished he believed it.

The sign affixed to the door read *Conroy Photography*. Justin rapped his knuckles twice into the center of it. Behind him, the unusual quiet of the street unnerved him. The absence of everyday sounds—like traffic, barking dogs or children at play—tightened already-tense muscles. Made him wish he had strapped his Glock to his side before he'd left his home. The thought disappeared the moment the door swung open.

Paige Conroy stood in the doorway, framed in the light from the room behind her. Gone was the woman he'd met that morning, a woman who'd exuded a surprising strength and professionalism. In her place stood a woman who unnerved him more.

Her hair hung down and fell in long, loose curls over her shoulder, nearly to her waist. The fingers of her left hand were tucked in the front pocket of a pair of faded jeans, worn white at the stress points and ripped at the knee. Old, comfortable jeans that fit her like a second skin, drawing his gaze down her long length of legs and to her bare feet. He took his time studying those feet, their red toenails and silver toe ring that he found ridiculously sexy. Enough time that when his gaze returned to her face, he found her frowning at him, her arms crossed before her.

"Sergeant Harrison, isn't it? Can I help you Sergeant Harrison?"

Her tone was ice cold, her stance forbidding. He'd expected this, had been prepared for it even. But he had not been prepared to discover that beneath her outward appearance of strength, in a face washed clean of make-up, was a frailty that had been missing that morning. Dark shadows and small lines of fatigue ringed her eyes.

The urge to pull her to him and offer comfort surprised him. She was unusually tall for a woman. He stood six-foot-three and even with her feet bare, she nearly looked him in the eye. He liked his women shorter—blonde and petite. Paige Conroy was neither, but the thought of her in his arms, their bodies lining up perfectly, chest-to-chest, pelvis-to-pelvis, warmed his blood.

"Sergeant?"

He raised the hand holding her purse before him. "I need to talk to you."

She uncrossed her arms and grabbed the doorknob in her right hand. Her eyes iced. Her back stiffened. He recognized her desire to close the door in his face. "Don't you mean you need to grill me some more?"

"I understand you've had a long day."

"I doubt it."

"There are some questions I need you to

answer."

She closed her eyes and sighed. Pushed the door open wider and motioned him in.

Their shoulders brushed as he stepped past her. She took an automatic step backwards. "I'm not certain I can tell you anything more than I've already told you."

Justin took a minute to examine his surroundings. Her studio should have felt cold, the immense sea of neutrals and cool contemporary lines, but she'd managed to give the place life. A splash of color here, a large plant there, it all worked together to create a comfortable space. All about him, wood beams, polished to a shine, stood out against walls painted bright white. Across the room, in the farthest corner, a stool sat before a black screen. Lights, some hanging from the ceiling and some attached to poles, surrounded the screen. Photographs, large black and whites lit from beneath, hung strategically about, commanding attention.

"Sometimes a little time is all that's needed to recall something new."

"I haven't remembered anything new."

Her face was set. Tension radiated out of her like a physical force. She made no move to hide the fact that she didn't want him there as she skirted around him and crossed the room to the sitting area centered before the large front window.

He waited until she settled into the corner of the couch before following. "Ms. Conroy, what was your relationship with Detective St. John?"

"He was my friend."

"That's it?"

"Yes."

Justin bent and placed her purse atop the table before her, alongside a stack of eight-by-tens compiled of tiny photographs. "During the course of our investigation, we have uncovered that you had a relationship with Detective St. John. Would you care to verify that?"

"Of course I had a relationship with him. As I have already told you, Lee and I were friends."

He nodded. And because he couldn't stand not knowing, he reached down and picked up one of the photo sheets. "Is this your work?"

Her feet hit the floor and she was off the couch like a shot. Her eyes locked onto his hands. "Please don't touch that. It has nothing to do with your investigation."

"The pictures are so small. What do you use this for?"

She raised her left hand toward the sheet, then stopped. Her breath released on a sigh. "They're called proof, or contact sheets. The pictures are so small because essentially it's nothing more than a copy of the negatives."

"Why do you copy the negatives this

way?"

"It's a roll's worth of film on one sheet. With it I can evaluate the quality of the negatives and choose which shots to enlarge."

"Don't most photographers use digital?"

"Unfortunately, yes." She held out her hand, palm up. "Sergeant?"

With her waiting impatiently at his side, Justin peered at the subject of the thirty or so pictures that made up the proof sheet. The woman sat on the floor, straight as a rail, her face away from the camera. All of her hair was pulled to the front of her body, leaving the camera with a clear, unobstructed view of her nude back. His eyes, as he was certain had been the photographer's intent, traced the woman's every curve, every vertebrae down to the cleft just above her buttocks and to the small, colorless butterfly tattoo therein.

"What do you mean unfortunately?"

Her slender brows drew together. A few seconds passed before she answered. "Artistically, film is the superior medium. There's a richness of color and depth that is lost with digital. Too many people rely on photo editing programs instead of an effective use of light and shadow." She cleared her throat. "Why don't you stop pretending an interest in my work and just ask me what you really want to know?"

Although she was wrong about his

interest in her work, Justin admired her fortitude. He handed her the proof sheet. "What is it I really want to know?"

"You want to know whether I slept with Leroy."

Her blunt statement took him by surprise. "Did you sleep with him?"

"Not recently."

"Could you please clarify that?"

"I could. I won't."

"I see." His lips curved. As perverse as it was, he enjoyed her spirit, her unwillingness to give him the easy answer. "You're the one who brought it up," he reminded her.

"Because you were afraid to."

"I wasn't afraid, I was..." His gaze slid down the length of her. "Distracted."

"Right, distracted." She curled her bottom lip between her teeth and bit down.

A jagged awareness shot into his gut. "Ms. Conroy—"

"There is no way that whether or not I slept with Lee is of any use to your investigation. I did not kill him."

"I haven't said that you did."

"You've insinuated it. You may be used to seeing death and dying up close and personal, Sergeant, but I'm not. What I saw this morning sickened me. I still can't get that image out of my head. I still can't even think about eating without my stomach turning. I didn't, I *couldn't* do something like that to another human being." Her eyes slid closed as she drew in a shaky breath. "Especially not Lee."

Justin couldn't pinpoint an exact reason, but at that instant he believed her. Not just about her relationship with the victim, but about her innocence as well. He had to admit that he never held much conviction in her being the killer. Not with the amount of strength it would take to hold down a man St. John's size while he fought for his very life. Unfortunate for her, he still had a job to do and in order to do it, he needed to know as much as he could about the victim.

"Tell me about St. John."

"I did that this morning."

"How long did you know him? How did you meet?" He stepped around the low table and walked toward her, firing off questions without allowing her time to answer. "Did it have anything to do with his job as a narcotics detective? Was it before or after his partnership with Preston? Why now, after more than two years, would he feel the need to look into his partner's murder investigation?"

All the color drained from her face. "Rick?"

Her hand reached out and settled lightly upon his wrist. She might as well have slugged him across the jaw. His muscles tightened, his blood warmed and, unlike the rest of him, his mind suddenly went soft.

"Are you certain?"

"Quite." Justin dragged air into his tight lungs, bringing with it the soft, subtle scent of her. A bolt of lust caught him right in the chest, then traveled downward. He looked at her hand, at the long, slender fingers curled about his wrist. Such a simple act of connection, a single touch, and with it she'd managed to throw him off kilter. His mind fogged. He fought the urge to cover her hand with his own.

Irritated by his reaction, he shook his head; forced his mind to clear. He damned his traitorous body's reaction to her and voiced his original question. "What was your relationship with Leroy St. John?"

"Friends, never more. We went out once, when I first met him, but the spark just didn't exist. We had no connection beyond friendship."

He felt the loss of her touch as she moved her hand from his wrist. He didn't like the attraction he felt for her, or his relief at learning she'd never been intimate with St. John. He didn't have the time for a woman right now. Especially not *this* woman. "How long ago did you meet him?"

"Six years ago."

"You would have been twenty at that time."

She stared at him, her displeasure evident in her posture, in the glint of fire that shot through her eyes. "You've done your homework."

He'd done his job. Checked out her story. Looked into her background.

Paige Louise Conroy, born in Boston, Massachusetts, twenty-six years before to Joseph and Elizabeth Conroy. Raised amidst wealth and privilege, she'd been expected to attend law school and follow her father and mother to one of Boston's most prestigious law firms. She had the smarts for it; graduated from high school at sixteen, college by nineteen. But instead of moving on to Harvard and marrying in her social class, as her parents had hoped, she'd opened her own photography studio and fallen for a cop.

"A year after we met, Lee got a new partner," she continued, as if background checks were a routine part of her life.

"Rick Preston."

"Yes."

"Is that how you met Preston, through St. John?"

"He and Rick quickly became friends. Lee decided that Rick and I would get along well. He introduced us."

She didn't elaborate further. She didn't have to. Justin already knew what happened next. They'd hit it off, Paige and her cop, hit it off well enough that they'd planned to marry. Only, before the big day ever came, Rick Preston was gunned down outside a local restaurant.

His hand unconsciously shifted to rest on his side. Taking a bullet. A cop's worst fear, his own worst nightmare. He knew the pain, the physical agony of it, but what about the emotional scars? How would someone, a woman like her in particular, get over witnessing her lover's shooting?

He never got the chance to ponder further as her voice interrupted his thoughts. "As for Lee reopening Rick's murder investigation, I didn't know he had. Not until you just told me."

She should have followed her parents' lead. She would have made a damn good lawyer. For that matter, she would have made a damn good cop. Chin high, shoulders squared and looking as if it hadn't cost her a thing, Paige had just answered every question he'd thrown at her moments ago.

In the order he'd put them to her.

"Do you have any more questions, or are we done?"

Justin frowned. In the space of a heartbeat the tough façade faded, replaced by the same vulnerability he'd glimpsed on his arrival. Before his very eyes she withdrew, closed in on herself. No matter how strong he believed her to be, she'd reached her limit. She wanted him gone.

He could tell himself that he didn't want to get involved, that he'd only showed up on her doorstep to glean some answers. His reluctance to leave told him something altogether different.

Without considering the why or giving his head time to list all the reasons he shouldn't, Justin crossed the room to a framed example of her work.

Portraits, he discovered as he moved about, she did portraits. But not your standard, run-of-the-mill headshots. No, her work could not be considered traditional. If he were to hazard a guess, he figured her goal was to get the observer to look past the obvious, to forget preconceived notions and see the true person that lay beneath. Yet in each case, the way she went about it differed. The end result—photographs as unique and individual as their subject. Some fun, some adventurous, and others oddly sensual.

Justin compared each new photograph to the one he'd studied first—the woman he'd discovered upon the proof sheet. Although he liked all of her work, saw the skill and beauty in each piece that hung in her studio, the woman with the tattoo remained his favorite. With its stark black-and-white contrasts and unique sensuality, he knew he wouldn't forget it easily.

Just as he couldn't forget the photographer easily.

Turning from the photograph before him, he crossed an expanse of oak flooring to the desk tucked against the wall. Another photograph hung centered behind the desk, this one color instead of her preferred black and white. The subject brought a smile to his face. "1959 Cadillac El Dorado."

She'd taken the photograph in what he could only describe as old-style, not showcasing the entire car, but its unique features. The rear quarter panel and chrome accents of the cotton-candy pink Cadillac sparkled, but it was the red, conical taillights that drew and held his attention. "I like this one."

When she didn't respond, he turned. "Ms. Conroy?"

She stood still as stone, watching him in a way that made his body warm. "Paige," she corrected automatically. With slow precision, she raised her gaze to meet his. "What did you say?"

Justin pushed away from the desk and walked toward her. "The Cadillac. Didn't I see that car parked in front of your building?"

"You noticed that, did you?"

"I tend to pay particular attention to things of beauty."

His words darkened her eyes to emerald. Color flashed across her cheeks.

Halting inches from her, he allowed his gaze to slide slowly from her head to her toes and back again. His fingers itched to touch her. Stifling the thought, he shoved his hands into his pockets. "Is it yours?"

"The photograph? Yes, it's one of my first, before I decided that portraits were more my style."

"I meant the Caddy."

"Right, the Caddy," she replied, a huskiness to her voice that hadn't been there before. "Yes, the Cadillac is mine."

He tipped his head. "Does your appreciation extend to all classic cars or just Cadillacs?"

The beginnings of a smile tipped the corners of her incredible mouth. "I love all the classics. What about you, what do you drive?"

"1969 Pontiac GTO."

"A goat," she said, using the nickname for the GTO. Her eyes narrowed. "Not a judge?"

"Yes."

"Stock or custom?"

"Stock. 400-cubic-inch Ram air V-8—"

"With a Quadra-jet carb."

Justin was impressed. This was a layer to Paige Conroy he hadn't expected. One of many he'd uncovered tonight. "You know your cars."

"I told you, I love the classics. Your goat, is it the standard package?"

He shook his head. "Ram Air IV, four-speed manual transmission."

Without conscious thought, Justin reached out and swept up a lock of hair that lay across her arm. She smelled like roses, he realized, as the gossamer soft strands curled

46

around his fingers. He'd always liked the smell of roses. "I brought her here, if you'd like to see her."

"I'd like that."

Justin crossed to the door, held it for her as she stepped out onto the sidewalk. He smiled at the sight of her Cadillac sitting at the curb, its top down in deference to the humid night air, before shifting his gaze to his own car, parked a few feet in front of hers and shining in the light from the street lamp.

Her lips parted as a startled gasp slipped free. Feet still bare, she walked to his car and slowly, one finger at a time, pressed down until her palm lay flat atop the front quarter panel. Even from his distance, he caught her tiny shiver of pleasure. "She's beautiful."

Justin watched, transfixed, as she moved around his car, each step forward followed by the gentle slide of her hand across the quarter panel. Down the side, across the rear spoiler and forward once more. Each stroke, each caress of her hand pushed his blood pressure up another notch until he had to steel himself from closing the distance and pulling her into his embrace.

Want consumed him. He wanted her hands on him, not just on his car. He wanted to taste her, feel her, to fist his hands in her hair and sink into her warmth. It'd been too long, far too long since he'd been with a woman—six months, ten days and twenty-two hours to be exact, and he missed it. He missed it more than he missed nicotine, more than he missed being able to draw a deep breath without the slightest twinge of pain.

She looked up and met his gaze across the expanse of the car. A smile curved her lips, brightened her face and lightened her features. Joy, pure, unadulterated joy sparkled in her eyes, warmed her voice. "How long have you had her?"

"About ten years now. I found her in a field behind someone's house with four flat tires and mold covering the front seat."

Disgust colored her features but her smile did not fade. Justin caught himself before he could return her smile. He shoved his hands into his front pockets.

It'd been a mistake coming here, a mistake he needed to quickly remedy. For years he'd chosen his women for their physical endowments and little else. He liked them blonde and stacked, girls who didn't expect more from him than a night of pleasure and tempted him in no other sense than the physical. Only since he'd faced down a bullet and lost, he hadn't been able to even consider enjoying a woman with the same carelessness as before.

This attraction, this connection he felt with the woman before him, was dangerous. With so much at stake, so much riding on him doing his job and doing it right, he couldn't afford to slip up. He couldn't risk another distraction. He had enough of those already, the pain in his side the largest one.

He drew in a deep breath, expanding his lungs, welcoming the accompanying ache as the slap of reality he so desperately needed. He had work to do, a murder to solve. He straightened and pulled his keys from his pocket, then shattered the intimacy by reminding them both of his reason for being there. "If I need anything else from you, I'll be in touch."

She blinked once. Twice. All the color drained from her face.

He hadn't meant to cause her grief, but he watched it wash over her. Guilt settled in, nearly choking him. He tightened his jaw and pushed it away. He couldn't get involved. He couldn't allow himself to care.

So he left her, standing beneath the streetlight, arms curled around her stomach. He called himself the worst kind of fool and cursed long and loud. And when he would have looked back, checked to see if she remained there, alone on that empty street, he turned a corner and accelerated, working through the gears with long-practiced ease.

CHAPTER THREE

Paige awoke with a start, the echo of her scream ringing in her ears. She sat up in bed and clutched the sheet to her chest. The smooth gleam of perspiration covered her skin. She shivered once in the moonlit room and pushed hair out of her face with fingers numb with cold.

It's only a dream, she assured herself, but the knowledge did little to slow her racing heart.

Death and dying.

Love and loss.

Images much too realistic taunted her shattered nerves.

Blood, so much blood.

She pushed her hand into her abdomen and doubled over, working the air in and out of her lungs. Her chest burned as if squeezed by a vise. Acid inched up the back of her throat.

"Breathe." She shifted to her knees, kicking frantically when the sheet snagged on her legs. "Just breathe."

Her breath came in ragged little gasps as she worked for composure. Her eyes swept the room about her, waiting, struggling with the

50

reality that she was awake. It had only been a dream.

Only it was more than just that, more than a nightmare. It was a memory.

"Why," she moaned, her hands fisting the lace coverlet. "Why couldn't you have stayed buried in the past?"

The answer came swift and vivid. Since she'd stumbled on Leroy's blood-covered body just twenty four hours before, thoughts of her past refused to fade into the background. Endless hours of restless sleep and more stress than any person should have to endure only made it more impossible to fight. Brick by brick, the wall she'd built around her memories began to crumble.

She closed her eyes and tried to push past the horror, past the memories struggling to break through, but they slammed into her with the force of a one-two punch. With no more strength to resist, her mind slipped into the past.

Rick. With little effort, she could envision him standing before her—his pale hair and eyes, his ruthless good looks. Young and foolish when she'd met him, he was the first man to ever cause her stomach to drop to her toes and her system to go jittery. Cocky, arrogant and quick to charm, he'd walked into her life and swept her off her feet. She'd allowed herself to be carried away by attraction and she'd fallen hard and fast.

It had nearly been her undoing.

By the time she realized she would never be able to compete with his job, she'd loved him completely. She withstood his sudden changes in mood and convinced herself that when he shut himself off to her, retreating behind a mask of cool indifference, it was nothing personal. She got good at accepting what little he gave her, even as she craved more. Good enough that his swift, brutal death nearly destroyed her.

Even though his life had brought her little more than frustration and pain.

"Never again," she whispered. "No more cops." Her breathing regulated, her stomach settled.

Until dark brown eyes flashed into her mind.

Stifling a groan, she scrubbed her palms across her face. She closed her eyes and waited for Sergeant Harrison's image to fade. When it remained wedged in place, Paige fumbled out from beneath her covers and staggered to her bathroom where she splashed cold water onto her face.

Because she could feel hot tears boiling up, she splashed her face a second time. It was nothing more than the need to reach out to someone. To feel the warmth of a man's arms around her, the soothing comfort of his voice in her ear. She was lonely, confused, and once again, she had all but witnessed a violent murder. Because she was too shaken to maintain tight control of her thoughts, her mind drifted again to Sergeant Harrison. He'd been the last person she'd seen before finally catching some sleep. It didn't have to mean anything more than that.

But she knew it did. For the first time in years, she ached for a man. A man with dark hair and eyes so unlike the blue she usually went for. A man with gentle hands, an inquisitive mind, and a gold shield upon his belt.

The realization brought Paige up short. She thought she'd changed, had gone out of her way to discard any and all representation of the woman she had been before Rick died. She'd grown stronger, more self-reliant. She refused to remain the same pathetic, hollow person who would allow others to choose her moods, her very thoughts.

Suddenly looking for affirmation, her gaze settled upon her reflection. She winced, not comforted by what she found.

Focused on the hollow cheeks and pale hue of the woman reflected back at her, Paige wondered just how much she *had* changed. She knew all too well how it felt to follow her heart and not her head. The mind-numbing ache of betrayal, that never completely went away. She had no desire to repeat her past, to experience that kind of pain again. So why did she fear she was doing just that—falling for a man she knew to be the epitome of everything she'd vowed to change about her life?

Sure, through the brief glimpses caught of the man behind the badge, she thought there might be something to Sergeant Harrison that she could care about. But twice now, immediately after showing pieces of himself, he'd closed off swiftly and completely. She'd been down that road before, knew the heartache of it. She wouldn't go down there again. For that reason, there was no room in her life for Sergeant Harrison. No room for him in her thoughts.

Paige exhaled slowly and reached for her toothbrush, avoiding her reflection. If she were to look just then, she just might catch a glimpse of regret in the pale, exhausted face that stared back at her, and that just wouldn't do. That wouldn't do at all.

* * *

Two hours and a half-pot of coffee later, Paige pulled her favorite black pantsuit from her large, walk-in closet. She dropped her bathrobe to the floor, pulled the pants up her legs and fastened them. She slipped into a black, tank-style camisole, followed by the snug, fitted blazer. She glanced in the mirror.

Immediately her mood improved. She appeared professional, together, just as she preferred to, as she needed to on a day like today, when she felt anything but together. The cool, collected exterior was a ruse, but a necessary one. She couldn't conduct business, convince people of her ability to get the job done, if they thought the slightest breeze would blow her over. She couldn't meet Lucinda Amelia Perenna presenting anything but her best.

Today was an important day for her, important enough to command the façade. Finally, after years of struggle, her work was receiving the recognition it deserved. Word of her talent, her ability to find and then showcase the unique individual within, had spread. It wouldn't be long now and she would have the success she strove for. She knew this, for last week she'd received the one phone call that would make it happen for her.

Enter Lucinda Amelia Perenna, an immigrant who married well and grew to become one of the most influential women in San Diego. Recently widowed, she'd taken over her husband's money and used it to speak out against racial prejudice. Ms. Perenna had power and spent her life in the public eye. She had connections, knew all the right people...

And she'd called *Conroy Photography* to commission her self-portrait.

It continued to addle Paige's mind. Her,

Ms. Perenna had contacted her! This was her chance. The chance she'd been working for, the chance to prove herself. For if—no *when*, she corrected—when she completed this assignment, delivering to Ms. Perenna a finished product both women could be proud of, she would know true success. Her name would make its way into the upper echelons of San Diego society and her business would grow.

She smiled as she slipped into a pair of black pumps. She'd dreamed of this moment for so long...since that day so many years ago when she'd first peered through a camera viewfinder and discovered why she saw the world so differently from the other girls her age. She'd fought self-doubt, ignored the criticism of those who set out to defeat her, for this very moment. This was the beginning of many wonderful things to come.

A smile on her face, heels clicking across the hardwood floor, Paige made her way to the stairs and down to her studio. Anticipation filled her as she crossed to her darkroom—the place she'd sought refuge in after Sergeant Harrison's departure the night before. Sleep evaded her and so she'd done the only thing she knew would relax her—she'd worked. Her worries forgotten amidst the task before her, she'd worked long into the night without pause. Now, she would view her end result.

Several eight-by-tens hung from the

drying line, but even from this distance, Paige easily identified her favorite. The nude of the woman with her back to the camera was her best work yet. It captured both the woman's disposition, turned away from the world about her, and the woman's beauty. The former was obvious upon first meeting Gabrielle Sumner. She'd grown up on the street, struggling to show the world she was more, then quickly building barriers against those unable to see past her circumstances. The latter, Paige knew her client would not expect to see.

Gently, still weighing each photograph's strengths and weaknesses, she removed them from the drying line. She stacked her favorites and carried them with her out into the studio in search of her briefcase. Along the way, she also collected her cell phone, proof sheets and a notepad. She shoved all but the phone into her briefcase, grabbed her car keys and headed for the door.

She was already in her car, sunglasses perched atop her nose and engine idling, before she realized she hadn't activated her building's alarm system. Digging the keys to the studio out of the depths of her briefcase, she aimed the wireless remote at the front of her building and pressed the arm button.

Then she saw it. Confusion wrinkled her brow. Her hand crept to her throat while she waited for her mind to process what was taped to her door. From her distance, she couldn't say for certain, but it looked an awful lot like a photograph.

She slid out of the car and skirted the hood. It did little good to assure herself that her eyes were just playing tricks on her. Fear settled in even as her legs propelled her closer and closer to the door. Her heart made a beeline for her throat. Her vision blurred. "It can't be," she said aloud.

She never got the chance to find out.

The explosion came out of nowhere, disturbing the quiet of the morning. Paige flew through the air like a rag doll and bounced off the unforgiving bricks of her building. Pain burst through her body, drove the oxygen from her lungs. She struggled to regain her breath, to pull the thick, hot air into her starving lungs. Glass rained down upon her, hitting her legs, her stomach. Something large and hot crashed into her face, just above her left eye. Her vision doubled, tripled.

Her world spun in circles, then went dark.

CHAPTER FOUR

Paige stood before the desk sergeant, lukewarm ice pack pressed against her throbbing head. Body aching, in desperate need of a place to sit down, she listened to the man's instructions and silently cursed her bad luck. Her ears rang from the percussion of the explosion. Her world had yet to right itself. To top it off, the man behind the desk informed her that multiple flights of stairs stood between her and her destination. Joy at being alive was swiftly replaced with an intense urge to cry.

Only a couple hours before, she'd awoken to pulsing red-and-blue lights and thick black smoke. She'd opened her eyes to discover a paramedic checking her vitals, and a uniformed cop pacing in circles about her. Confusion filled her, intensified by the brutal slash of pain that whipped through her when she'd attempted to sit up. She'd blinked away blood, then glanced about her.

Someone had blown up her car. Her cherished 1959 pink Cadillac lay in pieces. Glass and debris covered her. She'd wanted to scream, to cry. She'd settled on white-hot rage.

It coursed through her, sustaining her as she reported to the crime scene investigators all that she knew. It fueled her on the ride to the hospital, where they'd put five stitches in her forehead, slipped her a painkiller, and tried their best to admit her for observation. And it would carry her up those flights of stairs to the detectives she sought.

"Anything so I can sit down."

She shifted her ice pack over her eye and winced as pain shot through her temple. A promise that she had someone at home to wake her every few hours combined with not letting on about the extent of her pain got her released from the hospital. She didn't want to stay there. She wanted her own home, her own bed. Before she could have those things, she had one last thing to do.

Which is why she'd given the taxi driver the address to the police precinct instead of her home. Why she stood here now, in the last place she ever thought she'd set foot in again.

One step at a time, she worked her way up the stairs. It was slow going, relying on the handrail as well as her anger as she turned to the right, then to the left. Ten more steps, then another right.

The noise hit her first, intensifying the ache behind her eyes. She stopped in her tracks, centered in the archway of the detective's division as she waited for the pain to ebb.

The room was full of people, young and old, male and female. They sat behind desks squared off against each other and typed on computers. They milled about in groups, deep in conversation. Some were like her, with expressions that ranged from shock to rage, confusion and fear. A woman sat near one of the metal, institutional-style desks and cried. The man at her side—a detective Paige guessed—bent his head closer to his computer screen, as though ignoring the woman's distress would make it disappear.

Phones rang. People barked out orders. A man, his enormous belly hanging out below the hem of his shirt, began to curse loudly. Suddenly, he came out of his seat and pushed his weight into the desk before him. The metal screeched as the desk shifted, pinning the officer behind it against the wall before he could even cry out. To Paige's horror, onlookers began to cheer. Two detectives jumped across their desks and wrestled the handcuffed brute to the floor. His curses intensified in both pitch and ingenuity.

Noise brought a pounding ache to her left temple. She lifted her hand and then flinched as the swollen side of her head protested loudly to her touch. Second thoughts assaulted her. Unease climbed up her throat. Suddenly rage was not enough to carry her into this room. She didn't like precincts, couldn't handle the noise, the smells. She couldn't handle the memories.

Her heart began to race. Her breath hitched. A sudden, instinctive urge to flee assaulted her and her body began to tremble.

Paige turned away. Her sore leg protested loudly as she hurried back to the stairs on feet that felt somehow disconnected. Clutching the ice pack in her left hand, she grabbed hold of the handrail with her right and started down.

The firm, gentle clutch of fingers circled her upper arm, caused her to stop abruptly. Only her death-grip on the handrail kept her from tipping forward and onto her face for the second time that day.

"Paige?" a deep, male voice intoned.

Sergeant Harrison. The small part of her mind that still functioned clearly recognized the voice—latched onto it. She turned, her movements slowed by her intense feeling of unreality. She struggled to keep her thoughts focused, to clear her mind of the panic that clawed at her, but the harder she tried, the greater her anxiety. The walls began closing in on her. She couldn't breathe.

"Paige? Are you all right?"

Run! the voice in her head screamed.

Survival paramount in her mind, she stepped away from him, down two steps. When his fingers tightened and he refused to release her, she made the mistake of lurching from his grasp. Her world began to spin, the stairs to tilt out from under her. She stumbled, her high heels lost traction and a second wave of fear surged.

Just when she thought she was going down, she dropped the icepack, placed her left hand beside her right on the handrail, and managed not to plummet down three flights of stairs. Her knees promptly gave out and she sank onto the step.

Ignoring the curious glances they drew, Justin crouched before Paige and said her name. When she didn't respond, he pushed the hair that had slipped from her braid behind her ear and tried again. "Paige?"

Fear burned brightly in her eyes. His insides tightened. Anger clawed at him. Her clothes were torn and spotted with blood. Her blood, based on the appearance of her face. A deep purple bruise marked her left temple, the eye beneath swollen badly enough that she probably couldn't see out it. An angry red gash, held together with tiny black sutures, bisected her eyebrow.

Someone had hurt her and he wanted to hurt that someone. Justin glanced from the hands still clutching the handrail to the eyes that had yet to focus on him. "Who did this to you?"

She visibly flinched at his harsh tone.

He needed to calm down. His anger was not helping the situation. As far as he could tell, her pupils appeared normal, but something was very wrong with her. He didn't know what had caused it, but she appeared trapped by her own terror, leaving him to figure out how to calm her.

Fisting his hands at his side, he forced his expression neutral and his voice gentle. "Paige, look at me. You're all right."

She didn't respond for a long, long moment. "Sergeant...Harrison?" Recognition came slowly. Her face paled and she moved as if to stand.

"No." Hand upon her knee, Justin did his best to ignore the tight knot that lodged in his throat when she trembled. "Don't try to stand just yet."

"I have to get out of here."

Not before he knew exactly what had happened to her. "Who did this to you?"

Her hand probed the side of her face. "I...don't know."

He didn't accept that she didn't know the person's identity and he didn't intend to let up until he got the name from her. But strongholding her didn't seem like the most intelligent way to go about it. He needed to try a different approach. "What brought you here?"

She met his gaze, her eyes bleak, disconnected. "I came to see you."

Irrationally pleased by her statement, he reached out and gently swept her hair out of her eyes, again tucking the strands behind her ear. The smooth warmth of her skin registered just before she bucked away from his touch.

What the hell was he doing? He'd spent the night thinking of her, of that insane moment outside her building when he'd ached to touch her. Thoughts of her haunted his sleep. The way she'd smiled at him, just smiled, and he'd been so damned aroused so damned fast, it had been mind-boggling.

But she wasn't smiling now and she didn't welcome his touch. In fact, he'd be lucky if she fully comprehended who knelt before her.

"I have to get out of here," she whispered, a bit unsteady.

"In a minute." First, he needed some answers. Like what had happened to her and who or what filled her with such panic that she could barely string her sentences together? He wished he could say it was just his cop's mind refusing to let loose the puzzle, but it was more than that. Much more. That alone was a huge and frightening admission. One he would never make aloud.

"You say you came to see me. Well, here I am. Why don't we go upstairs to my desk and talk?" Without giving her a chance to refuse, Justin stood. He grasped her elbow gently and helped her to her feet, his hold tightening minutely when she swayed. "Come on, Paige. It's not far."

Her eerie silence unnerved him as they made their way down the hall, as did her unsteadiness when he helped her into the chair near his and Allan's desks.

"What happened?" Allan questioned. His grim gaze moved over Paige's face. "Was she assaulted?"

"I haven't gotten a clear answer yet." Justin studied her as he sat down behind his own desk. Her eyes weren't nearly as glassy, but beneath the hand he placed on her shoulder, her body still trembled.

He had just poured himself a fresh cup of coffee when the desk sergeant called up to inform him he had a visitor. Upon hearing Paige's identity, he'd naturally assumed she was here because she'd remembered something pertinent to the St. John homicide. That she might be here to report an attempt on her person never crossed his mind. Until now.

Justin took a deep breath to counteract the twisting in his stomach. He picked up his coffee and offered it to her, pleased when her fingers curled around the mug. "Drink this."

Slowly, the warmth of the mug in her hand began to penetrate Paige's fog. Like waking from a dream, her tunnel vision cleared and the room about her registered. With a snap, her eyes focused and told her she sat in the detective's division, near a pair of desks butted up against one another.

Her lower lip slid into her mouth and she bit down firmly as she realized she didn't remember getting here. She focused her thoughts, but all that came to her were bits and pieces of images and voices. Confusion filled her, along with the tiniest twinge of fear. What had happened to her?

Her head pounded as she reached back into the hazy recesses of her mind for a memory, any memory past standing in the archway. She recalled the explosion, the trip to the hospital, and the taxi ride to the precinct. Her stomach churned as she remembered the fear that washed over her as she'd stopped in the archway. She'd turned away, then...stairs...a familiar voice...

She *thought* those were memories, but she just didn't know. It seemed the harder she tried to reclaim the missing time, the fuzzier the memories became.

Paige closed her eyes against a surge of nausea. She dragged a series of shaky breaths into her lungs. Moments passed before the hum of voices from the room about her seeped into her consciousness. One voice in particular stood out from the rest.

She opened her eyes and studied the boots nearest her. Up denim-clad legs, past the badge, the shoulder holster, until she met his concerned gaze. "Sergeant Harrison."

Her mind hurt from the conflicting

emotions that suddenly assaulted her. Confusion. Relief. Desire. He looked so together, so in control at a time when she felt anything but. She clasped the mug tightly and fought against the impulsive urge to crawl into his lap. Like a small child needing comfort, she wished for a strong set of arms wrapped about her. His arms.

"Are you with us now?"

Humiliation coursed through her, driving any renewed warmth from her limbs. She shifted uncomfortably in the hard wooden chair and gasped aloud when her injured knee bumped against the side of the desk.

He gave her a long, considering stare, as if conducting some sort of assessment of her. "Drink. The caffeine will help."

She drank.

"How are you doing? Feeling any better?"

She wished she remembered what she had done, what continued to elude her. Her cheeks burned with embarrassment. "I'm sorry."

"For what?"

"I don't know what happened. Just now, I...can't remember."

"Why don't we begin with who hurt you?"

"I don't know." When it seemed as if he would argue, she quickly added, "It's not what you think."

"Tell me."

"I think someone tried to kill me today."

68

"You think?"

"My car, someone blew up my car."

Shock colored his features but he recovered quickly. "With you in it?"

"Close enough."

"Are you all right?"

"I'm better than my Caddy." Paige laughed without humor then scowled. Her spine stiffened against the shock of fear that washed over her, driving away all traces of embarrassment. "Oh my God," she whispered. "Someone tried to kill me."

She felt faint and weak, on the verge of another panic attack. Her fingers were like cubes of ice and her stomach had yet to settle. Willing herself to calm down, she adjusted her grip on the mug and brought it to her lips, pausing as she caught sight of the desk before her.

The nameplate read, *Sgt. J. Harrison.* Her mind, eager for something else to think about, grasped hold of the puzzle. John, she pondered, or perhaps Jason or Jeremy? Had he used his full name when he'd introduced himself to her? If he had, she couldn't recall.

Paige sipped the coffee, letting the hot liquid slide down her throat and warm her from the inside. She slid her gaze to the second desk, the one to her right. Allan, that one was easy enough, his nameplate read *Sgt. Allan Simmons.*

She continued to drink the coffee while mentally sorting through all the names she knew that began with a 'J'. Somewhere around Joshua, her thoughts came to an abrupt halt. Her gaze shifted back to Sergeant Harrison's desk.

Her brows drew together as she took in the clean, uncluttered desk. Except for the telephone and a few pens, nothing littered the top of his desk, not files, nor writing on the blotter. She thought of her desk at home, the stack of photos and scattering of papers that covered it. She had the same blotter, an over-sized calendar, yet where his remained free of anything harsher than a stain to indicate the place his mug sat, hers was covered with scribbled notes, phone numbers, and doodles jotted down while on the telephone.

Something tickled her brain.

"How long ago did this take place?" Sergeant Simmons asked, pulling her from her thoughts. He held the same notebook as yesterday, his mouth set in a thin, tight line.

"A few hours ago. Around eight this morning."

"Did you report it when it happened?"

"Yes. I spoke with a...I think his name was Sullivan."

"Sullivan?" Sergeant Harrison asked. "Tom Sullivan, from the crime scene unit?"

"Yes. They were already there when I

came to. Someone from a neighboring business must have called in the explosion."

His gaze sharpened. "You lost consciousness? You should be in a hospital."

"I don't like hospitals."

"I don't like that we're only hearing about this now," Sergeant Simmons replied. He swiped up the phone and punched in a series of numbers. "Yeah, this is Simmons, let me talk to Sullivan. When he gets back make sure he calls me. That scene he's working involves my witness from the St. John homicide."

Sergeant Simmons' words drove home the reality of her situation. Her insides knotted tightly. She closed her eyes and tightened her grip on the coffee mug in her hand.

"Paige."

She startled. Her heart climbed into her throat and lodged there.

"Maybe you should start at the beginning. Tell us what happened this morning."

"I left my car on the street last night, which I don't normally do." Mindful of her bruises, she rubbed at the ache in her temple. Every heartbeat banged like a gong in her head, making it hard to concentrate. She kept her focus on Sergeant Harrison, grounded somehow by his nearness.

"After you left, I couldn't sit still so I worked until I was exhausted enough to sleep, and then went straight to bed." She glanced down at the warm mug in her hand, grateful to have something to hold onto. "I had an appointment this morning. I gathered my things and went out to my car."

"An appointment with whom?" Sergeant Harrison asked.

"Lucinda Amelia Perenna."

"The matriarch?"

"Yes. She wants to hire me to take her portrait."

He nodded. "Go on."

"I started my car. That's when I remembered that I had forgotten to set my security system. I dug out my remote, then I noticed the photograph taped to my door. I got out of the car to take a closer look at it."

"A photograph?" Sergeant Simmons commented as Harrison simultaneously asked. "What kind of photograph?"

"The same photograph that you showed to me yesterday."

Sergeant Simmons set his pen down and retrieved a file from atop his desk. From it he removed a photograph and held it out to her. "This photograph?"

"Yes."

"Are you certain it was the same photo?"

"Yes, I'm certain. It's my engagement photo. I'd know it anywhere."

His interest piqued, Sergeant Simmons straightened in his chair. "What happened to the picture? Did you touch it?"

"No, my car blew up before I got to it." The fear of seeing that photo returned, along with it, the remembered pain of crashing to the ground. Paige began to tremble. Coffee sloshed back and forth in the mug, then slipped from the edge and onto her knee. She rubbed at the stain absently.

"I think I hit the door before landing on the ground. I don't recall exactly, just the debris raining from the sky and the pain. Something hit me in the face and I passed out."

"What do you think are the odds our shooter left a viable set of prints on that picture?" Sergeant Harrison asked, his attention focused on his partner.

"Not good," Simmons replied.

Dread settled in the pit of her stomach. Paige shook her head, and immediately regretted it when pain stabbed her temple. She drew a deep breath. "There is no photo."

Two sets of eyes locked onto her. Simmons spoke first. "You just said there was a photo taped to your door."

"It was there before the explosion, but not when I came to. I asked both Sullivan and the paramedic, but no one recalled seeing anything taped to my door."

Sergeant Simmons gave her a dubious, narrow-eyed look. "I see."

"I know what I saw."

He dropped the photo back into the file on his desk and set it aside. "So you say."

"You don't believe me." She was surprised by how much that hurt. "You still suspect me of killing Leroy, don't you?"

"I believe in the evidence, Ms. Conroy, and until I have evidence that proves otherwise, you will remain a person of interest."

"You actually think I would blow up my own car to divert attention from myself?" Paige didn't give them a chance to respond. Suddenly, irrationally angry, she surged to her feet, pressing both hands upon the desk before her and grinding her teeth to keep the dizziness at bay. Her stomach lurched abruptly. She waited to make sure she wasn't going to be sick before turning to the one man she thought she could reason with.

"Are you a good cop, Sergeant Harrison?"

He gave her a curious look. "It's what I do best."

"Good. Then I at least have the comfort of knowing you'll find this person after they kill me, too."

"Paige."

Everything inside her went still. "This attack on me is connected to Leroy's murder and not because I am responsible for both acts. You're wrong about that."

She pinched the bridge of her nose. She'd faced her demons today in search of help. Paige hated police stations, resented the fact that she'd had to step foot in one again after so many years, but she'd done it. And for what? So they could accuse her of staging her own accident and lying about ever seeing the photograph?

"Why would someone want you dead, Paige?"

"I don't know."

"Is there anything you're not telling us about the events of yesterday morning? Something Leroy St. John told you, something you saw?"

"I told you everything."

"You're sure?"

"Yes." Under different circumstances, she might not have blamed them. She had no proof, just her word that she had seen the photograph. But her life was in danger. Someone had killed Leroy and blown up her car. She knew the two events were connected. The same way she knew the photograph had been there and that the uncluttered desk before her was important.

For a long, tense moment, Sergeant Harrison's dark gaze locked with hers. She caught a flash in his eyes that she didn't understand, then they went cool and disconnected—cop's eyes.

Her heart lurched. Her knees went weak.

"What do you want me to do?" he asked.

"I want you to believe me."

"My personal beliefs don't mean much if I

can't back them up with something concrete."

Pain, along with an odd sense of betrayal filled her. "Something more than the word of your prime suspect, you mean."

She straightened, prepared to walk away. His hand atop hers stopped her retreat.

Paige jolted with surprise, her gaze drawn to the top of the desk, to the sudden warmth of her fingers beneath his. She remained before him, frozen in place, unable to breathe as sparks of electricity shot up her arm.

She blamed it on the noise and the disturbance, on her morning and her unease over being in a police station after so many years. She blamed it on her concussion, anything, but the man before her. Not this man, who didn't believe in her.

"I don't know what to tell you. I have to follow procedure."

She stared down at him, pulse racing. "Of course you do. In the meantime, I'm supposed to do what? Sit back and wait for the person who failed to kill me this morning to try again?"

"You don't know for sure that he will."

"I don't know that he won't." With as much composure as she could muster, she pulled her hand out from under his, turned on her heels and limped from the room.

It wasn't until she reached the glass front doors that she caught her breath. She stepped to the side, out of the way of the flow of traffic, and wrapped her arms about her middle. Acid pooled in her stomach, her pulse galloped. She needed a few moments to pull herself back together.

Never had a man unnerved her so. Just one touch, just one look from those dark eyes of his and she was lost. Her knees knocked, her insides turned to jelly, and all reasonable thought left her. Even his occupation, her personal aversion to his job, didn't lessen his effect on her.

Tightening her arms Paige stared out at the parking lot. As her gaze settled upon a bright orange GTO, sunshine glinting off the polished rear bumper, she accepted the truth. She was in danger. Not just from a faceless assailant she feared would steal her life, but from a dark-eyed detective she feared would steal her heart.

And give it back to her in tiny little pieces.

* * *

Paige had barely cleared the archway before Allan turned to Justin. "Mind telling me what that was about?"

The accusing edge to his partner's voice set knots of tension settling across Justin's shoulders. He pushed aside his guilt over how hard he'd been on Paige, and focused on his partner. "What do you mean?"

"You want me to spell it out for you?"

"I guess you're going to have to because I have no idea what you're getting at."

"You were with her last night."

The accusation was clear, tossed between them like a gauntlet.

"Damn it, Justin, I don't like being left in the dark!"

"Are you asking what happened or accusing me of something?"

"I can guess what happened."

It was a struggle to stay calm. "You can, huh?"

"You have a reputation with women. You see one you want, you go after her. You crossed the line."

"I didn't."

"You crossed the line and got involved with a suspect. What's wrong with you? This is a tough case. I need you to be objective and you can't do that if all your thoughts are centered below the belt."

Anger began a slow burn inside him, rising to an icy rage. He'd done nothing wrong and never expected Allan to jump to such an unsubstantiated conclusion. "You'd think after all these years you'd know me better than that."

"You should have filled me in."

And told him what? That upon first meeting Paige Conroy he'd felt a connection with her that he'd never before experienced? That he had left work and made it all the way home before the urge to see her became too strong to ignore? That he'd actually showered and shaved in anticipation? Justin didn't think so.

He ran a palm over the knotted muscles in his neck. The bond between him and Allan was ironclad. They shared not only their professional lives, but their personal ones. This thing with Paige Conroy, whatever it was, Justin couldn't share. Because he didn't understand it yet himself.

It didn't really matter, because nothing had happened. He hadn't touched her. "If there's something you need to know, I'll tell you."

"Meaning mind my own business."

"Meaning there's nothing to tell."

Allan shook his head and sighed. "You've made a mistake."

Maybe, but it was his mistake to make. He stood, grabbed his worn, brown leather jacket off the back of his chair and pushed his arms into the sleeves with more force than was necessary. "Look, I appreciate what you're trying to do here."

"No, you don't."

"You're right, I don't."

"You're going after her, aren't you?"

Never before had he been so aware of a woman. Damn it, he'd spent the last twenty-four hours trying to banish her from his thoughts. But she'd gotten under his skin. How the hell had that happened? "She's in trouble."

"She could *be* trouble."

"Yes, she could be."

"But you'll risk it, our investigation, your job?"

Justin's thoughts veered to the courageous woman who stood before him yesterday, the green eyes that had locked with his as she denied any involvement in St. John's murder. He pictured the panic ridden woman who'd collapsed on the stairs, so obviously in pain, yet still managed not to break down. He scrubbed his hand across his face as he recalled how quickly he'd changed all of that by refusing to vocalize his belief in her innocence. Just before she'd turned away, he'd caught the welling of tears in her eyes.

Justin leaned forward, palms flat against the top of his desk. "I believe her, Allan."

Allan sighed audibly. "What can you do?"

What *could* he do? He knew all of what Allan said to be true. He was taking a risk he couldn't afford to take. The stakes were too high. Justin risked the very thing that defined him—his job. He'd been wise to walk away from Paige last night, wiser to let her walk away today. The only result of his getting involved, would be damage to his credibility.

So why even think about doing this?

"Justin?"

Allan sat unmoving, waiting for an

answer. Justin didn't have one for him. He didn't know what he could do to help. He just knew he had to do something. Like most cops, he didn't believe in coincidence. "Give me twenty minutes."

Allan mumbled something unintelligible under his breath. He pinned Justin in place with a look. "She may already be gone."

Justin smiled wryly. "Where's she going to go, Allan? She has no car."

Five minutes later, Justin's grim prediction proved to be true when he found Paige near the glass front doors of the station. She stood looking out toward the parking lot, arms hugged around her middle as if protecting herself from something only she could see. Sunlight streamed through the glass and across her face, emphasizing the dark bruising that marred her left temple, the brutal gash that bisected her eyebrow.

Frustration coiled his muscles like tightly wound springs. Her appearance, the fact that fear remained evident in her gaze, should have quelled his need for her. Diminished it at least.

It didn't.

He fisted his hands at his side to keep from reaching for her. He didn't want to feel attraction, didn't need the added protective urge that coursed through him. The circumstances were bad, the timing rotten. The fact that the feelings existed and he couldn't do anything about them had his jaw tightening painfully.

He expelled a frustrated breath and crossed to stand at her side. "I'd like to help."

She came alive at his words, beautifully, surprisingly alive. "And do what? Hold my hand?"

Justin blinked at the immediate change in her. He took a moment to study her before deciding he liked her like this, standing firm as temper sparkled in her eyes. Holding her own, even as her body trembled from a combination of fear and pain. Her head had to ache like the devil, yet she didn't crumble. Instead, she used her discomfort to fuel her anger and fight back.

She was really something, this woman who'd gotten to him on a level no woman before her had ever managed.

"If you want me to."

Turning abruptly, she faced him. He reached out and curled his fingers around her upper arm when she swayed.

"What..." Her lashes fluttered before she steadied herself. "What are you up to?"

"I have to be up to something to want to help you?"

Her eyes narrowed as emotions played across her face: anger, confusion, suspicion. "Not fifteen minutes ago I asked for your help and you turned me down."

He smoothed his palm down her sleeve and took her hand in his. Felt the same zing of electricity as the last time he'd touched her. "Now I'm offering it."

Paige visibly jolted. Her mouth opened, then closed. Her voice was unsteady as she finally said, "I don't need you to hold my hand."

"No?"

"No."

"Well then," with his free hand he pulled his business card from the inside pocket of his jacket and placed it into her upturned palm, sandwiching her hand between both of his. "In case you change your mind."

She glanced from him to their joined hands and back again. "Do you believe me?" she whispered.

He'd hurt her, he realized. In refusing to accept her word that what happened to her this morning was connected to her friend's murder, he'd clearly wounded her.

Releasing the card into her palm, he raised his hand and gently brushed his knuckles over her forehead, around her bruise and down her cheek. "I believe you."

The corner of her mouth turned up in the slightest of smiles even as she bit down on her lower lip. Justin sucked in a breath and worked to push it past the ball of need that whipped through him quietly, painfully, overriding his better judgment, his self-control. He shouldn't get involved, couldn't let himself care. But knowing it didn't stop him from saying the words that sealed his fate.

"I believe you. I don't think you had anything to do with St. John's death."

"What about my car?"

"If you aren't guilty of murder, why would you destroy such a beautiful piece of American engineering?" Her fingers squeezed his and he swept his thumb across her knuckle. "I'll find whoever's responsible. In the meantime, if you need to talk to me, about anything, my number is on the card."

As if they had a mind of their own, his fingers slid farther down her face. Reason told him to stop. Risking everything, his career, his reputation within the department for one little taste of her wasn't smart. He knew attraction faded and then disappeared. Knew love was nothing but a fabrication, a fairy tale he didn't buy into.

Slowly, his eyes never leaving hers, he trailed his fingers down her neck to settle at her throat. Beneath his thumb, her pulse skipped. She didn't pull away, as he half expected her to do. Maybe if she had, he could have resisted, tamped down the desire that burned in his gut. But she didn't. She didn't move at all. She just gazed at him, her features softened, her cheeks colored.

Need slammed through him, driving away the last of his resolve. He knew all the reasons why he shouldn't do this, but with the scent of her surrounding him, the soft feel of her skin beneath his fingertips, he no longer cared. In a matter of seconds, he made the conscience choice to push objectivity out the window.

Easing closer, Justin lowered his head.

CHAPTER FIVE

"Harrison, you old dog!"

Pain exploded along Justin's left side, driving the air from his lungs and forcing him to release Paige abruptly. He bit back the curse that echoed in his head as his nerve endings sang out in protest. His stomach cramped, his lungs wheezed. It was all he could do not to double over and empty his stomach on his boots.

Impervious to his pain, the officer who'd jovially slapped him on the shoulder continued. "Two days back and already the ladies are all over you."

A single bead of sweat trickled down his temple. He settled his hand upon his ribs and drew deep breaths in through his nostrils and out his mouth. White spots danced across his field of vision. His ears rang, making it near impossible for him to understand the words of the young officer at his side.

"I hope you're not looking for sympathy from the rest of us," the man exclaimed with a grin that quickly faded as he turned toward Paige and caught sight of her injuries. "Oh jeez, I'm sorry. I thought...I automatically assumed..."

Justin struggled to pull himself together enough to speak but the words wouldn't come. Helplessly he watched as Paige, her face pale and creased with confusion, stepped away from him. Her gaze locked with his, she raised her hand and pressed her fingers against her lips. The lips he'd yet to taste.

"I'm sorry," the officer repeated before he made his hasty exit.

Justin didn't move a muscle. Carefully, Paige bent to retrieve the fallen business card. Her hand shook hard enough she made two swipes before her fingers curled around it. A soft groan slid past her lips as she straightened and her hand lifted to her temple.

He envied her freedom to acknowledge her discomfort as he struggled against his own. Justin couldn't let anyone see the clawing ache that tore at him. He couldn't risk anyone asking questions. Holding himself totally still, he drew each shallow breath carefully, unable to do more than watch as Paige continued to walk backwards, each step taking her farther away from him.

"I have to go," she stated, her voice raw and unsteady, her breathing as ragged as his.

He'd just come close to screwing up. Big time. Yet he couldn't work up the emotion to be glad he'd been interrupted before taking that last step over Allan's proverbial line.

"Paige."

She stopped her retreat. For a moment, a heartbeat really, he thought she would reach out to him, renew the connection so abruptly broken.

"I can't...breathe in this place."

Disappointment sliced through him, tensing muscles already screaming out in pain. With the assault his injured side had just taken, he could do no more than watch as she slipped out the door.

He let loose a string of imaginative curses.

"That good, huh?"

Justin turned his head in the direction of his partner's voice, surprised to find Allan not more than ten feet away from him. From his nearness and the pinched expression he wore, Justin knew Allan had witnessed all that had transpired over the last ten minutes.

He waited as Allan crossed to stand at his side. Watched, as irritation turned to concern. "You aren't going to pass out on me are you?

God, he hoped not. "Is it that obvious?"

"Only if you know what to look for."

"Is anyone else looking?"

After a quick but thorough scan of the area, Allan replied, "No."

Justin doubled over. Hands on his knees, he drew air greedily into his lungs, and forced himself to hold it until he'd worked through the worst of the pain. This was agony, this stabbing ache that incapacitated him. Far worse than when he pushed too hard at therapy, worse than when he slept wrong. It was the worst pain he'd felt in weeks.

"Jesus, Justin, are you certain you're all right? Maybe you should—"

"Don't say it." His pain reduced to a dull ache, he straightened slowly. "I don't want to hear how I should have waited a few more weeks. I'm fine."

Disbelief colored Allan's features.

"I'm fine."

"You're a fool."

"Allan."

Allan raised his hands in surrender. "You didn't hear it from me." He turned away and abruptly changed the subject. "We should offer her a ride."

Justin followed Allan's gaze out the window and to the parking lot. Paige stood with her back to them, sunlight glinting off the red highlights in her hair. "I thought you were worried about me crossing the line?"

"You've already done that." Allan's voice held no accusation, just resignation. Justin flinched anyway. "I want to know why Sullivan didn't call us. I also want a look at the scene before they've cleared it. I'm willing to give her a lift, so I can do that. When we're done, I think you should let this go."

When he didn't immediately reply, Allan turned, his expression serious. "I mean it, Justin. Don't see the girl while on the job. Breaking policy just now wouldn't be your smartest move."

Hand still upon his side, Justin had to agree. Too-close scrutiny would be damaging to him at this point in his career. He couldn't afford to raise any red flags or attract too much attention. He needed to back off. Concentrate on what needed to be done to discover the identity of a killer. He needed to consider his career first and his uncommonly strong attraction to Paige second. He needed to be smart.

"Say good-bye to her, Justin."

* * *

Paige stood just outside of the yellow crime scene tape and studied the after effects of her violent morning. Glass from her shattered front window, and other miscellaneous debris, littered the ground directly in front of her building. She did her best to remain emotionless as crime scene technicians photographed and gathered what appeared to be the contents of her trunk. She failed immensely.

Exhausted defeat pulled at her. Tears burned the back of her eyes. Her head spun— the injury and the stench of burned rubber a lethal combination. Turning away from the destruction, she fought back a wave of dizziness.

What had she done? What could she possibly have done to make someone want to hurt her? What crime, real or imagined, had she committed against someone to make them turn against her this way? Why her? Why now?

Her head began to pound as the questions circled her mind. Too many questions without any answers. The answers, she feared, had died in that hotel room yesterday morning along with Leroy. Whatever had brought him across the country to see her, whatever he had to tell her face-to-face, had been enough of a threat to someone that they'd killed to keep him quiet.

Now, that someone wanted her dead, too.

She crossed her arms over her chest and rubbed her upper arms when a chill moved through her. Her gaze sought out and located Sergeant Harrison as he walked alongside his partner, surveying the scene behind the police tape.

She was scared, she admitted to herself. Really scared. Of the threat to her safety, as well as her growing desire for the man before her. Just looking at him now, her heart rate skipped, jumped a few beats before taking off in a race that had nothing to do with fear and everything to do with memory. He'd touched her today, in more ways than one. She had no business wanting him, but she did. To be held, stroked, comforted. It had been a long time.

In an unconscious move, Paige touched

the tips of her fingers to her lips as she recalled the feeling of being in his arms, the heat of his body and the gentle strength of his hand upon her neck. Beneath the warmth of the pre-summer sun, she took a moment to wonder, had his lips met hers, would his kiss have been soft and searching, or hot and passionate?

Her breath shallowed as she studied his strong, clean-shaven profile. The sharp, masculine cut of his jaw. The pulse-altering way he filled out his button-fly jeans and brown leather bomber jacket. She had vowed years ago to stay away from men like him, to never again make the same mistake with a man so obviously all wrong for her. But that didn't stop her admiring gaze from lingering, or her thoughts from scattering when he turned and caught her staring.

The dimple in his left cheek winked as his lips curled in an intimate smile.

It was a good thing he didn't use that smile very often. The quick curving of his lips and flash of dimple was a powerful package that triggered an even more powerful punch. Heat flooded her limbs. Her heart beat wildly against her ribs.

"Ms. Conroy." The man who'd identified himself as Tom Sullivan a few hours previously, ducked under the stretch of tape and moved to stand at her side. "I see you've received medical attention. What's the verdict?"

She didn't react for a full minute. His words were clear, she heard every one. Trapped as she was in the web of sexual electricity that sparked between her and Sergeant Harrison, she just couldn't seem to form her response. "Five stitches...and a concussion."

If he realized the reason for her stuttered reply, Sullivan didn't let on. "Those can be bad news. Do you have someone to stay with you for awhile?"

"Yes," she lied.

Sergeant Harrison's dark eyes remained steady on her. Her body grew warm as her own measured the broad span of his shoulders. Her eyes moved lower.

Her gaze hardened. The pounding in her temples intensified.

His hand lay against his side as he moved overly carefully around the burned-out shell of her car. In a sudden flash of clarity, she recalled his quiet, strained expression before she walked from the station. His quick intake of air that signified pain as the young officer slapped him on the shoulder and exclaimed, *"Two days back and already the ladies are all over you."*

Two days back?

His clean, uncluttered desk sprang to mind and suddenly the fog she'd felt trapped in since the explosion cleared. Cold realization slammed into her. The gravity of her error pressed down upon her.

"I..." She'd really stepped into this one. Chest tight, she pushed a hurried explanation from between her lips. "I need to sit down. Please excuse me."

Her pace hurried, she sidestepped the police tape, moving away from Sullivan, from the wreckage, and around the corner of her building to a rarely used side entrance. Memory echoed along with the pounding beat in her head.

Two days back...I hope you're not looking for sympathy from the rest of us...

She'd managed to forget. The shock. The horror. She'd pushed it aside, at least for a while. Suddenly, memories of her past flooded her. A chill snaked up her spine.

How could she have been so blind? It had been right in front of her the whole time. Only she'd been too distracted to see it. Her stomach ached. There was such a terrible pressure there that she pressed her right hand against it.

Body trembling, she stood before the door she'd just unlocked and stared blindly at the keys nestled in the palm of her left hand. She struggled to focus her thoughts, to bring her last vestige of energy together and to face this new turn of events. But as it had for days now, the urge to hide away, to run from that which she feared most won out. She turned the handle of the door.

"Are you all right?" Sergeant Harrison

voiced from just behind her.

With her thoughts so inwardly focused, she hadn't heard his approach. "Of course." The tremble in her voice said otherwise. "I just need to sit down."

"I'll come with you."

"No." Her stomach ached, her head swam—she thought she might get sick. "Thanks for the ride home."

"Paige?"

When his hand settled upon her shoulder, she sucked in air against an undeniable longing and turned abruptly. Her above average height of five-eleven combined with her heels put her at eye level with him and gave her an unparalleled view of the stricken look that crossed his face at her next words.

"Two days back," she said with conviction.

He recovered quickly. "I've had a bit of time off."

"Please, don't tell me."

"Paige, I—"

"I don't want to know." She already knew. It all made sense now. The exact details didn't matter for they didn't change what she had to do. "I can't do this again."

"Let me explain." His hand shifted to her face, circled her eye. The tips of his fingers slipped into her hair as his thumb wiped across her cheek.

She closed her eyes and briefly drank in

the pleasure of his touch. "I don't even know your first name."

"Justin."

"Justin, that's nice."

He stepped closer.

"I don't date cops." Her words stopped him cold, as she knew they would. His lips thinned and his hand fell away. "Whatever this is between us, it could have been good. But I won't make the same mistake twice." She reached behind her and pushed the door open. "No more cops," she whispered with a shake of her head.

He didn't respond, just stood his ground, hands in his pockets.

"Good-bye, Justin."

The warm rush of humid air greeted her as she pushed through the door and into her studio. Without turning to see if he'd left, Paige closed the door behind her. With a low groan, she dropped to sit upon the bottom step of the stairs leading to her living quarters. She pulled her hair from its braid and ran her fingers through the strands to ease the strain on her scalp. She toed off her shoes and unbuttoned her blazer. She fought the urge to cry.

Justin. His name was Justin. After years of yearning, of searching for someone who could arouse her both physically and emotionally, she'd finally stumbled upon the man. His name was Justin and he too closely paralleled the one part of her life she would never repeat.

She'd done the right thing in ending it before it could even start. She'd done the right thing.

So why did she feel as if she'd just been tossed against the side of her building for the second time that day?

* * *

Not until he crossed the threshold to his home and locked the door behind him, did Justin give in to the strain of the day. His body ached, screamed in protest of the crack on the shoulder the young officer delivered and the stiff, unyielding stance he'd maintained since the incident. He'd held tough, showed little weakness and no complaint, and he'd paid dearly for it.

His shoulders sagged beneath the weight of his exhaustion as he moved with uncharacteristic slowness through his kitchen, to the desk situated in the corner of his living room. Dropping his duplicate copy of the St. John file onto the glass-covered mahogany, he melted into the executive chair. With careful, precise movements, he released and removed his shoulder rig from his side. He opened the center drawer of the desk.

The lone content of the drawer rolled forward and bounced off the handle, stopping label up. Justin stared down at the small, brown bottle and frowned. His name, printed in bold script, stared back.

He hated that bottle and its little white pills, hated everything it represented. Weakness and pain were his enemy, his inability to make it more than forty-eight hours without medication, his curse. He worked hard, did everything and more than the therapist prescribed and yet every day the ache persisted—a constant reminder of his vulnerability.

Hell, he should be happy to be alive, with all his faculties intact. What was muscle and nerve damage compared to paralysis, even death? So what if he had days so bad that he questioned his ability to continue working the job he loved. He could always put in for a transfer. After all, a cop who rode a desk was still a cop, right?

His fingers tightened on the prescription bottle of pills. "I'd rather be dead," he admitted aloud.

Justin set his jaw. Frustrated and worn out, he palmed a pain pill. He needed the rest the prescription narcotic would bring him, no matter the muddled senses and loss of concentration he knew from experience he would suffer tomorrow. Without sleep, the pain would have a tighter hold on him, become even harder for him to ignore. If the price for that sleep was loss of mental acuity and a bad attitude, so be it. His mood was already just this side of foul.

Scowl firmly in place, he swallowed the pill dry. He flipped open the case file he'd brought home with him and began reading through what little information he and Allan had managed to gather. Though he knew the meager contents backwards and forwards, the impending arrival of Detective Jon Brennan, St. John's partner from Boston, drove him to take a closer look. There had to be something there, something he'd missed. He resolved to find it.

With single-minded determination, he dove into the file. An hour later, he'd only made it half way through the information when the telephone at his right rang. His thought processes interrupted, he answered abruptly. "Yeah?"

"I always did like a man with manners," a female voice responded dryly.

Justin smiled, genuinely happy to hear from the most important woman in his life. "Hey, Mom, how are you?"

"I'm glad you asked. I'm doing wonderfully. And I assume you are as well. You're back to working with Allan, is that right?"

"I'm back on active duty, yes."

"That's wonderful, dear. I know how eager you are to get back into the swing of things. You're taking care of yourself, staying safe? You know I worry about you."

"I know you do, Mom, but you don't need to. I'm fine."

"Good. That's good."

Sudden, uncharacteristic silence came from the other end of the phone line. Justin waited, at once uncomfortable. Something was wrong with this. One thing about his mother, she didn't call often, but when she did he needed to be prepared for one whirlwind conversation. Thelma Kincaid tended to store her thoughts, file them away and then spill them upon him about once every two or three weeks in the most exhausting conversations he ever engaged in.

He always looked forward to those calls.

"What is it, Mom? What's the matter?"

"Nothing's the matter."

She paused just long enough for him to know she was lying. Anxiety tightened the muscles in his side, shot pain down his arm. The urge for nicotine swamped him. Justin leaned back in his chair and waited for her to get to the point.

"I just called to see if you'd meet me for dinner Thursday night?" she continued after a moment.

"Of course I will." Her voice was too chipper, her cadence hesitant. She had something to say all right, and the longer it took her to come out and say it, the more uncomfortable he became. "Spill it, Mom, you know you want to."

"You always did know me too well. Okay, here goes. I met a man. His name is Nicholas and he's asked me to marry him."

"Shit!"

"I've agreed."

He scraped his fingers through his hair. "Aren't you a bit old for this?"

"I am fifty-seven years old. I am not dead."

Her steely tone told him he'd hurt her feelings. The knowledge did nothing to improve Justin's rapidly disintegrating mood. He slid open the desk drawer on his right, then slammed it shut when he remembered he didn't smoke anymore.

Why did she keep doing this? What was the point of constantly setting herself up to fail? He loved his mother, would do anything for her. Which is why he felt the need to protect her from herself.

All his life he'd watched her go through men. She chased love, hunted after it like her life just wasn't complete without it. When she found it, at least what she believed to be true love, things were good. But it never lasted, and in the end, she always wound up hurt.

It was after her second failed marriage, when he was but twelve-years-old, that he vowed never to love, never to risk his heart. Thelma Kincaid might believe in love everlasting and commitment, but he'd witnessed firsthand just what that brought her— heartache and pain. As a result, Justin kept his encounters with women light and carefree. Never remaining with any woman long enough for her to get any ideas about the future.

"Mom, when are you going to learn?"

"What would you have me learn, Justin?"

"It's okay to be alone," he assured her. He refused to admit that he might also be assuring himself. "There's no shame in it."

"There's no shame in wanting more, either. I don't know about you, but I do not wish to die alone, with only my own arms about me."

His throat tightened painfully. A few months ago, he would have brushed aside her concerns, never believing such a thing possible. "I'll hold you, Mom."

"I'm more concerned with who will hold on to *you*," she replied passionately. "Your aversion to love is not normal. Random affairs are not healthy."

"I don't have affairs—"

"Of course not. Affairs require some modicum of intimacy. You won't even give a woman that much."

Her words hit with unerring accuracy. Had the subject been different, less personal, he might have smiled at their identical temperaments. Instead, he could only listen as she continued, her tone and attack becoming that which only a mother could deliver.

"Listen to us, snapping at each other like children. We've always been close, Justin. Haven't we always been close?"

"Yeah, Mom, we've always been close."

"Yes. Maybe too close, but I feel I can tell you this."

"Mom, I—"

"I was wrong to turn to you after your father left us. Wrong to make it your sole responsibility to keep me happy. I'm sorry for doing that. You were too young. You were struggling with your own pain."

"You did your best."

"I'm not so sure. What I did, taught you nothing but the pain of loving someone. It's not all pain, Justin. It's joy, excitement, and the most wonderful thing anyone can experience. To love someone, to have someone return that love is…it's…"

"Temporary," he supplied, then immediately regretted his comment.

"It's a risk, certainly, but what is life if not a risk?"

"I'm a cop, Mom. In my line of work, risk can get me killed."

"You're also a man, Justin."

He didn't know what to say to her. She didn't give him the opportunity.

"Just tell me, are you happy?"

Was he?

"I'm happy," he assured her. He wondered whether either of them truly believed it.

"Fine. Good." She offered no further argument. "Dinner. Thursday night, eight o'clock."

"I'll be there."

Justin pushed his thumb and forefinger against his closed lids as he hung up the phone. He reached out blindly and closed the case file. Trying to get anything done after that conversation would be a waste of time. He couldn't think past the hurt he'd just caused his mother, by not showing proper enthusiasm over her engagement. If he hadn't been in pain, already angry about his own limitations, perhaps he could have managed to feign happiness for her benefit. But with fatigue pressing down on him, he just couldn't get overly enthused about something history told him was a washout.

Thelma Kincaid married. *Again*. He could hardly believe it.

Pushing out of the chair, Justin headed for his bedroom. He changed into a pair of sweatpants and dropped atop the bed. He stared at the ceiling as his mother's words played in his head.

"It's not all pain."

You could have fooled him. He'd been there, holding her as she cried, comforting her as best he could. He'd witnessed firsthand the effect her 'true love' had on a heart. No way he'd risk his own.

"I don't want to die alone…"

Stretching his left arm above his head, he moved his right hand to his side as his thoughts shifted to how close he'd come to doing just that. Through the thin material of his shirt he fingered his scars—the round, puckered mark near his shoulder and the larger, jagged line at his side. His lids drooped, his body relaxing as the medication began to take effect. As his pain eased, his mind drifted back to how he'd gotten them.

He'd been unstoppable, mixing long hours on the job with late nights with the ladies. He'd been impulsive, insatiable and invincible.

At least he'd thought so.

Veterans of war say you hear every bullet that passes you, but not the one that hits you. Justin could verify that statement. It had been the worst day of his life, both professionally and personally. And it had only gotten worse. He'd been strung out, wrung dry and feeling far more than his thirty-five years. To this day, he wondered had he been at the top of his game, would he have made such a perfect target? He would never know.

The worst part of it was that it hadn't even been one of his cases that put him in the line of fire. He'd simply been in the wrong place at the wrong time and faced with a man with too little money to support a growing drug habit.

His memory, whenever he allowed himself to recall that fateful day, played the events out before him as if they'd happened to someone else. He watched, like viewing a film in slow motion, as he pulled his police issue beater into the strip mall in search of a pack of smokes. In his mind's eye he saw himself exit the vehicle and start across the lot toward the convenience store. He'd been reaching for his wallet when the front door of the store swung open and a disheveled man in a hooded sweatshirt stepped out.

The next few minutes were a mixed blur of images and impressions. He saw the man's face, his shifting eyes and hardened expression as he spotted the shield clearly visible on Justin's belt. As a trained observer, the best at what he did, Justin should have spotted the .38 aimed at his chest before he felt the burning pain in his side. He should have gotten the drop on the guy, or at least gotten out of the line of fire. Instead, he'd gone down hard and fast.

Although difficult to believe, luck had been on his side that day. He lay there, unconscious and vulnerable, a perfect target, yet the shooter had cared more for his next fix than for finishing him off. Cash in his pocket, the man simply ran off. The store clerk, left unharmed, called for an ambulance, and then worked to slow Justin's bleeding until its arrival.

He came to in the hospital, surrounded by the unsettling silence of the intensive care unit, agonizing pain in his lung and an empty room. The bullet had torn into his shoulder, just below his clavicle, causing muscle and nerve damage. It hadn't stopped there. From the amount of damage, the doctors concluded it then ricocheted, puncturing his lung and fracturing two ribs before coming to rest. The combination of blood loss, exhaustion and a two-pack-a-day nicotine habit resulted in pneumonia. Blind luck was credited for keeping him alive.

The fight back was long and hard, the endless nights alone the most difficult to face. What he wouldn't have given for someone to have been there for him, just once during those long agonizing nights of recovery when pain and doubt would assault his already weakened senses and cause him to question. Would he recover enough to return to active duty, to the job he loved? Would he suffer any lasting consequences? Would he ever find the peace he used to in his solitary lifestyle, or would he forever hear only the silence of the night?

As that very silence settled around him, Justin answered the questions that had plagued him so those six months before. Hours of therapy repaired his mobility enough to return to active duty. Occasionally, he still experienced weakness in his left arm, but it wasn't anything he couldn't work through. As for his solitary lifestyle, more than once during those first few weeks of recovery, he'd almost died. Alone. Lonely.

Again, Thelma's words played through his mind. He didn't want to die alone any more than his mother did. But marriage, commitment, these things went against every lesson life had taught him. He didn't want marriage or commitment. He just wanted companionship.

He wanted Paige Conroy.

When had she done it? When had she stolen past his defenses? He didn't get involved. Sure as hell never became hung up on one woman, the way he seemed to be hung up on Paige. What was it about her that he couldn't seem to shake her image from his mind? And why her and not any of the other women he'd known?

Sleep pulled at him, but his mind refused to shut down. He fisted his hands as her image came to him, beaten and bruised for sure, but still able to rattle him like no other. Her smile, her scent—not perfume, but something far more subtle that he had yet to place. The way she said his name, her voice like a caress against his flesh, just before cutting him off at the knees with four little words.

"I don't date cops."

Frustration burned like acid in his gut.

His shoulder throbbed. He pushed the heel of his palm into his chest and rubbed. Stopped suddenly when he realized his focus centered above his heart, instead of his side.

Disgusted, he set his jaw and told himself to stop acting like a fool. He didn't know the woman well enough to feel anything stronger than frustration, perhaps resentment. His reaction to her sudden dismissal was ludicrous, what should he care that she didn't want to see him again?

But he had to admit he did care. He cared a great deal. And in his melancholy mood he couldn't shake the unfairness of the situation he found himself entrenched in. Paige Conroy didn't date cops. With her past, her firsthand experience of the worst side of law enforcement, he couldn't blame her. But hell, it wouldn't surprise him to learn he bled blue. He was all cop.

He didn't know how to be anything else.

CHAPTER SIX

She dreamt of echoing gunfire and the stench of death. Of sunny days, quiet evenings, and pain far greater than that of the flesh. Paige leaped into wakefulness with a jolt that caused her stomach to lurch. She stared at the darkened ceiling above her, heart skittering in her chest, nerves snapping and popping as her temple pounded.

It had been two days since her concussion diagnosis. Two days of nausea and lightheadedness and, contrary to popular medical belief, two days of insomnia. She slept in fits and surges, dozing off only to awaken abruptly when the demons of her mind chased her into alertness. She kept waiting for it to end, for her life to move forward, for her body to heal. Yet her pain persisted.

She nearly accepted it, this new ripple in what once had been a very stagnant life. She turned a blind eye to her bruises, her discomfort and, in a vain attempt to feign normalcy, she worked. But work took concentration and concentration became impossible with her boarded-up front window casting the room in darkness, even at the brightest hour of the afternoon.

Mindful of the stitches at her brow, Paige pushed her fingers into her hair and away from her face. She pulled her knees to her chest and allowed herself a moment of dejection. She yearned for someone to confide in, to talk to about her nightmares, her worry and her fear. She might be an independent, self-reliant woman, but she wished she had someone to lean on.

Her eyes searched through the darkness to the sofa upholstered in pale, muted tones and tossed with pillows in varying shades of green. The urge to curl into the corner of it, to dial the telephone and reach out for reassurance was strong. In the past, whenever she needed someone, whenever her world fell apart and she needed a shoulder to cry on, she'd gone to her father. Closest to her in temperament and personality, he understood her in a way that her mother never would. He was her rock, the one person she could count on to always be there for her. He would be there for her now. All she had to do was pick up the phone.

She couldn't do it. She couldn't risk exposing her father to any of this. There was no guarantee that by his standing at her side, she would be any safer. Stronger, perhaps, but the risk to him far outweighed the promise of temporary stability. She would have to face this—alone.

Knowledge brought an ache, deep down in the center of her being. When had she done this? When exactly had her search for independence, her escape from the pain her complete reliance on Rick and his subsequent death brought her, managed to alienate her from the rest of the world? In the past three years, she'd not just become self-reliant, she'd become lonely.

And so, in the darkness of the midnight hour, when she could no longer deny what during the light of day she possessed the strength to ignore, Paige had nowhere to turn. She blinked against her pounding headache and accepted the truth. She couldn't sleep, couldn't work, couldn't even eat—not from the return of lost memories or the discomfort of her injuries, but from fear. Fear that coursed through her like a living, breathing entity. Fear that grew stronger with each passing day until even her security system provided little reassurance. Swallowing past the lump in her throat, she admitted she had never been more afraid.

Until the sudden, unmistakable burst of breaking glass from her studio pushed her terror to a new level.

Paige realized she was on her feet only when the movement brought about a surge of nausea. She fisted her hand against her abdomen and listened, waiting for the din of her alarm, for any further hint as to the basis of the sound. It couldn't be an intruder. There was no way past her security system, no way in without triggering the alarm.

"Get a grip," she whispered. But the silence that hung throughout her building failed to calm. Her discomfort shot up another notch. Skin prickling, she glanced over her shoulder and located her telephone. Two days before, she'd placed Justin's business card alongside it. Absently she wondered if he'd had late night phone calls in mind when he'd given her the card.

Seconds later, the ominous creak of dry hinges as her darkroom door swung open had her whirling back toward the stairs. Her heart stopped. When it started again, it was skipping beats. Breath heaving, Paige slowly backed up and picked her keys off the bedside table. She depressed the alarm button on her security remote once, twice, biting back panic when her system failed to respond. With a last searching glance through the darkness, she snatched her phone up and tiptoed toward the bathroom, the only room in her house with a door that locked.

Her sudden indrawn breath and gasp of pain sounded unbearably loud in the silent room. She fought against the urge to crumple to the floor as her weight came down upon something unidentifiable in the dark and her injured knee twisted painfully. The relative safety of a locked door overshadowing any concerns about noise, she quickened her pace, limping noisily toward the door a few feet away.

Finally, she was there, twisting the lock and backing against the cool tile wall. She punched in the number.

"Nine-one-one. What's your emergency?"

"Someone's in my house."

* * *

The dark atmosphere of the dimly lit bar fit Justin's mood. At this late hour, occupancy was sparse and continued to dwindle as couples paired up and made their way to the door. That suited him. He didn't want laughter and camaraderie. He wanted to be left alone to unwind, to think. And this was just the place to do it, complete with frosted mugs and enough nicotine in the air to let him know that they didn't always follow the smoking ban.

Justin drew the secondhand smoke into his lungs, welcoming the burn as he lifted his mug toward his lips. He fought a sigh when the burn took on an edge sharp enough to bring tears to his eyes. A fitting end to a day that had started out bad and gone downhill from there.

The mirror before him reflected the bartender's moves as he placed a neon-pink drink before a doe-eyed blonde at the opposite end of the bar. A small part of his brain acknowledged the inviting smile the blonde sent him, but his energy remained focused elsewhere.

He awoke that morning to a clawing ache in his side and weakness in his left arm. A scalding hot shower helped ease the pain but did little to soothe his foul temper, so that by the end of his shift, with no telephone records, no coroner's report and no Detective Jon Brennan, Justin snapped and bit at everyone who dared speak to him. Which left tensions high, relationships strained and a partner who'd taken about all of him he could take, eager to return to the solitude of his home and the loving arms of his eight-months-pregnant wife.

Which in turn left Justin more than a bit envious.

Yet his day had been far from over. A glitch in the precinct's voice mail system that left everyone unable to retrieve their messages, combined with him having left his cell phone on his kitchen counter, meant he'd missed the call from his mother informing him of a change in the evening's plans. So by the time he retrieved his cell, changed his clothes and stepped through the door of the pre-determined restaurant to meet his mother for dinner, he was over an hour late.

Pushing his fingers through his hair, he gave his reflection an acrid smile. As lousy as his day had been, nothing could have come as more of a surprise than when, over a plate of prime rib, he discovered not only did his mother's new beau not put him off, but he actually liked the man. Justin still couldn't wrap his mind around it. Nicholas Parsons, corporate CEO, seemed like a decent guy. With manners as impeccable as his suit, he'd been funny, attentive and appeared to genuinely care for Thelma. In fact, throughout the meal, Parsons hung on Thelma's every word.

Maybe it was stress and frustration making him soft, but the evening gave him hope. Something about the couple, the shared intimacies and the joy that shone through whenever his mother looked at the man she planned to marry just felt...right. For his mother, of course, he reserved his hope for his mother. He wouldn't consider the possibility there just might be someone out there, a partner, for him. He didn't want a partner. He wasn't the marrying kind. He knew first-hand that attraction dulled, need faded. And love? He didn't believe in the emotion. Not between a man and a woman. Not the forever kind. In the end, someone was always left hurting, bleeding as the other moved on.

No, he decided, setting his jaw. Marriage wasn't for him. Still, he thought of Allan and Suzanne and wondered. What it would be like to have someone he could care about. Someone who cared about him in return.

Out of the corner of his eye, Justin

watched the blonde, frothy pink drink in hand, sashay her way to him. She slipped onto the stool at his side and leaned forward in just a way to give him an unobstructed view of what not long ago would have attracted him like a moth to a flame.

"Hi, my name's Candi, with an 'I.'"

Her voice was too throaty, her line too obvious, and the hand she placed high on his thigh had absolutely no effect on his heart rate.

"What's your name?"

He slid her a look and said nothing as she leaned even closer so that her breast brushed his arm. The overpowering scent of her perfume engulfed him.

"You do have a name, don't you, handsome?"

The trill of his cell phone stopped the none-too-subtle brush-off that hovered on the tip of his tongue. He managed to dislodge her hand before answering. "Harrison."

"Justin?"

"Paige?" The reception in the bar was touch and go. The line crackled and hummed. Yet the strain in Paige's voice came through loud and clear. As did her fear. Any thought of unwinding faded away as quickly as the blonde at his side and the noise about him.

"You gave me your business card," she reminded him unnecessarily. "You said to call...if I needed anything."

The tremble in her voice tightened his chest. Tossing a few bills on the bar, Justin slid off his stool, shoved through the bar door and out into the parking lot. Immediately, the reception cleared. "Paige, has something happened? What's wrong?"

"I...need you."

"I'm on the way."

*　*　*

With the glow of the pulsing red and blue lights bouncing off the darkened buildings and drawing him like a lighthouse beacon, Justin could only assume he'd arrived at the correct destination. He pulled his GTO to the curb, angled between the two police cruisers, and raked his gaze across the scene. It would help if he knew what he was looking for. But demanded explanations had been the farthest thing from his mind when Paige called, and something she hadn't voluntarily offered.

I need you.

He should be ecstatic, happy as hell to hear her utter the words he'd hoped for from the moment he'd first laid eyes on her. Instead, fear—cold and dark—slid through his veins. Paige needed him. But not for the myriad of erotic images he could call to mind with only the slightest effort. No, her tone, the knife-sharp edge of alarm, told him everything he needed to know, driving him from his stool and halfway to the exit before she uttered more than his name. Paige had called for the badge, not the man behind it.

Pushing away the lingering disappointment, Justin popped the trunk of his car and removed his shoulder holster and sidearm from the leather duffel he habitually carried within. He took a few moments to fasten his Glock into place. A few more to pull himself together.

Previous visits allowed him to piece together what little he could garner in the darkness. The flicker of reflection from the tape cordoning off the front of the building remained unchanged, as did the glass that littered the ground. The broken front window was boarded from the inside, keeping curious eyes from what stood behind it. Keeping him in the dark.

With nothing to go on, no visible sign as to Paige's recent trauma, he could only imagine what brought him to her. Something he preferred not to do since experience gave his imagination a much too graphic picture.

"Help you?"

Shield clipped to his belt, he faced the uniform suddenly at his side. "Paige Conroy." *Is she Okay? In one piece? Broken and bleeding?* He left the melodramatic questions unspoken and worked to remain focused. "Where is she?"

"Second floor. She said something about a friend coming. I guess that would be you."

"I guess it would."

Her studio was lit up like the sky on the Fourth of July. Once inside, a cursory glance provided no more clues than the exterior of the building. Again, with the exception of the two cops at the base of the stairs, everything appeared the same as on his last visit. Nothing seemed out of place, missing or broken. Everything appeared nice and tidy. Too nice and tidy, he decided as his scalp prickled. The need to see Paige, to uncover the urgency of her situation, drove him up the stairs.

On the second level, he stepped into what he knew to be her living area. Where her studio was a sea of neutrals, of cool professional lines, the upstairs he found to be more personal. Its pale upholstered furniture stood out against the cherry hardwood floors and forest green walls. Spacious and open, one room artfully blended into another while remaining discernible by the unique placement of furniture. Windows covered two walls of the space, and potted plants sat everywhere, so lush and overgrown that they resembled small trees.

Yet it was not the homey atmosphere, the myriad of artwork, both hers and others, that drew his attention. Even the over-sized bed, complete with netting that hung from the ceiling to attach to the four posts couldn't compare to the woman pacing before it.

In place of her usual business suit, Paige

wore silk boxers and a tee—testament to the fact that she had either been pulled from bed or on her way when her evening abruptly turned. Her hair hung down, long and silky around her shoulders, dark ends swishing a few inches above her trim bottom as she abruptly turned and started in the opposite direction.

The sight of her did what the blonde at the bar had not. That quickly, cold fear turned to hot desire. His body tightened, his pulse tripped along at an increased rate. Since she had yet to notice his arrival, he took a few moments to just look at her, to see with his own eyes that she was in one piece.

As he watched, she continued her journey, back and forth before that grand bed. Despite her cool dismissal of him two days before, he wanted to gather her close and channel that pent up energy into something more fulfilling. He closed his eyes against the wave of longing, only to feel her in his arms, to hear her pleasure as he slipped inside her.

"Sergeant, what can I do for you?"

Justin blinked once, twice, to clear the sudden, unbidden image from his mind. Damn, he was hard as a rock. He tried to moderate his breathing, forced each deep breath as he strode for calm. "I'm here for Ms. Conroy," he informed the lone officer at his left.

She turned at the sound of his voice, and like every time their eyes met, something hot and dangerous sparked between them. They stared at each other for a long, intense moment as the air between them buzzed and crackled. Hunger rose like a white-hot wave to wash over him.

He didn't stand a snowball's chance in hell of finding calm anytime soon.

Setting his jaw, Justin faced the uniform. "What can you tell me about what happened tonight?"

"Break-in, or so she says."

"You don't believe her." He didn't phrase it as a question. The man's tone held the answer.

"Sir, there are no signs of forced entry and nothing missing. In fact, the alarm system was tripped by the first on the scene." In a move guaranteed to press his importance, the officer settled his hands upon his utility belt and flared his chest. "Ms. Conroy admits to being overtired and overstressed. What with her last altercation barely two days ago, she's letting her imagination get the best of her, hearing things that aren't there."

Unimpressed, Justin leaned forward and checked the name on the man's severely starched uniform. "It could be, Officer Carlton, that she's justifiably afraid and hearing things that are there." He met the man's glare. "What with her last altercation just two days ago."

Carlton's self-importance still firmly in

place, he puffed his chest out a few more inches. The lines of his face settled into a frown.

"Why don't you take off, go file your report. I'll handle Ms. Conroy." For a good sixty seconds, the officer held his ground. Twenty more, he looked as if he might argue. And then, just when Justin thought things were going to get ugly, Officer Carlton turned and headed for the stairs. Justin didn't wait any longer. He crossed the room to Paige.

She looked terrible. How long had it been since she'd gotten any sleep, something to eat? In the four days he'd known her, she'd dropped enough weight that her cheeks no longer appeared sculpted, but hollowed, the vibrant green of her eyes, dulled.

As predicted, she had one hell of a shiner. Varied in shade from black to raspberry, it covered her left eye from just above her brow to her cheekbone. He could tell her, from personal experience, that her bruise would turn a hideous shade of green before fading. Instead, he chose to keep that bit of information to himself.

"How are you doing?"

She curled her bottom lip between her teeth and studied him as if considering her answer. "I'm better than when I called you."

"Some of your swelling has gone down. Does your head still hurt?"

She stiffened her spine, pulled her strength around her like a blanket. "Not much."

Justin tucked his hands in his pockets, determined to remain cool and detached, the competent professional, just as she wanted him to be. He nearly broke out in a cold sweat from the effort to keep from reaching for her. He wanted to touch her, hold her. She didn't appear to need his support, definitely wouldn't welcome it. The desire was there, just the same. "What happened tonight?"

"Someone broke into my house."

He had to hand it to her, even faced with Carlton's patent disbelief, she held tough to her belief of an intruder. She must have heard the officer's comments, but she didn't back down. He admired that about her. "Go on."

"I woke up, heard someone downstairs."

"The sound of the intruder woke you, or something else?"

"Something else."

"You don't know what?"

She worried her bottom lip between her teeth. "No."

"What exactly did you hear?"

"The first sound, I'm not sure..." Her eyes closed, as if returning to the moment. "Breaking glass, I think. Then, I heard the darkroom door. It squeaks."

"That's it?"

"Yes."

"I'll be right back."

The moment he left her alone, Paige felt vulnerable once more. She wrapped her arms about her middle and fought the urge to pace. He wanted to know what woke her. She wasn't about to admit to him the truth.

For days she'd walked a tightrope of anxiety and stress. Jumping at shadows, starting at the most minor, out-of-place sound. She'd taken to sitting with her back to the wall, alert, aware, even in the privacy of her own home. Always, no matter how she tried to fight, sleep pulled at her and when she could go no longer and her lids would droop, her muscles relax, she would sleep. And dream. Horrifyingly realistic dreams of pain and death, of eyes in the dark, watching her slumber, silently moving closer and closer until they hovered just above her.

A shiver worked through her muscles. She shook the returned images from her mind. Justin didn't need to know the truth. She wouldn't admit that bad dreams roused her from sleep tonight—every night—only to leave her alone and frightened. Longing for him.

At the echo of his booted feet ascending her stairs, relief surged. The sharp edge of her anxiety smoothed. She straightened, mentally brushing aside all hint of vulnerability and weakness. It was insane, really, her inability to brush aside thoughts of him as easily. She'd only known Justin a few days, most of that time

125

spent trying to prove to him that she was not what he thought, yet sometime in all of it he'd become her lifeline. It grew increasingly difficult to keep her thoughts from drifting to him. Always to him.

Right now, she had enough on her plate without trying to analyze why.

"Your locks don't appear to have been jimmied," Justin said as he stepped before her. "And the board covering the front window doesn't seem to be disturbed."

"That's what Officer Carlton said, too."

"Your security system, it's code protected?"

"Yes."

"Who besides you has the code?"

"No one."

A frown creased his brow. "Did you remember to set the system tonight?"

"Yes."

"You're certain?"

"The uniformed officers tripped it when they arrived."

"Not before, when you heard the noise?"

"No." Like the uniforms before him, he hadn't found any sign of a break-in. The first hint of doubt settled in. Her arms found their way back around her middle. "Look, I'm sorry."

"For what?"

The compassion in his gaze didn't help her sudden feelings of guilt. "For interrupting your evening."

"You didn't."

Their voices blended, rolled over each other as she continued to speak even as he replied. "For getting you out of bed for this."

"You didn't."

"I just let my imagination get the best of me."

"Paige, you didn't."

His words finally penetrated. She didn't what? Didn't get him out of bed? Interrupt his evening? She stopped babbling. Her eyes, as well as her mind, focused on the man before her.

He wore black. Jeans and a snug knit shirt tucked into the waistband, topped with a blazer-style jacket of leather. He was dressed to go out, dressed to please the eye and stir the blood. He definitely stirred something in her. Heat crawled up her torso, warmed her from the inside-out. She raised her hand to the base of her throat where her pulse beat wildly.

"I don't believe imagination got the best of you."

"You're the only one who doesn't."

His eyes were dark and unreadable as he studied her. "It's okay to lean on someone, you know. We all need to at times."

It wasn't good to make it a habit, the way she had been doing lately. "I've never felt so out of control."

"You look pretty together to me."

Because he saw what she wanted him to see. On the inside, she was slowly falling apart. She needed to get a grip before she forgot herself and asked him to hold her. Or just closed the distance between them and rested her head against the warm solace of his broad shoulder. She ached for comfort, longed to be pulled against the hard planes of his chest. Wrapped in his strong embrace, while his calloused hands stroked her back.

Expelling a breath, she studied him through a veil of dark lashes. He was a cool one, the way he controlled that lean and muscled body. She would bet he never felt vulnerable, stripped and exposed as she did right now. Just his presence in the same room calmed her, restored a bit of her peace. Imagine the comfort of his embrace.

As her legs suddenly went weak, Paige forced away the thought. She couldn't get involved with him. Couldn't let herself care.

She dragged in a shaky breath. "I'm sorry I've wasted your time."

"I never said you were wasting my time."

She'd been so afraid, coming out of a nightmare then hearing someone move around downstairs. So sure of what she'd heard, certain of someone in her studio. Now...

Maybe it had been a dream, or the panicked imaginings of an exhausted mind. "I must be overreacting."

"It would be understandable."

She closed her eyes against the kindness in his voice. Snapped them open at the brush of his finger beneath her chin. He tipped her face to his. "Then there's the broken bottle in the darkroom. Imagination doesn't explain that."

Relief filled her. She wasn't losing her mind, after all. "Thank you."

"For what, doing my job?"

"For answering my call, even though you were probably busy with something else. For believing in me. Again."

"We aren't going to start this again, are we? I wasn't busy." He lifted his hand and traced his fingertip along her jaw. "I had dinner with my mother earlier. On my way home, I stopped off for a drink. That's where I was when you called."

The caress of his fingers across her skin made her pulse trip. "I'm glad." She wasn't supposed to care where he went or who he spent his free time with, but had to admit to being thrilled he hadn't been on a date. Just the thought of him touching another woman the way he touched her now made her stomach clench painfully. "I'm glad you weren't busy."

"It wouldn't have mattered." His fingers continued to dance down her neck before settling at her throat. "Busy or not, I would have answered your call." His free hand slid around her waist, eased her closer until his warm breath brushed across her lips. "This is where I want to be."

Longing swamped her. Her pulse thundered in her ears. She lifted her hand, placed it against the center of his chest. "Justin."

His lips brushed against hers lightly, gently and her mind clicked off. Her body reacted immediately, instinctively. Her blood heated. Her bones melted. Sensation shot through her like lightning bolts.

His kiss was as hard and demanding as the body pressed against her. His hand moved from her neck, fisted in her hair and dragged her head back as his mouth continued to seduce. His taste seeped into her. Something between a moan and a sigh slid up the back of her throat. She knew she should pull away. She told herself to pull away. Instead, she parted her lips and surrendered.

Her mouth moved eagerly on his, exploring, discovering his taste. She couldn't breathe. The heady, male scent of him surrounded her. Her head spun. Fire burned inside her belly. She felt the pull of desire, the heat simmering between them. Felt herself go wet. The ache of need was more than she could stand. She gave herself up to it.

Palm flat against his chest, her hand streaked up, slipped beneath his jacket and skimmed down his side. Her fingers curled into his shirt. From somewhere deep inside, sanity returned. Alarm bells chimed in her head like a gong. Her body tightened as a chill ran the length of her spine. She pulled her mouth from his, pressed trembling hands against his shoulders and staggered back, out of his arms.

"Paige..." His voice hoarse, and tinged with confusion, he reached for her.

"I can't do this. I'm sorry." Struggling to reign in her reeling emotions, she turned away.

The intensity of what they'd just shared rocked her foundation. Never before had she felt anything so powerful, experienced anything so right. When he touched her, when he pulled her to him he made her forget everything but him. Gone was her fear, her anxiety. In its place raged need stronger than she'd ever known. Longing so powerful she'd been helpless to resist. Until the placement of her hands upon his smooth washboard of muscle registered. Reality slammed back into place.

How could she have forgotten so quickly? The one thing she feared most was there, right there beneath her right hand, beneath the cool polymer of his Glock. The memory of him holding that same side of his body as pain stole the warmth from his eyes settled in. Followed quickly by the remembered pain of loss.

"This is wrong," she said softly.

"I want to take you home tonight," he replied as if he hadn't heard her protest.

"You ask too much of me."

"It's too much to want to protect you? Too much to believe you should be safe?"

Her body still vibrated from his touch. When her eyes darted to the bed near her and his followed, a flood of heat arrowed from her breasts to between her legs.

"It doesn't have to be that way. As much as I would love to carry you to that big bed over there, it doesn't have to be like that. Let me keep you safe."

Safe. She would feel safe with Justin. No longer alone, no longer afraid. But who would keep her safe from him? Being with him felt so right, so natural, and powerful. That was dangerous. She'd been that route before, had stood on that precipice of pain and loss and she was in no rush to return. This time, she didn't think she would survive.

"No."

"Paige—"

"I can't, Justin," she argued, hating the waver in her voice but unable to control it.

He slipped his left hand into his pocket and sighed. "I don't think you should stay here. You're alone, vulnerable. The businesses around yours are all closed for the night."

A chill worked through her at the reminder. "Do you think whoever was in my house will come back?"

"Probably not. Still, I think you should

reconsider."

"No."

Frustrated, he scrubbed a hand over his face. "Are you always this hardheaded, or is it just me?"

"I'm sorry, Justin. It's just..." She ran her tongue over her dry lips, then immediately regretted it when she discovered she could still taste him. "I can't get involved with you."

"*You* called *me*. Not the other way around."

"That was a mistake. I shouldn't have called you. I should have let the responding officers do their job and left it at that."

"A mistake?"

"I can't get involved with you...without letting you matter. I don't want you to matter to me."

An emotion she couldn't identify came and went in his gaze. "I see. If you won't reconsider, then you need some form of self-protection."

The muscles in her spine went taut. Justin continued talking, unaware of her growing tension.

"I can't believe I'm even suggesting this, do you know how to use a handgun? My back-up weapon is in my trunk. I could show you how to use it safely."

"I hate guns."

"You need to be able to protect yourself."

"No."

"Damn it," he growled, right hand fisting against his thigh. "I can't help you if you won't help yourself."

Her body began to tremble. She took a small step backward. "You don't understand."

Eyes narrowing, he studied her face. His hand unclenched as the temper faded from his dark, brown eyes. "Paige," he assured her softly, "knowledge reduces fear."

The pain in her stomach increased even though his words were meant to soothe. He didn't understand. She would have to make him.

On legs suddenly weak and unsteady she crossed the room to her roll-top desk. In the center drawer, just beneath a scattering of unopened junk mail, she found it. In the exact spot she had placed it years before when forgetting was paramount.

The knots in her stomach tightening with every passing moment, Paige removed the black plastic case and set it atop the desk. The lid slid open easily and there it sat—more firepower than a woman like her needed. Rick's voice played back in her mind as with practiced skill, she checked the chamber, the safeties, then locked the fully loaded magazine into the handle.

Guns don't kill, P.C., people kill. Even so, you've got to respect the weapon, respect the power.

Respect the power. She respected it all right. She knew guns, how to break them down, clean them and put them back together. She knew how to shoot. She also knew firsthand the deadly force they were capable of.

Sometimes, Paige thought, *knowledge only feeds fear.*

Surprise rippled through Justin at the skilled way Paige handled the handgun. She'd gone so pale, seemed so shaken by his offer of a gun, he'd assumed her fear stemmed from naiveté. Yet her movements appeared second nature, as if demonstrated by one who handled such power daily. Her body might tremble with emotion, but her hands were steady, competent.

Questions ran through his mind. What was a woman with such unbending animosity toward violence doing with a nine millimeter Beretta stashed in an unlocked drawer? Or, perhaps more importantly, where had she gotten it? He knew, for he'd gathered all the information he could find on her just a few days before, that she had no license for such a weapon.

His whole body tensed. Just what other surprises did she have up her sleeve? "You do know that I could arrest you for possession of an unlicensed handgun."

"You won't."

"What makes you so sure?" She wouldn't

come home with him and he knew better than to suggest he spend the night on her couch. What if he was wrong and her intruder returned to finish the job? If she spent the night in a holding cell awaiting arraignment, at least she'd be safe.

"You just offered me the use of your sidearm."

He'd offered her his back-up weapon. Damn it, since when did he put his neck on the line like that? He'd always done things by the book. He respected the law he swore to uphold. He didn't break rules or push boundaries. At least not before he met her.

"Where'd you get the Beretta, Paige?"

She sighed audibly, returned her attention to the gun in her hand. "It's Rick's old service pistol. It didn't help him much, did it, Justin?"

He didn't have an answer for her. She didn't wait for one.

"I hate guns. I hate being afraid, but I hate guns more. I won't use one. *Ever.*"

"Then why did you keep it?" he asked with a casualness he didn't come close to feeling. "Why have it at all?"

Her responding laugh was humorless and filled with irony. "I don't really know. So I never forget?" As she spoke, she removed the magazine, replaced the weapon and closed the lid of the box with a snap. "Like I could ever forget."

She squeezed her eyes closed, opened them a heartbeat later. He had the sudden, uncomfortable feeling that as she stood before him, surrounded by darkened windows that looked out at a mild San Diego night, it was not him she saw, but another man and another city.

"The thing about knowledge is that it can sometimes work against you. I know all too well the damage that can be done even with the smallest caliber handgun."

Her words, the pain in her voice and the far-away look in her eyes, twisted him up inside. He knew better than to go to her, but closed the distance between them anyway. "I'm sorry," he said, brushing the tips of his fingers across her cheek.

Her hand reached out for him, settled lightly against his left side, just below his sidearm. "What about you, Justin? Do you know, too? Is that what happened to you?"

Her words splintered through him. He swore softly and stepped back, forcing her to drop her hand. "That doesn't matter now."

"I think it does. I think it matters a great deal."

What could he say that wouldn't add to the fear already churning through her? "Paige, please, we need to discuss getting you out of here."

"I'm not leaving. I won't be driven from my own home."

"You shouldn't be alone."

She lifted her chin, determined to show him strength even while her hands shook. "I'll be fine."

Frustration wound deeper. He rolled his shoulder where his muscles knotted painfully. "Listen to me—"

"You aren't going to tell me are you?"

He set his jaw.

"Why not?"

Because she mattered to him. Because the truth about what happened to him six months ago would hurt her, push her away and he didn't want that. Not when he ached to draw her back into his arms, ached to have the sweet, potent taste of her swimming through his system again.

Too late he realized his silence had the same effect on her. Already, her eyes were going cold and distant as she pulled her emotions tightly under control. Only this time, it wasn't fear she wanted to keep at bay, but him.

The knowledge stung. It didn't matter that by distancing herself from him— emotionally and physically—she was probably doing him a favor. He'd already spent enough time thinking of her when he should have been concentrating on his job. Recalling the scent of her, the feeling of rightness that filled him when he held her in his arms. When he was supposed to be reestablishing his place in the department.

He needed to remember that any further involvement with her would be a colossal mistake. That he couldn't afford the distraction Paige Conroy represented.

Still, the ache in his chest as she withdrew even further took him by surprise.

"Tempting as your offer is," she said quietly, as she eased across the room. "I won't go home with you. I can't sleep with you, Justin. You say it doesn't have to be that way, but you and I both know that's the way it would be." Her arms slid around her middle. Her gaze met his. "You're a risk I can't afford to take."

CHAPTER SEVEN

The first forty-eight hours of any investigation are critical. After those first crucial days, trails tend to go cold. Once cold, dead isn't far off.

One-hundred-and-two hours after Detective St. John was gunned down in his hotel bed, Justin sat on a case colder than Becky O'Riley the night he tried to go a little too far in the backseat of her daddy's '79 Chevy. The first forty-eight hours had been and gone long ago. Were he to get them back, he was less than certain they would be any further enlightened about what brought a Boston narcotics officer three-thousand miles to his death.

At least the dead man's partner had finally decided to grace them with his presence. Sitting at the apex of the desks, feet propped just to the right of Justin's coffee mug, Detective Jon Brennan didn't do much to boost any hope for closure. Tall and lanky, he wore his otherwise ordinary brown hair short, its bleached tips slicked forward into spiky disarray. With cold blue eyes, he scanned through the crime scene photos once, before tossing them atop the desk, the corner of his mouth kicked up into what could only be described as a smirk.

Justin set his teeth. He shot his left hand out and stopped the photos before they slid off the desk and onto the floor.

"Detective St. John died no more than three hours before his body was discovered." Unaware of Justin's growing antagonism, Allan continued to bring Brennan up to date. "Cause of death is a single shot to the back of the head. By the starburst pattern of the wound and the bruising present, it appears he was held face-first into the pillow and shot point-blank. Ante mortem bruises present on the upper arms indicate St. John struggled briefly with the shooter. Since it would take considerable upper body strength to overpower a man of St. John's size, we believe our shooter is a man, but the total lack of physical evidence at the scene leaves us without much to go on."

"Execution style, quick and easy," Brennan stated, his tone cool and detached, as if the man they discussed was a stranger.

For someone who just lost a partner, Brennan didn't appear overly upset by the loss. Justin fingered his side. He shook his head. Detective Jon Brennan was either made of ice, or heartless.

His face a mask of indifference, Brennan continued. "Any sign of a robbery?"

"No." Allan shifted through the ever-growing pile of papers before him. "The room didn't appear to be searched. His cash and credit cards were still in his wallet."

"Did he place any calls?"

"Telephone company records show he placed one call to Ms. Conroy. The conversation lasted two minutes, ten seconds."

It was not the hotel's practice to log local outgoing calls. In order to verify Paige's statement, they'd had to arrange for the telephone company log. "Just enough time to plan to meet," Justin pointed out, speaking up for the first time since introductions had been made.

Brennan's chair groaned in protest as he lifted his feet from the desktop and straightened, his attention shifting from Allan to Justin. "So this Ms. Conroy, she's the last person to see St. John alive?"

"Not exactly," Justin replied bluntly.

"What does that mean?"

"Paige Conroy didn't walk into that hotel room until four hours after the telephone call. By then, Detective, your partner was dead."

"That doesn't make any sense. What time did he place the call?"

Justin shuffled through his notes even though he knew the few facts of the case by memory. "Three-fifty a.m."

"So for whatever reason, St. John felt it

142

important enough to wake her, but not important enough for her to meet with him right away?"

"I wondered about the same thing," Justin replied. "She stated your partner claimed it was urgent he speak with her. So why didn't they meet right then? Why did St. John apparently go to bed after placing the call?"

"What did he have to tell her? What was he doing in San Diego?" Brennan asked.

Allan quirked an eyebrow. "We hoped that you could tell us the reason behind his trip."

"I have no idea."

"None?" Justin asked with derision. "You were partners for the past two years."

In the first show of emotion since his arrival, anger flared briefly in Brennan's eyes. His jaw clenched tight enough to bring out the white line of a faded scar along his left temple. "Leroy didn't talk much."

"Great." Allan's frustration rose to match Justin's. "Just wonderful. Let me just vocalize what I'm certain my partner would like to know as much as I would. What exactly are you doing here?"

"Making certain you two give this case the attention it deserves."

"You arrogant, little sonofa—"

"Justin," Allan warned.

"If you're so worried about our handling

143

of this case, where have you been for the last three days? What kept you from arriving on Tuesday as planned?"

Brennan shrugged negligently. "Something came up."

"Something came up? That's rich, really." Justin rubbed at the tight muscles in the back of his neck as he pondered the man before him. Jon Brennan was arrogant, condescending and a tad too dispassionate when it came to the murder of his partner.

"Here," Justin stated as he made up his mind. He dug one of the larger files from the pile on his desk and dropped it before Brennan. "Let me introduce you to your partner. Leroy St. John, age thirty-three. Graduated from the academy at twenty, top in his class, moved through the ranks quickly, made detective in record time. Worked robbery for a while but switched to narcotics when his sister's kid OD'd on bad smack at the ripe old age of ten."

With a flick of his wrist, the file flipped open and a few years' younger version of Detective St. John beamed up at his partner. "He was a good cop, dedicated, made an impressive number of arrests." All morning the sensation that he was missing something ate at Justin. It flared to life again. "None of this means squat right now because what I need to know, you should be telling me. What was the man like, on and off duty? Did he make friendships that lasted a lifetime? Was he careless, did he make a habit of sticking his neck out? Did he do that here, in my city, right before he had his head taken off?"

Justin placed his elbows on the desk and leaned in. "Or was he the type of man who took his time, muddled through, working out all the details before he made his move? 'Cause I gotta think he's the latter. Otherwise, he just left Ms. Conroy swinging in the breeze. And if I'm right, we're missing something here. If I'm right, St. John spent the time between his one call and our witness's arrival, getting his ducks in a row. Are you following me, Detective Brennan?"

Jon Brennan surged to his feet. The raw scrape of his chair across the floor echoed throughout the room. "Don't talk to me as if I'm ignorant."

"Don't walk into my precinct and insinuate I don't know how to do my job."

Ever the mediator, Allan piped in. "Boys."

Brennan's hands clenched into fists. He stared down at the file for a moment then said through his teeth. "You've got one problem, Sergeant."

"And what's that?"

"From what I've heard so far, you didn't find any so-called ducks in that hotel room. You didn't find jack shit."

True enough. Justin moved his pinching shoulder holster to a more comfortable position.

145

He didn't have time for this. Not the constant delays that meant he was losing ground on the St. John homicide fast, or his growing dislike of the victim's partner. His patience had run out within five minutes of meeting the man, but anger wasn't going to solve their problems. He needed to keep a level head. "Let's go back to the beginning on this, shall we? What have you brought us that we can use?"

Hands digging into the top of the chair he'd vacated, Brennan stood motionless as his gaze swept the squad room before him. After a moment, he shifted the angle of the chair and sat. "Upon receiving notification of Leroy's death, I went to his apartment. It had been tossed and not very professionally."

"Any prints?" Allan asked.

"Hundreds. We're still sorting through all of them. It'll take a while. He wasn't exactly a tidy housekeeper."

"Do you know if there was anything missing?" Justin questioned.

"Hard to tell."

Hard to tell because of the mess, or because Brennan hadn't taken the time to get to know the one man he should have known best?

Justin shifted his gaze to his partner. After ten years of working side by side with Allan, he knew his partner's furrowed brow meant he was thinking, turning Brennan's answer over in his mind. For most people that

146

expression meant confusion. For Allan, it meant contemplation. Justin knew this because partners, no matter how short a time together, grew tight. They learned each other's ins and outs, their strengths and weaknesses. They learned each other's quirks. That's what happened when you spent hours together on the job, relying on each other to cover your back no matter the situation.

And with that bond came communication. Partners talked about everything. They learned things about each other, the most personal things. Right now, if anyone asked, Justin could tell them what Allan and his wife, Suzanne, planned to name their baby, even though the decision had only been made the previous evening—Jessica for a girl, Andrew, a boy.

Leroy didn't talk much.

Partners communicate. They share a bond not unlike marriage. They know things about one another no one else could. It didn't make sense that St. John and Brennan's partnership would be so much different.

Justin rubbed at eyes that felt like they were filled with sand. He considered Allan's opinion, voiced just that morning that he was taking this case far too personally. He knew the dangers of taking a case home with him, spending even his off time turning it around in his mind. But some cases chased you like a rabid dog and bled over into your personal life.

For him, this case was that one.

What about for Detective St. John? Did he have a case like that?

"Did you find any files?" Justin asked. "Any notes or paperwork?"

"About what?"

"The Preston homicide."

Brennan's brow wrinkled. Justin could all but smell his skepticism. "You think Leroy's death is linked to his obsession with Preston's murder?"

"The only case St. John was actively investigating that had any link to San Diego was Preston's murder," Allan supplied.

"Which you should know. You were his partner, after all."

Brennan ignored Justin's barb. "If he had any new information on Preston's murder, Leroy didn't share it with me."

"Apparently he chose not to share this information with anyone," Allan replied dryly.

"What about at his apartment? Did you find any files?" Justin reiterated.

"His home computer had been wiped clean. We found nothing there." As if he'd only just recalled possessing the item, Brennan reached into the case at his side and withdrew an oversized manila envelope. "I did recover something of interest from a locked drawer of his desk." He passed the item to Justin. "A curiosity, really. Not much there to necessitate a lock."

Justin opened the envelope carefully and dumped the contents across the top of his desk. He separated the papers and lined everything up in no particular order. "Curious."

"What have you got?" Allan shifted to the front edge of his chair and took the photograph Justin passed him. An identical photograph to the one found in St. John's hotel room. "Curious indeed. What else?"

"One key chain: a silver bullet, no keys. A newspaper article regarding a drug bust. A transcript of Paige Conroy's interview after Preston's murder, complete with notes in the margins. Copy of Preston's autopsy report, a photo of two grown men dressed head-to-toe for Halloween. The one on the right looks like Preston, the other could be St. John." Justin held the shot up for his partner to see.

"Superman and The Lone Ranger?"

Justin shrugged. "Who knows." He picked up the final item. "And a wedding invitation," he began to read. "Mr. And Mrs. Joseph Martin Conroy request the honor of your presence at the marriage of their daughter Paige Louise to Detective Rick Preston..."

"Detective? The man's rank is on his wedding invitation?" Allan shook his head. "Was she marrying the man or the job?"

"The man was the job," Justin replied laconically. It seemed he and Preston had a lot

149

more in common than just Paige Conroy.

Why did that leave an uneasy feeling in the pit of his stomach?

"You're right, Detective," Allan leaned back in his chair and placed his hands behind his head. He stretched from side to side. "I don't see anything here important enough to require it be kept under lock and key."

"There's a reason. You don't just lock up a bag of trinkets for no reason." Justin shifted the items around once more, as if seeing them in a different order would help them tell their story.

"You do if your name is Leroy St. John," Brennan replied dryly. "The man didn't always make sense."

"Perhaps he did, but only to those select few that knew him best."

"Speaking of which." Allan tipped his head toward a spot behind Justin's shoulder. "Justin, it appears you have a visitor."

"I'll take that as my signal to go stretch my legs." Brennan nearly tipped his chair over backwards as he stood. A grin split his face as he caught it. "See, too many hours on a plane has made me clumsy."

Justin swiveled his chair to follow Brennan's retreat. He opened his mouth, prepared to offer a rather non-complimentary opinion of the departing detective, when he caught sight of his visitor.

Paige. The cool professional was back.

Hair piled atop her head, donning a suit and a pair of dark sunglasses, she stood just inside the archway, a leather computer case clutched in her left hand. Until that moment, Justin had managed to keep thoughts of her to a minimum. Just that quickly, the memory of holding her in his arms slammed into his brain—the warmth of her body against his, the taste of her lips. Desire shot through his system with the force of a mule kick. His pulse jumped into high gear, his gut tied into knots.

The calm control she exuded as she turned and started in his direction came as a surprise after her attack of anxiety during her last visit. She walked with the grace of a high-fashion model. Tall and elegant, she crossed toward him and his partner.

"You seeing her outside the capacity of this investigation?" In a way only Allan could, he kept his inquisition both casual and cautionary.

Several pairs of male eyes tracked her progress with keen interest until her destination registered and they met with Justin's icy stare. "She doesn't date cops."

"Do you blame her?"

They both rose as Paige neared. "Hell no."

"Why do I get the impression you won't let it go at that?"

Justin threw one last narrowed-eyed glance at his partner before she stepped before them. He faced her, unable to judge her intent through the dark lenses.

"It's good to see you again, Ms. Conroy," Allan stated politely. "How are you?"

"I have a bit of a headache, actually." She tipped her face in Justin's direction. "I need to talk to you, do you have a minute?"

"Sure." Justin motioned to the chair Brennan had left vacant.

"Um..." He couldn't be certain, but he got the distinct impression that her eyes left his. Paige shifted the case she carried from her side to her front. Her right hand joined her left at the handle momentarily before she dropped it to her left side once more. "Somewhere else. If you don't mind."

"Not a problem." She was wound tight as a spring, as evidenced by her steely posture and the fact that she clutched her case so tightly, her knuckles were white. Justin wondered whether her discomfort extended from seeing him again after last night, or if she'd had yet another incident. Perversely, he wondered which he would find most unsettling. "There's a conference room, this way."

She didn't move. Not immediately and not in the direction he indicated. Instead, Paige turned back just as Allan prepared to sit down.

"Sergeant Simmons, I think you should hear this as well."

Brilliant slashes of sunlight shone through open blinds, warming the room and its occupants. Though the table centered in the space could easily accommodate twenty, no one sat.

Standing just inside the closed door, Paige watched as dust particles danced in the ray of light. She was running on sheer nerves and had been for days. She couldn't eat, couldn't sleep, and thanks to the pictures she had in her possession, she was chilled to the bone. Cold— the way no sweater or blanket could warm. Cold and filled with a healthy dose of fresh angst.

She couldn't grasp what she'd done to wind up in the center of this mess, whom she'd hurt. In her exhausted state, she couldn't grasp much of anything, except that she was quickly running out of options. Burying her head in the sand and pretending everything would be okay no longer seemed like a viable solution. So this morning, she'd decided it was time to take matters into her own hands. Time to stop sitting idly by while her world fell apart around her.

Wiping her damp palms on her slacks, Paige moved the short distance to the table where she placed her laptop case. She removed her dark glasses and with a deep breath, turned and faced the detectives at her back. "Justin." He'd come up behind her and stood only inches away. The heady male scent of him made her senses spin.

153

She hadn't slept well last night. Plagued by thoughts of him, she'd lain awake, imagining what it would feel like to have that perfect mouth take hers again while his hands slicked over her bare flesh. To wake up wrapped in the comfort of his arms, his scent warming every breath she took. Unable to control herself, her gaze settled on his mouth. The chill that had thickened her blood all morning thawed. Her body heated. Her breasts tingled.

The man kissed like a dream. Desperate, demanding yet controlled and gentle. Her mouth went dry and for one insane moment she wanted him to kiss her again.

Here.

Now.

But the answering heat, so clear in his gaze the night before, was gone. His eyes were sharp and assessing as they scanned her face. His voice held accusation. "You didn't sleep."

"I've been having a problem with that." The even press of his fingers against her shoulder made it difficult for her to concentrate. As did the deep bite of need that streaked straight up her spine and tensed every raw nerve. She edged sideways so he no longer touched her. "Last night was worse than normal."

"The mind can only handle so much. You need to let it out."

The smooth baritone of his voice wrapped

around her like a blanket, promising heat, comfort. She was a fool if she took it. "How do you do it?"

His dark-chocolate eyes held hers as he skimmed his knuckles over her left cheek. "Smoke, or I used to."

That wasn't what she meant. Paige looked at him, at the concern that now filled his gaze and wondered just when the cool indifferent cop had been replaced by this compassionate man. When had her world flipped upside down, leaving her to question everything she believed to be true?

"We all have our vices, our ways of diminishing stress before it can take over our lives. You need to find yours."

"Normally I work through a crisis." She could really use that cool, indifferent cop right now. The one who would listen to what she'd come to tell him and remain calm and detached, emotionless, at a time when she was anything but. Where last night Justin's presence soothed the ragged edges of her fear, today it drove home the hard reality of what was happening to her. "Staying busy helps."

"It doesn't appear to be helping this time."

"No, it doesn't."

Paige closed her eyes, struggling for control. She knew, without a doubt, that the photos she carried changed everything. There would be no turning back. No restoring the order to her utterly boring life. Not until this man was caught. This nameless, faceless man who slowly pushed her closer and closer to the edge.

No, she corrected, taking a deep breath and forcing herself to relax. It would take more than a few threats to send her over the edge.

She hoped.

Still needing that cool, emotionless detective, she turned her attention from Justin to his partner. "Sergeant Simmons, I don't know if Justin has mentioned anything to you about my break-in last night?"

"He did and call me Allan."

His attention appeared hung up on her face. Suddenly self-conscious, the urge to hide behind her sunglasses flared to life. She'd done her best to camouflage her bruising under a few layers of makeup. Had believed she'd done a credible job. His distraction made her wonder if she shouldn't have just left it alone.

"Okay. Well, Allan, last night there seemed to be some question about whether or not someone had been in my home. This morning, I received proof."

"What kind of proof?" Justin ran his hand through his hair and then shoved it into his front pocket in a move she was beginning to understand indicated his level of tension.

Briskly, she unzipped her laptop case.

Without glancing at them, she passed the photos she'd printed just that morning to Justin. His steady stream of expletives, spoken under his breath, brought the tiny hairs on her arms to attention.

"Where'd you get these, Paige?"

"When I checked my e-mail this morning, I found them."

Justin fell silent, a muscle flexing in his jaw as he flipped through the photographs one by one, studying each one individually before passing them to Allan.

"Look at the way the body's positioned," Allan said as he studied the first picture.

"Body?" Paige couldn't stop the shiver that passed through her. "That's not just any body."

"It's you," Justin growled.

"Yes. You have to stop this guy." The irony of this latest threat hadn't escaped her. The fact that this man had used photographs against her—a photographer. "I don't know how much more of this I can take."

"The message is clear," Allan began, taking the remaining photos from Justin and shuffling through them. "He took the time to manipulate her, but left her unharmed."

"Is it? I'm not certain I'm getting it. If he wants me dead why—" Shock slammed through her system as his words registered. "Wait a minute. What do you mean by manipulated?"

157

"Did you eat or drink anything out of the ordinary last night?"

"No. No, of course not. Why?"

The expression that settled onto Justin's face had Paige stepping back. Tension pulsed off of him in waves. His hand fisted against his thigh.

"Why?"

Allan looked up from the photographs in his hands. "These pictures are similar—"

"Frighteningly similar."

"Yes," Allan agreed. "To the shots we have from the St. John homicide."

"Leroy." Nausea rolled in her stomach as she saw him again, stomach down, sheet tangled around his legs.

It hadn't registered. Not when she opened her email and discovered them, or later as she'd developed them. She hadn't realized just what about those photographs froze her heart with fear. The thought that someone had been in her home, standing over her bed for God knew how long before she came awake was terrifying enough. But now...

The images shifted in and out of focus— images of her, deep asleep, face buried into her pillow, sheet riding low on her hips. Shock snapped across her nerve endings.

"N-no." Her gaze swung between the two men. "The similarities don't mean anything." They couldn't mean anything. This put a whole new spin on things. One she couldn't accept. "I did not sleep through some…" What was the word she wanted? "*Person* positioning me like the body of one of his victims. That's just how I sleep."

Justin and Allan's swift exchange of looks spoke as loudly as their silence.

"I've always been a stomach sleeper. The rest is just coincidence."

"I believe this goes a step beyond coincidence," Allan replied gravely.

"No." The trembling started in her knees and worked up her legs. She circled her fingers around Justin's bicep. "It's not possible."

"Paige, listen to me." Justin spoke softly but firmly, his hand settling over hers. "There's no other explanation. The photos are damn near identical."

"How can that be?" She closed her eyes, opened them. "I don't understand any of this."

"You need to—"

Paige jumped as his cell phone trilled loudly.

Justin pulled the phone from his pocket and flipped it open. "Harrison," he intoned automatically.

"Anthony Sullivan here, you asked that I call you as soon as I had something on Ms. Conroy's car bomb."

His timing couldn't have been more unfortunate. Too much acid churning his stomach already, Justin prepared for more nerve-racking news. "What did you find?"

"Okay, technical jargon aside, the bomb was not designed to do major damage. You saw the scene, I'm sure you noticed the building itself suffered no structural damage beyond the shattering of the front windows."

"I noticed. Exactly what does that tell you?"

"Not much on its own. The vehicle tells us that the bomber placed the device on the rear floorboard of the car. That, along with the fragments collected, and I can tell you that this was not your run of the mill, rig-it-to-the-ignition car bomb. This one had a remote trigger. Pretty short range actually, your guy had to be no farther than a half mile from Ms. Conroy when he detonated."

One by one, Justin's muscles coiled. His shoulder screamed. He stared at the fear shining in Paige's green eyes and fought back rage. "Close enough to watch."

As if she heard both sides of his conversation and couldn't ignore the significance of Sullivan's words any more than he could, Paige straightened. She removed her hand from his arm and wrapped her arms around her waist.

"He never intended to kill her, Sergeant Harrison. He just wanted to send her a message."

"I think she got that message, loud and clear."

"Let me know if there's anything else you need from me."

"Yeah, I will." With a flip of his wrist, Justin disconnected. He didn't replace the phone in his pocket just yet, but used it as something to keep his hands busy.

Damn, some days he really missed smoking. He closed his eyes and imagined tapping a cigarette from a pack and lighting it, savoring the smooth taste as it filled his lungs and calmed his nerves.

He wasn't happy with the direction of the case. No matter how hard they tried, they hadn't come up with squat. Not on the St. John homicide, or whatever the hell was going on with Paige. She'd come close to dying the other day, damn close. Discovering that the bomber's intent had not been to kill her did nothing to stop the uncomfortable sensation climbing up Justin's spine.

A game was afoot. A game Paige had no idea she was playing. Justin didn't doubt for a minute that destroying her car, breaking into her house in the dead of night and taking pictures of her while she slept, then making certain she knew he'd been there by e-mailing her the photos, was some sick bastard's idea of a good time. He also didn't doubt that eventually, the man would tire of the game. He would end it, and when that happened, there would be no warning and very little chance of stopping him before it was too late.

Something had to be done. Paige needed to realize just how serious the risk to her life was. She needed to understand that from that moment, all bets were off.

He opened his eyes, refocusing on the woman before him. "The report on your car bomb came through. Seems our boy likes to watch."

Her spine stiffened, the arms around her middle tightened, but she remained silent.

"He was there?" Allan asked. "How do they know?

"Remote trigger."

"I'm afraid I don't follow you," Paige said.

"The crime scene techs discovered pieces of a remote trigger in the debris. Whoever this is, whatever his motives, he's sending you a message, Paige. Whether you figure that message out or not, I don't think that matters to him. All that matters to him at this point is making you as uncomfortable as he can. He's out to break you, to push you over the edge."

She blinked. "You don't believe in holding things back do you?"

"Would you prefer I lie to you?"

"No." She appeared adamant about that much. "What is a remote trigger?"

Her ability to handle the information

without tears or histrionics impressed him. In his years on the force, he'd seen people break down over much less. Not Paige Conroy.

She was afraid, he knew, and not unfeeling. That much showed in her inability to get a decent night's rest. He'd been unhappy to discover that when she removed her dark glasses, her features were more drawn than the night before. Still, not many women he knew could function at anywhere near normal with a madman terrorizing them. Yet here Paige stood, exhausted, but facing her problems head on, with courage and intelligence.

"Have you ever wondered why your car didn't blow when you first started it? Why you got out and walked away before it exploded?"

"I hadn't thought about it."

"Our boy was watching you that morning. From across the street, from down the block, who knows for sure? The point is he never planned to kill you, just scare you. He made the bomb small, to prove a point maybe, and then he waited and he watched for the right moment to key the trigger."

"He put the picture on my door, so I would get out of the car."

"Yes, then he stepped over your unconscious, bleeding body to remove it."

"Justin," Allan warned as Paige's features slackened.

Justin bit back the anger that had

simmered all morning, only now reaching a full, rolling boil. Fear for her well-being clawed at him, tore great holes in the wall of indifference he wore for his partner. He wanted, no needed more than anything, to drag Paige into his arms and tell her everything was going to be all right. Five, even ten minutes before he might have, now, he wasn't at all certain it wasn't an outright lie.

"He knows you, Paige. Well enough to know that photo would draw you. Well enough to get into your building without setting off your alarm."

"He has her code key," Allan supplied.

"That would be my guess."

Paige shook her head in denial. "That's not possible."

"Of course it is," Justin continued, his tone less harsh but still tight. "Most people use something familiar to them. Something easily remembered. If this guy knows you, it wouldn't be difficult for him to figure out what that code is."

"He wouldn't have enough time. The system's too fast, it..."

"What?"

"Last night before I called 911 I tried my wireless remote. I hit the panic button multiple times, but the alarm never sounded. I assumed it was the remote, that it was damaged in the explosion. But if it's the system..."

"Then he could get in."

"That doesn't play for me," Allan stated. "He would have to know that the system had been damaged and how would he?"

Justin kept his gaze locked on Paige. "At this point the how doesn't matter as much as the why. He watched you, while you slept, as he pushed the button and blew up your car. And he'll keep watching you. He'll keep at you until he finally has what he came for."

"Which is?"

"You, Paige. He wants you."

Her face went sheet-pale. "Dead, isn't that what you mean? He wants me dead."

Justin took a deep breath into his lungs, and held it even as his recovering injuries protested. He wouldn't let it happen. He'd do whatever it took to keep her alive. "St. John came to San Diego. He came to see you, Paige. And whoever took him out has set his sights on you."

"If he wants me dead, then why not just kill me?"

Much as he hated admitting it, he had no answer to that particular question. Paige didn't wait for him to think one up. She took a deep breath and broke the uncomfortable silence.

"So I'm giving him exactly what he wants. This is a game to him and I'm playing right into his hands."

"We don't know that," Allan reassured.

"I'm scared aren't I?"

Allan moved about the room as he spoke. "The key to all of this is to stay one step ahead of his game."

"How is that possible when we don't have any idea what his next move will be?"

"That's why you came to us." Although meant to encourage, Justin could tell that his words fell short of their goal as Paige lifted her gaze to meet his. He brushed his fingers over the back of her hand. "We'll figure it out, Paige."

"I have to believe you or I'll lose my mind," she admitted softly. "I have to believe you, so I will."

She had great confidence in him. Confidence he wasn't at all certain he had earned.

"In the mean time," Allan continued, "I suggest you get the hell out of Dodge. Do you have someone you can stay with for a while, just until this blows over?"

"No. At least not anyone I'm willing to put in harm's way."

"Go back to Boston."

Her spine went stiff as a rail at the firm command in Allan's voice. Color returned to her cheeks, a spark of fire to her eyes. "That won't do me any good. You said he knows me, that this centers around me. If that's true, then how do you know that's not his plan? If he knows me, he knows where I'd run to."

Although Justin preferred her anger over the cold fear of a few moments ago, his nerves remained fractured. Paige needed more than anger to survive this, she needed protection.

Undaunted, Allan continued, "There has to be someone you can stay with. Anyone who would offer to help you hide out, someone this guy wouldn't know about?"

"She'll be staying with me."

Paige's eyes grew large as saucers. Her mouth dropped open, but no argument broke loose.

The firm grip of his partner's hand upon his arm drew Justin aside. "I hope you know what you're doing."

Warning, along with a note of concern colored Allan's words but failed to pull Justin's attention away from Paige. She messed with his head but good. To the point that things he never imagined could come out of his mouth did. Like asking her to go home with him. Twice. To his home, his sanctuary, the one place he never invited a woman.

She crawled under his skin, swam through his bloodstream. Bullied her way past his defenses until he was left with no defenses where she was concerned. No one, not ever, got past his cop barriers, the thing that kept him alive. Yet she had.

Thoughts of her ate at him, chased him whether awake or asleep. He hadn't been able to push her from his mind since meeting her. It made no sense. Even now, his mind kept wandering back to the previous evening, to the mind-numbing feel of her in his arms. To how well their bodies aligned. Just the memory had his pulse racing, his blood heating in anticipation.

"Justin?" Allan's voice broke through the fog of his mind. "I hope you know what you're doing."

"So do I."

CHAPTER EIGHT

"She'll be staying with me."

Justin's words circled round and round Paige's head as she watched the two men converse, their voices dropped to an octave she was unable to hear. Not that she would have made sense of anything past the five words still spinning through her mind. Words spoken with enough authority as to invoke no argument.

Uncertain that her legs would hold her up any longer, she sank into one of the chairs about the table. Her gaze settled on the window across from her and the dancing dust motes. Her left hand tinkered with her sunglasses. Her head throbbed in time with her heartbeat.

Within the course of a week, everything had changed. Her life was a puzzle she couldn't sort out. Things she'd always known about herself, she suddenly questioned. Emotions she thought she'd reined under control years ago ran free, muddling her thoughts, confusing the issues. She felt a connection to Justin, a connection she didn't want to feel. He was a cop, the type of man she knew she should avoid.

Still, she knew she was out of options.

169

She was going home with Justin. Fear of their mutual attraction aside, he seemed to be the only option available to her. He would help shoulder her burden. He would keep her safe. Common sense told her any threat he offered paled in comparison to the threat from her faceless assailant. The knowledge did nothing to ease her discomfort.

It was only temporary, this glitch in her routine, this confusion she called her life. Soon enough things would level out. The answers would come, the case would close, and she would move on. Back to her studio and her photographs, back to evenings spent in the darkroom instead of curled in the corner of her bed. She closed her eyes and pictured it, only to be struck with one last thought. When that time finally came, how much of herself would she be able to salvage?

With a sigh, Paige folded her arms upon the top of the table and dropped her face onto them. Her life was a puzzle all right, one of those five-thousand-piece numbers with raw, uneven edges and no picture on the box cover to guide her.

The door to the room clicked open. At the same time, the chair on her left pulled out and someone eased into it. She didn't need to look to identify who sat beside her. The jolts of electricity that wracked her body whenever Justin was near told her.

"I'm not any good with puzzles. Somewhere in the middle, despite my eye for detail, those pieces become nothing more than a multitude of odd shapes and sizes that don't fit together no matter how I turn them." Straightening in her seat, she met his gaze. "I've been turning everything over in my head, but none of it makes sense."

Especially her overwhelming urge to ask him for comfort.

As his hand reached out, cupping the side of her face. Paige closed her eyes then opened them. She shouldn't feel so drawn to him. Even if she could handle his career, she knew what kind of man she wanted in her life and he wasn't it. She wished she were different, wished she could enjoy him, his nearness, the electricity and heat they generated, the connection they shared without letting him matter. Without letting him in too far. Without the pain.

She couldn't.

She wished she could forget about him. Go home to her boring life, to her staid career, and have things back the way they used to be. Before one phone call turned her world around. Before she walked into that hotel room and discovered Leroy dead. Before she'd looked up into the most intense pair of brown eyes she'd ever seen.

She couldn't.

171

Reaching up, Paige removed Justin's hand from her face. When her fingers began to curl around his, she released his hand abruptly and stood. She needed space, needed to put distance between them and pull her reeling emotions back under control. For whenever he was near, control was the very last thing she possessed.

As her gaze flitted about the room and the knowledge that they were alone settled in, she took a step in retreat.

Justin's dark brows drew together. "Are you okay?"

"Of course." His white shirt buttoned up the front, and tucked into his jeans. The top few buttons hung open, revealing tanned skin lightly sprinkled with dark hair. Heat licked through her veins and she was struck with the sudden desire to work the rest of his buttons free and push his shirt off his shoulders, revealing the rest of his broad chest to her gaze. "Where's Allan gone off to?"

"He went to see one of the techs about those photos of yours." He watched, a curious look upon his face as she plucked her sunglasses from the table and turned them end over end in her hand. "Are you sure you're okay?"

She laid the glasses back down, raised her hand to the pounding in her temple. "Of course."

He said nothing for a moment, his eyes on

hers. Finally, he motioned to her laptop case. "Most likely they're going to want to take a look at your computer, see if they can trace who sent the photos to you. By the looks of it, you already knew that."

"I didn't know for sure, so I brought it along."

"Any passwords or special security features they're going to need to know about?"

The ache behind her eyes was becoming unbearable. She pulled the aspirin bottle from the pocket of her suit jacket and struggled against the child-proof cap. "No." Her fingers fumbled. She forced her eyes to focus and tried again, but lack of sleep made her clumsy. Frustration ground her molars together, a move she immediately regretted when her head pounded harder. "Are you any good with these?"

He took the tiny bottle she offered him, fisted his free hand, propped the lip of the bottle lid against the edge of the table and brought his fist down atop it. The lid snapped free, flipped into the air and landed unceremoniously in the center of her laptop case. "Two?"

She held up three fingers.

A frown furrowed his brow even as he dropped the caplets into her waiting hand. "When did you last eat?"

"What day is it?"

"Shit." Justin pushed to his feet. He crossed the room to the water cooler on the opposite wall and filled a paper cup, waiting until she swallowed the caplets to comment further. "I can be at your place by six. I'll pick up something to eat on the way. Anything particular you want?"

"My life back."

A muscle in his jaw ticked. "I know you don't want to come home with me. But Allan's right, you need to get out of your place."

She did want to go home with him. More than he understood. He would make her forget, quite easily in fact. Worse, he made her want...much more than he was offering. "What if you never find this guy? I can't hide forever."

"How about we focus on today and leave tomorrow for tomorrow?"

"Like a puzzle? One piece at a time?"

"Exactly."

He would be very good at puzzles. Patient, competent, willing to do whatever it took to arrange the pieces into order, slowly building one on another until the complete picture came into focus. After all, wasn't that what investigative work was like?

Paige looked up into those amazing dark-brown eyes of his. Circled in thick, black lashes, they were creased at the corners in a way that told her those few wicked grins he'd sent her way were far more normal for him than the sober look of contemplation that colored his features now. Swamped by the urge to smooth those frown lines from his brow with the tips of her fingers, to ease the grim line of his mouth and work the corners up into a dimpled smile, she shoved her hands toward her rear pockets. They slid over the smooth fabric of her pocketless slacks, leaving her fumbling.

His frown deepened. "I know what you're thinking, you know. And you're wrong."

The lump in her throat made swallowing difficult. "What am I thinking?"

"Making choices that keep you alive does not make you weak. It would be much simpler to just give up and let this bastard win."

"I could stay where I am, refuse to run and face him."

"You could die in the process."

The thought sent a ripple of alarm through Justin. What if she refused? He couldn't hog-tie her, couldn't make her come with him. He understood her ill-ease, for he felt the same stirrings of discomfort as she at the low hum of sensual awareness that circled about them like a hungry shark. Even right now, he had to fight against the urge to haul her into his arms. And not to ease the clawing panic clearly visible in her eyes. No, his motives were not that heroic.

Against his better judgment, he allowed his gaze to drop, to caress the shape of her body outlined by her suit. He knew just what that suit of hers covered for he'd had his hands all over her just the night before. A high, tight rear-end, slim hips, endlessly long legs that would pull him deep into her warmth. Desire shot straight to his stomach, swirled there. The palms of his hands began to itch.

Paige wore her clothing like armor, each piece carefully chosen to broadcast an image, a strength she alone believed she lacked. She'd have chosen this one to disguise the fear he knew filled her. To tell him, in no uncertain terms, that she could handle anything thrown her way.

Anything.

Even the need to turn to him for help.

God, she impressed him. Aroused him, challenged him as no other before her had done. He scrubbed a frustrated hand across his face and focused on the cool green gaze of the woman before him, the woman his brain told him to stay away from. He'd yet to fully recover from his injury. The last thing he needed was to get involved with a woman who screamed commitment. He was a loner. He didn't do commitment.

His body wasn't listening. He wanted Paige. Above him, below him, it didn't matter. He knew it was bad timing, but he wanted her just the same. And he would have her, sooner or later. If he had to keep his hands in his pockets, pants zipped until the threat that chased her was destroyed, he would. He could.

"Suppose I promised not to do anything

you don't ask me to do?"

She eased out a breath. "What if I said, it isn't you I worry about?"

Shock and awareness filled him, stole his ability to reply. Heat surged through his limbs, tingled in his side. A groan slid past his clenched lips.

He curled his fingers around her upper arm and urged her closer. Drew the scent of her greedily into his lungs. "How do you expect me to ignore a comment like that?"

Enough color flashed into her face to tell him she hadn't meant to reveal that bit of information to him. "I don't."

"Flanders said he'd see what he could do about tracing the origin of that e-mail."

Allan's voice brought Justin's head up. He discovered his partner, just inside the door, eyebrow raised in silent question.

"He needs Ms. Conroy's computer."

Blood hammering, Justin could only nod. Reluctantly, he released his hold on Paige, who immediately turned away and retrieved her sunglasses from the table. She slid them into place.

He had the strongest urge to call her on it, to question who exactly she was hiding from, him or his partner.

"Brennan's back and looking for us," Allan stated as he slipped past Justin and lifted the case off the table.

"Right." Justin followed his partner to the door, stopped before following him out into the hall. He needed to get back to work, back to the job and away from Paige. He needed to focus his thoughts and couldn't seem to do that when she was near. But they hadn't settled this, hadn't solved anything.

Hand on the doorknob, he glanced over his shoulder in her direction. "It's not safe to stay at your place. Paige?"

"I know. I know I can't stay there."

"You should be fine for the next few hours. I'll pick you up after work. Six o'clock."

The seconds ticked by, ten, twenty, before she replied softly, "Six o'clock."

* * *

Paige's stomach rolled painfully as she stood before the building that had been her home for the last two years and felt a sense of dread spread through her at the thought of entering. Her body ached with fatigue, sorrow, and a sense of violation stronger than the rest of her emotions combined. In her right hand, she held the cell phone she'd replaced on her drive back from the police precinct, in her left, the key to the side door of her building. In her heart, she held the knowledge that she would never again feel the sense of homecoming crossing the threshold used to offer her.

In the years since her move to San Diego,

she'd made the place hers. Her home. Her success. The building before her, nothing more than a converted warehouse to others, was so much more. It housed her dreams, her hopes and fears. Within these walls, she'd known laughter and tears, loss and acceptance, and recently, the thrill of a job well done. It represented everything she wanted, all that she needed.

Until evil crossed its threshold, infesting its walls like cockroaches.

When the hair on the back of her neck stood on end, Paige knew it wasn't the taste of cold fear on her tongue that caused it. She didn't need to see the curious looks she drew to know people watched her. The charred curbside to her left and the yellow tape caused quite a stir amongst the people who lined the sidewalk. Busy with the comings and goings of the businesses surrounding hers, they watched her now, as they had before. Unlike any other time, today she found she preferred their stares to the cool interior of her building.

Pressing trembling fingers to her temple, she fought against the urge to look over her shoulder. She wanted to be strong, to close the distance between her and her building and slip inside, shut the door behind her and keep reality at bay. But she no longer had that option. Her steel doors were not enough to keep the man chasing her out, how could she hope they would ever keep the world out? How could they ever keep her safe again?

The squeal of brakes as a panel truck pulled to the side of the road spun her on her heels. Filled with a heightened sense of extreme caution, she watched, throat dry, as the driver swung his door wide and dropped to the curb before her. Eyes to the sun, she couldn't make out his features, even with her dark-tinted sunglasses.

"Ms. Conroy?"

What the man lacked in height, he more than made up for in width. He had the build of a fireplug; round and solidly muscled. Ill-ease skittered along her spine, weakened her knees. In his hands he held a clipboard, the pages of which rustled when the wind picked up.

"Are you Paige Conroy? I got an order here to replace your front window."

Her gaze left him to lock onto the name on the side of the truck. She read and re-read it. Was that the place she'd called? Uncertainty crawled over her. With her state of mind over the past few days, she couldn't recall.

"Lady?"

His hand tucked into his pocket, reaching toward something just out of her sight. Her breath backed up in her lungs. Her muscles bunched and tightened.

The creak of hinges in need of oil echoed through her mind and drew her gaze back to the truck. A second man stepped onto the street. Nausea cramped her stomach painfully. Fear left a cold, metallic taste in her mouth.

"Marv, we got the right place or what?" the second man asked.

A click to her right brought her head around faster than was intelligent in her weakened state. Paige's world spun once and then blessedly stilled. She expected to find a pistol aimed at her middle, a knife, anything but a silver ballpoint pen.

She blinked with surprise.

"Lady? Is your name Paige Conroy or not?"

Mortification threatened to drown her. Taking a deep breath, she willed her heart to slow. "Y-yes."

"Thanks be for small favors," the man mumbled under his breath. He raised his voice, aimed his words at the man still beside the truck. "This is the right place."

As the second man began to unload the truck, the first shoved the pen in her direction. "Sign here," he instructed gruffly.

Tears of humiliation threatened. For a minute there, she'd been so afraid, she thought she could actually choke on the feeling. Paige took the pen he offered, relieved when he held the clipboard in place for her. The state she was in, just signing her name to the authorization form felt like more than she could handle. Her hand shook. Her teeth began to chatter.

The knowledge that she was going to break down pushed her to close the distance between her and her side door. It took three tries before the key slid into the lock. By the time she stumbled into her building, the first tears wet her cheeks. She barely made it to the top of the stairs before her knees gave out and she crumpled to the floor in a heap.

* * *

He found her sprawled at the top of the stairs. Literally at his feet. Had the unlocked side door not triggered caution in Justin, he likely would have tripped over her prone form.

"Paige?"

Throat tight, her name escaped as no more than a whisper of sound in the too-silent room. He visually searched for a wound, for a breath he was unable to discern from his height. He drew his weapon.

"Paige?"

The absence of walls left him with an unobstructed view of what lay about him. Or, more importantly, what wasn't about him. A laundry basket lounged in the recliner to his left, towels folded neatly and stacked to its rim. A half-full coffee mug and black cordless telephone sat propped upon the center cushion of the couch, a pale green afghan pooled on the floor before it. Bright sunlight illuminated it all, leaving no shadows, no monsters, no threat to Paige's physical being at all. Just Paige, lying inert at his boots.

Satisfied that no threat hovered, Justin squatted at her side. With only the slightest hesitation, he used his free hand to push aside the collar of her blazer and press reassuring fingers to her carotid artery. Her pulse beat strong and steady. Relief cut like a knife.

He draped his forearms across his knees, Glock hanging loosely in his right hand. It took a moment to catch his breath.

She was asleep. Not wounded or dead, just drained. The knowledge that she had run out of steam didn't surprise. The fact that she appeared to have barely made it up her stairs before sleep claimed her, did.

Her face angled toward him, a few strands of her hair stuck in the black tips of her stitches. Her right arm cushioned her head, her left arced away from her body, keys inches from her slackened hand. Justin trailed his fingers across her brow, brushing the hair away from her eye. He traced the line of her jaw. Her lips parted and her breath brushed across his knuckle as he followed the shape of her mouth with his thumb.

Good God, she was beautiful. And strong, stubborn, driven—things that he never imagined he could find so alluring. Still teasing himself with the feel of her beneath his fingertips, he trailed his hand down her throat toward the gentle swell of her breast above the neckline of her blazer. His palm itched to continue on, to cup her. He wanted his hands on her, wanted his mouth on her.

He fought back the urge by reminding himself that Paige had wants of her own. She wanted her life back. The life she had before St. John's murder, before the threats and the fear. The life she'd had before him. It would do for him to remember that.

Instead, he chose to recall the taste of her. Her throaty moan of approval as his mouth had taken hers. The way her body had strained against his, seeking release, a release she craved as badly as he. Emotion pulled at him, threatened to drown him. Scared the hell out of him the way those photos had just a few hours ago.

He hadn't known a man could want like he did. He wanted her even though she made him wish for things he'd never even considered, things he wasn't certain he even believed existed. He wanted to risk, to reach for that ever-elusive something that snaked through him whenever she set those green eyes on him.

Damn, but just admitting that to himself made him wonder if he'd lost his senses completely. He'd been trained not to risk. In his line of work, risk could get him killed. Yet ever since that fateful evening some six months before, the feeling that he was missing out on something in life ate at him.

Her eyelids eased open. He went from staring into her sleep-softened face to staring into the endless green of her gaze. A smile curved her lips, lit her up from the inside out.

"Justin."

He didn't know which he liked more, the way she said his name, or her smile. His pulse kicked into high gear. Desire sucker-punched him in the gut. "Were you expecting someone else?"

She sat up slowly, her fingers moving to his jaw. Her gaze slid to his mouth as she traced his smile, dipped her thumb into his dimple. "Hmm...your smile is incredible."

"Is it?" He held perfectly still, worked to draw oxygen into his suddenly deprived lungs as she eased her body closer and closer. Her thigh pressed against his, her breasts brushed his chest.

"So is your mouth," she murmured, her voice like a caress across his flesh. Leaning into him, she used her teeth to nip at his lips, following the sharp bite with a swipe of her tongue.

Leave her alone, the voice of reason whispered, but he ruthlessly shoved the thought aside. Blood pounding, mind reeling, he settled his left hand at her waist, slid it up to cup her breast through her jacket and captured her moan with his mouth.

She met him stroke for stroke, her mouth eager. Desperate. Hungry. Her fingers slipped through his hair, then raked down his back, sending a sharp arrow of lust through his gut. She grasped his hips and molded her body to his, straining against him until time and place lost all importance and Justin could think of nothing past peeling her clothes from her body and driving his flesh into hers. Again and again.

When she arched back, pressing her pebbled nipple into his palm, he caught it between his thumb and forefinger and pinched lightly. A moan slipped from the back of her throat and she pressed even harder against him. He kissed her longer, deeper, settling his body atop hers as she melted to the floor beneath him. Her mound cupped his erection, her heat searing him through the barrier of their clothing. He pulsed in response.

Anticipation filled him, sharp, biting and blissfully painful. The sensation of her skin against his was one he couldn't deny himself the pleasure of experiencing any longer. Yet, when he shifted his right hand toward the buttons of her blazer, he realized he still clutched his Glock in that hand.

Shock slammed through him with brutal force, brought him to his feet. Damn it, he was supposed to protect Paige, not devour her. He prided himself on control, yet one touch, one stroke of her fingers across his flesh crushed his restraint. His job was to keep her safe. Instead, he'd nearly taken her like an animal, like a horny teenage boy lacking the finesse to coax her to her bed.

He bit back a curse. Pulse hammering, he turned away from Paige and re-holstered his weapon as he fought to control his ragged breathing, and the knife-sharp edge of self-contempt.

After a few moments, sanity returned and he could breathe again. Justin slid his hands into his pockets and faced her, ready to do the only thing he could do.

CHAPTER NINE

Paige pulled her knees to her chest and did her best to ignore the heat that still infused every cell of her body. She drew a shaky breath into her lungs and fought against a surge of embarrassment as the realization of what had just happened hit her full force.

Caught in that blissful place between sleep and wakefulness, it had seemed only natural to reach for Justin as his handsome face slowly came into focus before her. He seemed to have stepped from her sleep-induced thoughts into her reality and she was helpless to keep from testing to see if his lips were as sweet as she remembered, his body as warm.

Her memory couldn't compete with reality.

Paige buried her face in her knees and groaned aloud. Mortification balled in her stomach at the knowledge that she'd nearly had sex with him on her floor. Thank heavens one of them had regained their senses before they'd made a big mistake. For surely their joining would have been a mistake. Cataclysmic, but a mistake nonetheless.

"Paige, I'm sorry. I—"

She held up her hand, thankful when his words halted. Uncertain she could handle words just yet, she didn't want to hear his apology.

He believed her to be strong. She knew otherwise. A strong woman would hold to her promise to keep her head where he was concerned. A strong woman would face him, not hide. Her body still flushed, nerve endings screaming at the thought of how close she'd come to discovering the magic those calloused hands of his could work upon her naked flesh.

Oh, God! Something hot and liquid pooled in her stomach.

She squeezed her knees tighter to her chest. Grief drove her. Grief, along with a healthy dose of fear. It had to be. She'd read somewhere that sexual intimacy was the most popular way of reaffirming life. Surely that's all she sought now, all that drove her into his arms. She couldn't be falling for him, couldn't trust her heart on a cop again. She was still trying to glue the pieces of her life back together after the last time.

Never again would she settle for a relationship where she was anything but an equal partner. No more secrets kept under the pretense of protecting her fragile sensibilities. No more giving all of herself to someone who wouldn't give all of himself back. Better to be weak, to feel drawn to a man simply because he allayed her fear, than to take an active role in setting herself up for pain.

Feeling as though she had a handle on her emotions, Paige lifted her face from her knees. She focused on Justin, standing a good ten feet away from her, his mouth curled in a tentative smile. Beneath the shoulder holster molded against his ribs, his white shirt hung a bit crooked, his tails untucked. When her fingers began to itch with the remembered feel of his warm skin beneath her palms, she knew, quite certainly, that she didn't have a handle on anything.

Instead, her emotions had a handle on her.

She felt off balance, her unease growing higher and higher with every passing hour she remained with him. No matter how strong her will, she knew going home with him would change things between them. She struggled enough against her intense attraction to him, once under the same roof, it would be impossible to resist. "I think I'm going to stay here."

His smile faded. "Running away? I wouldn't have thought that was your style."

"Actually, it's exactly my style." At least it used to be. Running away from her problems is what brought her to San Diego in the first place.

Gathering her courage, Paige moved to her feet. She pressed her hand against her stomach where a hard ball of need remained.

"I'm not sorry I kissed you. I'm also not sorry that you had the intelligence to end it."

"About that—"

"It was a smart move. That kiss was…a mistake," she managed over a suddenly dry throat.

"A mistake."

"Yes." She reached up and pulled the pins from her hair. The long length fell free about her shoulders, the loss of its weight helping to ease the tension in her neck. "A mistake I can't afford to make right now."

His mouth thinned to a grim line. "I see."

"I'm not ready for this."

"This?"

"You. I'm not ready for you, for a relationship with you." She cherished honesty, gave it to him now. "I don't know that I will ever be comfortable with your job. Not after living through the worst of it. I won't go through that again."

"I never said I wanted a relationship."

"Then what?" What else did they have if not the beginnings of a relationship? "What are you looking for? What is this between us?"

"Sex," he replied simply.

Numb with shock, a moment passed before she could speak. "Right. Of course."

"Paige—"

"No, you're right." She straightened her shoulders, and tried not to let his words hurt.

Hadn't she just told him she couldn't handle a relationship with him? Why should it matter that he hadn't been looking for one?

Swallowing past the tightness in her throat, she forced herself to hold his gaze. "Then it's a good thing you ended things when you did. I'm not very good at sex without something more."

"You're an all-or-nothing sort of woman," he said matter-of-factly.

"That I am. That's why I think I should stay home."

Slowly, he closed the distance between them. "You don't think we can keep our hands off each other while under the same roof?"

She could still feel the weight of his body atop hers, the press of his arousal against her center, and was painfully aware that her body wanted more. It took everything she had not to lift her hand and settle it in the center of his chest, savoring his warmth beneath her fingertips.

"You do?" The thickness to her voice startled her. "You think we can keep our hands off each other?"

Her throat tightened as all hint to what he felt left his face. Had she not witnessed it herself, she never would have guessed that moments ago, hunger had deepened his intense brown eyes to near black.

"I'm prepared to do whatever I have to do

192

to keep you safe," he said with quiet emphasis. "You are not staying here. You and I both know it is not a good idea."

She did know. Just as she knew spending long hours in his company would be a mistake that would lead to certain disaster. Everything inside her screamed to walk away, but there was no way to do that. As easily as someone had gotten into her home the night before, she wasn't safe staying. It was only a matter of time before her mysterious someone returned, and the next time, he may not be happy just taking pictures.

Just the thought of being alone when that happened froze the blood in her veins. Wrapping her arms around herself, she scrubbed her hands over her upper arms, trying to ward off the chill that had been with her for hours. "Maybe I should check into a hotel."

"He'd find you. The same way he found St. John."

"I'll use a false name, pay with cash."

"I won't leave you on your own. If you prefer we stay in a hotel, fine."

Paige closed her eyes and pressed her fingers against her pounding temple. "You'd stay with me?"

"Yes."

Resistance gave way to compliance. "All right, I'll stay with you at your place. I just need to get some things together."

Pausing to kick off the high heels that somehow managed to still be on her feet, she snatched them up and strode toward her bath and the large walk-in closet it housed. With each step, the sense that something about her home seemed a bit 'off,' grew. Halfway to her destination the feeling grew so great that she stopped and skimmed her gaze around the living area, searching for anything out of place, anything that would explain the sudden prickling of her skin.

Nothing stood out.

But the eerie sensation remained. The small hairs at the back of her neck lifted and she reached out to smooth them. Her heartbeat quickened into a gallop. She wondered if she would ever again feel comfortable in her own home?

Irritated, she shifted her heels to her other hand, and scanned the room a second time. Froze, then took an instinctive step back as she focused on a spot on the floor, not three feet in front of her.

Her ring. The ring she kept stuffed in the back of her panty drawer, in a shoe box filled with memories she didn't wish to revisit but couldn't seem to part with.

In her mind, Paige relived her hurried dash across the room the night before. Her muffled cry of pain as she stepped on something unseen in the dark and twisted her injured knee. That something was her ring.

Only, she hadn't left her ring in the center of her room. She hadn't left it on the desk at her left or the bedside table. Not anywhere near its final resting place. She hadn't even seen the ring since she'd tucked it into that box in her drawer.

Two years ago.

A cold knot formed in her stomach. Bile crawled up the back of her throat. Her feeling of violation increased tenfold as she watched the sun reflect off the diamond she'd always felt too pretentious. Someone had been in her home last night. And he hadn't been satisfied with just standing over her bed, taking her picture after all.

"Justin." She couldn't stop shaking. She hugged herself tighter, backed away from the ring and in the direction she'd come. The urge to race to the bathroom and lock herself inside swelled. To hide from the reality of what her world had become.

"Justin."

"What's the matter?" he asked quietly, his voice directly behind her.

She spun so quickly she collided into his chest. Her heels slid from her hand, landed with a thud on the oak floor.

His fingers tightened around her elbow as she teetered. "What's the matter, Paige?"

"Last night..." She forced her voice to

remain calm even while anxiety tore her up inside. "He did more than take my picture last night."

He slid quickly, seamlessly into cop mode. A hard intensity descended over his face. His shoulders stiffened. "How do you know that?"

"There."

"Where? I don't see what you're pointing at."

Taking hold of his upper arm, she walked the few steps and pointed at the floor. "There. Do you see it? It shouldn't be there."

He crouched down to get a better look, but she noticed he didn't touch it. "This is yours?"

"Yes."

"I'm guessing this isn't where you normally keep it?"

"You'd be right," she replied as his eyes came back to her. "I keep it in a shoe box, shoved in the back of a drawer."

He quirked an eyebrow. "You don't keep it in a jewelry box?"

"No. I don't wear it." Her heartbeat quickened to a gallop as she looked past him and focused on the ring on the floor. "The only way it got out of that box is if someone besides me took it out."

"Your intruder?"

"I stepped on it last night. I didn't know what it was at the time. I didn't care, I just..."

She took a deep breath to steady herself. "I locked myself in the bathroom after hearing someone in my studio. On the way there, I stepped on something."

"This ring."

"Apparently, yes"

He straightened. "That would mean your intruder did more than take your picture, he also searched your place."

A headache started just behind her eyes. Her throat went bone-dry.

"Have you noticed anything else out of place?"

She dragged an unsteady hand across her forehead. "No."

"Paige?" Justin leaned toward her, his gaze intense. "Is the ring significant in some way?"

"It's the engagement ring Rick gave to me."

* * *

One hour later, Paige sat in the passenger seat of Justin's GTO, wishing she could enjoy the ride. Under normal circumstances, she found the rumble of a powerful engine calming, its throaty purr reassuring. On a different occasion, she would appreciate the car's classic lines. Heck, she might even encourage him to open it up and show her what *The Judge* had. But tonight, thoughts of her own safety kept her mind too busy to enjoy anything of her drive across town. She was on the verge of a breakdown and the police traffic softly crackling from the radio hidden beneath the dash only sharpened her anxiety.

Taking a deep breath, she blew it out slowly and tried to ease the knots still sliding through the pit of her stomach. She didn't want to think about the man after her, but couldn't seem to stop. How could this have happened? What did it say about her that she slept through someone searching her house? It had been bad enough knowing he'd been close enough to take her picture, but this? Someone had gone through her belongings. Slowly, meticulously, all while she slept just a few feet away, blissfully unaware.

Her eyes stung with the threat of tears. She was a grown woman who lived alone. While her security system provided a relative amount of solace, she was not naturally a heavy sleeper. She couldn't wrap her mind around how now, when she was most vulnerable, she could have dropped her guard so completely.

Perhaps Justin and Allan were right and she had ingested something that kept her from waking? That would mean her intruder had been in her home on multiple occasions. Once, to drug her food or water, and a second time to search. She didn't want to believe it, refused to believe. But at the same time she had to wonder if even her exhaustion was great enough to overtake her fear and cause her to fall into a deep, healing sleep.

Which coincidentally gave her intruder the perfect opportunity to search her home.

Thankfully the whine of the engine as the RPMs spiked kept Paige from circling back over that train of thought. Her eyes focused on the scenery outside her window as Justin downshifted and turned into a residential neighborhood. Immediately the smell of freshly cut grass and damp earth swarmed her senses. Unable to resist the temptation, she rolled the window down further and drew deep breaths into her lungs.

It wasn't what she expected, this little piece of suburbia. Justin lived surrounded by kids and dogs. And neighbors who were home in the evenings, not just nine-to-five on weekdays like hers. When he'd invited her to come home with him, she'd naturally pictured an apartment or condo. She'd never pictured the home he referred to as a pretty little stucco with flowers that bloomed along the drive between the houses.

As he pulled the car into the attached garage, she turned her attention away from the dove-gray home with white trim and concentrated on its owner. She watched the way the shadow caused by the closing garage door played across Justin's face, emphasizing the firm line of his lips, the masculine cut of his jaw. The photographer in her wished for her camera, wanting to capture the searing intensity of his gaze as his eyes locked with hers. The woman in her wished she could push caution aside and slide across the seat, straight into his arms.

When he pulled the keys from the ignition and shifted in her direction, she sucked in air against an undeniable urge to do just that. The tight confines of the car made it impossible for her to draw a breath without tasting his scent. All her senses were heightened—touch, sight, smell, sound. Whether from awareness or fatigue, she had yet to decide.

"Ready?" The deep tenor of his voice tangled her thought processes. He pulled her bag from the backseat and pushed open his door, stopped when she didn't immediately move. His eyebrow raised in silent question. "Paige?"

She licked her dry-as-dust lips. "Ready."

Paige followed him through the connecting kitchen door, her thoughts on the long-legged detective before her and not the room about her. That changed as they moved to the living room.

Bachelor was the only way to describe his decorating style. His couch, the most god-awful brown plaid she'd ever laid eyes upon, sat in the center of the room. She walked around it, her hand trailing along the back, and decided he'd chosen the piece not for its aesthetics, but for its comfort. Oversized and well padded, it called to her, urged her to ease into its depths and succumb to her exhaustion.

One side of the room was lined with bookshelves and they were filled from top to bottom. Next to the bookshelves sat a television, its angle telling her that when he chose to watch, he sprawled on the couch, not in the leather recliner at her right. A desk occupied the other corner of the room—mahogany if she wasn't mistaken. Its glass-covered top held a top-of-the-line personal computer and a telephone.

"The bedroom is that way," Justin said, pointing at the door to her left. "You can have the bed. I'll take the couch."

"Okay."

"Would you like something to drink?"

"No, thank you."

Where were the bits and pieces of his life? The bookshelves held only books, no sculptures or family snapshots. No paintings or pictures of any kind decorated the bare walls. The only photographs to be found in the room littered the top of the coffee table.

"Do you always bring your work home with you?" she asked as the need to sit down before she fell down pushed her to the corner of the couch. She sank deeply into its cushions, fought the urge to sigh out loud.

"No," he replied matter-of-factly. His gaze dipped to the coffee table and hers followed. "This case is a first for me on many levels."

She hadn't meant to look too closely, knew instinctively that she wouldn't want to see the images captured in those photographs. Then she caught a glimpse of honey-blond hair and a smile that could only belong to one man.

Leroy.

The photos that littered the table before her shared the same subject—Leroy St. John. Spread out before her she discovered candids of him smiling and laughing, mixed with shots from the scene of his murder. Grisly, bloody shots immortalizing his death as accurately as the others immortalized his life.

Grief, sharp enough to steal her breath, swelled inside her. She reached out her hand toward the photo nearest her.

Paige's small sound of distress kicked Justin into action. Leaning before her, he began gathering up the photographs. "I'm sorry. You shouldn't have to see those."

Her hand settled lightly over his, stilling his movements. "He was a good man."

She hadn't spoken more than a few words since finding that ring over an hour ago. Even with the tension growing tighter and tighter inside him with each passing minute, he didn't find much relief when it was the St. John homicide that finally broke her silence.

Her fingers curled around his momentarily before she pushed his hands away and picked up one of the pictures. "He didn't deserve this," she said, her voice barely above a whisper.

In her hand, the photograph trembled.

Justin's throat tightened.

Face drawn, she focused on the image she held. The image of a man she once knew and cared for. It stirred him, a mixture of sympathy and guilt because instead of urging her to rest, as he'd planned to do, he was going to take advantage of the opening she'd just given him.

Circling the coffee table, he sat on the opposite end of the couch. "Tell me about him."

Her mouth thinned and she replaced the photograph on the coffee table. She remained silent for so long he didn't think she would answer him. "Lee was a quiet, down-to-earth man. A bit reserved. Some people mistook him as arrogant, but he wasn't. Not a bit."

Her voice broke, her hands continued to shake as she shifted through the photos before her, unconsciously separating those depicting his life from those of his death. The latter she shoved aside.

"He was a good man, loyal and honest, a good friend. He only had a handful of close friends, but the ones he had could count on him for anything. He was always coming to my rescue." Her hands stilled, her voice wavered. "This time it got him killed."

As difficult as tears were for him to handle, Justin decided he would prefer them to her all-too-focused gaze and stony expression. He feared for her, the way she denied her grief, buried it inside. Feared that her reluctance to allow emotion to break through, her obvious belief that such things were a weakness, would lead to her undoing. How far would she push herself in her quest to prove her strength? How much more could she handle before she broke?

And when she did, would she allow him to help her put the pieces back together?

Did he want her to?

"You are not to blame for what happened to him," he assured her.

She raised a trembling hand, pressed it against her temple. "I know that. In here, I know that." Her hand moved to cover her heart. "It's here, that hasn't gotten the message yet."

Unable to resist any longer, he reached for her. He bit back an oath as fingers of pain rippled down his side at the exact moment Paige pushed herself further into the corner of the couch, just out of his reach.

"Don't. I can't hold myself together when you look at me with compassion. I can't hold myself together if you touch me. And the only thing I have left that I am absolutely certain about, is the need to hold myself together."

"You don't have to hold yourself together."

"I do. If I fall apart, everything around me falls apart. When that happens, he wins. He can't win, Justin." She closed her eyes against the tears glittering there, pressed her fingers to her lids. "He can't win."

His throat tightened. He wanted to comfort her, to pull her against him and hold her. She sat not three feet away from him, looking as if she might shatter like glass if he touched her.

His hands far from steady, he raked them through his hair and stood. He needed to shift his focus off the woman before him and onto the case, the insight she could give him into the mind of Leroy St. John. "What was he like on the job?"

She opened her eyes, blinked with surprise. "The job?"

"As a narcotics detective. What was he like on the job? Do you know?"

"He was more than a cop—"

"I need to know, to understand the man on and off duty." And he needed her to tell him. If he ever hoped to break her from the nightmare she remained trapped in, to solve the homicide and give back her life, he needed to understand the victim. Since St. John's good-for-nothing partner provided no answers, Paige would have to. "Do you know his partner, Jon

Brennan?"

"No."

Odd, Brennan's quick exit today, inferred they knew each other. "You're sure?"

"Lee grew distant after Rick's death. He was there for me when I most needed him, but only if I called him. At the time, I'd been too caught up in my own pain to wonder about his distance. I always assumed that like me, he needed time to heal. Then, I moved away. I have no idea who Lee partnered up with after Rick's death." She pushed her hair out of her face, twisted it in one fist and tossed the mass over her shoulder.

Momentarily distracted, Justin watched it tumble and spread across the back of his couch. The image of all that cinnamon-brown hair spread across his sheets, draped across his chest sprang to life inside his mind. Blood pooled in his groin. He fisted his hands against the fierce, urgent need that threatened to engulf him.

Blinking, he struggled to pull air into his lungs. "And your knowledge of St. John's work habits?"

"Are all second-hand, told to me by someone other than Leroy."

"Preston?" He didn't wait for her response. "Tell me."

She stared down at her hands, gripped in a white-knuckle clench on her lap. "He had great instinct, but no real talent for gathering evidence. He tended to jump the gun. He'd be right, more than nine out of ten times, but he wouldn't always have the proof to back it up. Rick always said Lee didn't have the right stuff to be a cop."

"Yet Preston remained partnered with him."

"Leroy St. John was the type of guy you wanted covering your back because he was always calm. I don't know how much truth there is to the other things Rick said, but I do know that for fact. No matter the situation, Lee remained composed. I always wondered if their Lieutenant partnered them on purpose."

"What do you mean?"

"They were total opposites, Rick and Leroy, in every aspect imaginable. Lee believed in people. He was dedicated, loved what he did."

"Rick Preston didn't?"

Eyes closed, she shook her head. "I don't want to talk about Rick."

"Paige."

"No, Justin!" Her lips were pale, her eyes bleak as she propelled to her feet. She swayed once before regaining her balance.

"I know it's painful."

"You have no idea."

Every instinct he had screamed to tread softly. It would take a blind man not to see that she was hanging on by a thread. Her eyes

207

appeared darker than normal, filled with torment. Something inside him shifted. Something sharp. Painful.

Her gaze swept over the coffee table where the photographs remained. In spite of her denial, she sucked in a deep breath and began to speak, her voice lowered to a pitch he had to strain to hear. "Rick Preston was charming. People liked him. If you asked around, everyone was Rick's friend. But no one really knew him, not even me."

Justin set his jaw. He rubbed at the back of his neck as his muscles began to tighten. He could see her remembering. The way her gaze turned inward, the way her eyes seemed distant. Something in her tone told him he wouldn't like what she had to say.

"Rick could charm the spots off a leopard. Slick, and incredibly smart, he could ease his way into new situations—make everyone believe he was their newest, most trusted friend and walk away unscathed. He never let anyone get too close, never showed himself. Not even to me."

The tumble of words caught him by surprise. The more she said, the less he wanted to hear. She'd once loved this man, given her heart to him? Twin feelings of rage and jealousy twisted his stomach muscles into a nasty, clenching knot.

"You don't have to do this, Paige. Not

tonight."

"He was arrogant and moody. He'd shut down, shut me out completely, and then tell me to stop overreacting when I broached the subject. He controlled me like a master puppeteer and I let him. By the time I came to my senses and realized I couldn't marry him, that I couldn't spend the rest of my life as the woman he molded me into, it no longer mattered. Someone killed him."

She was peeling away some of the layers, and finally Justin could see exactly what fueled Paige's need to stay away from him. Without knowing all the details, he'd naturally assumed that it was her fiancé's violent death that caused her hesitation. He'd been wrong.

"I'm not that woman anymore, Justin." Her voice strengthened, her shoulders straightened. "At least, I keep telling myself I'm not. Then I look at you and I want."

The air became heavy, hard to draw into his tight lungs. "What do you want, Paige?"

"I look at you and I *want*."

"Me."

"Yes."

Blood pounding, he walked to stand before her, curled his hand around her upper arm and drew her close. "Paige."

Her fist came up to settle in the center of his chest, creating a barrier between them. "Do you know how much that scares me? I look at the gun and the badge and I remind myself what it was like—the secrets, that whole part of his life that he kept hidden from me. I look at you and I force myself to remember Rick."

His temper spiked, but he managed to keep his voice even. "I'm not Rick."

"Aren't you?"

"I would never expect you to be anyone but who you are."

"Because you don't want anything from me but sex."

Her cool, matter-of-fact tone caused him to flinch. He wanted to argue against the cold, crass way she summed up his interest in her but couldn't. After all, he'd told her exactly that just a few hours ago.

Paige sighed. "It's not what you want from me that makes you similar. It's how you define yourself."

She shifted minutely so he had no choice but to drop his hand, then she stepped away from him. She spoke with quiet, but desperate, firmness. "I'm not that woman. I *can't* be."

CHAPTER TEN

Paige leaned against the doorjamb, steaming mug of coffee in her hand, and studied the man across the living room. Barefoot, dressed in jeans and a San Diego PD T-shirt—her only indication he had moved at all since the evening before when exhaustion and heightened emotion drove her to bed—Justin sat in the center of the couch. Late-morning sunlight slanted through the front window, emphasizing the circles of fatigue that ringed his eyes, the shadow of beard stubble across his cheeks. His thick hair was mussed just enough to make her fingers itch to smooth it.

Although the newspaper lay open to what from her vantage point appeared to be the classifieds, he didn't seem to be reading. In fact, he seemed preoccupied, as if he couldn't see past the thoughts running through his mind to focus on the words printed on the page before him. Or notice her studying him.

She'd told him about Rick.

Slowly, in an effort to cool the too-hot liquid, she raised her mug to her lips and blew softly. Last night, he had pushed her for

211

answers and she'd given him the cold, unadulterated truth. Then, like a wounded animal, she'd gone off to lick her wounds.

In the light of day, after a night of deep, dreamless sleep that erased the mind-numbing fatigue that had plagued her for days, she felt stronger. The wall around her memories of Rick had crumbled. The pain those memories invoked, ebbed. Sleep brought about mental clarity, as well as the ability to face what just yesterday all but crippled her.

She was not the woman she had been three years before. She knew what she had to do. The time had come to face the facts. Since the day she'd first felt the warmth of Justin's touch she'd told herself he wasn't what she wanted. She couldn't handle his job. Couldn't risk getting involved with him. But it seemed she already was. She could continue to make excuses about why she felt about him the way she did, but deep down she knew it was all a lie. It wasn't fear that kept pushing her into his arms, but something far more powerful.

She was falling in love with Justin Harrison. The acknowledgment tightened her throat, gave her heart a jolt. Even so, she needed to face it. To deny her feelings would change nothing, not the pain of her past or the uncertainty of her future. It wouldn't clear her present confusion. She wasn't a fool. She knew better than to delude herself into believing a future existed for them. It didn't. In the end, he would leave her.

Shattered.

Broken.

Staying away from him seemed like the logical thing to do. She needed some time, space to do some thinking. But with a killer out there, somewhere, wanting her dead, space was not an option.

Biting her lip, she tried not to think about the next few days spent in his house. She never sat idle for long, especially not when she worked through a problem. So the thought of days spent in his company, with nothing to keep her busy, unsettled her. If only she had thought to pack her camera. Even her digital could have provided enough distraction to keep her thoughts off her growing desire for the man not ten paces from her.

She closed her eyes and worked to purge thoughts of him from her mind. It didn't help. Every breath she took drew the warm, male scent of him deeply into her lungs. If anything, her closed lids worsened her present situation. Without external stimuli, her mind brought back how desire darkened his eyes when she told him she wanted him. Heat climbed through her system, spread down to her breasts. Her pulse beat thick and fast.

Paige jerked her eyes open and forced the image from her mind. Only to find Justin focused on her.

"You look well rested." His eyes traveled from the top of her head, down to her painted toenails and back again. "How do you feel?"

She forced her breathing to even out. "Better than I've felt in days."

"Good." His fingers took up a drumming rhythm against the closed file folder just off to his right. "Look, I want to apologize for last night. I pushed you pretty hard."

"You were just doing your job."

"Yeah, my job."

His grave tone and averted gaze had her frowning. "What's wrong?" When he didn't immediately respond, she continued, "You look tired, Justin. And you've been staring blindly at that same page of the newspaper since I came out of the bedroom."

"I've been going over the case most of the night. Looking for something, anything I might have missed the first thirty times."

"Did you find anything?"

"I wish I could say I had. About two this morning I finally accepted the answer is not here."

Several moments passed as she considered what he meant. "Where does that leave you?"

His sigh was audible. He pushed both hands through his hair leaving it even more messed and standing on end, then dropped them to hang between his knees. "Spinning my wheels. Going nowhere fast."

Paige crossed to the couch and sank into the corner, leg tucked beneath her. She dropped her gaze to her still-full mug. "Where does it leave me?"

Good question, Justin thought, and just one of the many he'd spent the night contemplating. Unfortunately, it was also one he hadn't found an answer to. He settled his hand over hers, felt the air between them warm and shift when she linked her long, slender fingers with his. Color tinted her cheeks. The faintest shadow of desire flared in her eyes.

She wore a pair of those jeans with the waistband that sat below her navel. Her shirt hugged her small breasts and ended just above that waistband, teasing him with a glimpse of pale flesh. With her feet bare and her hair hanging loosely, she looked comfortable, at home in his living room. A thought he should have found unsettling but didn't.

A hot ball of need settled in his stomach. He needed to decide just what to do about Paige Conroy. And fast. He wanted her physically, but was he ready for something more, an emotional relationship? Did he even know how to go about having one?

"Justin?"

Somehow, the warmth of her hand in his stole his ability to think straight. The unique

215

smell of her, mixed with the soap from his bathroom, sent his head spinning. He fought the urge to drag her into his arms, to touch her, taste her.

Because desire was there, clouding his logic, he took a quick, mental step backward and removed his hand from hers. He busied himself with the task of refolding the newspaper and placing it aside, deliberately ignoring the flood of questions in her eyes.

She blinked once, curled her hand back around her mug. "When I awoke this morning, I realized I've been too busy pretending this isn't happening to me to give much thought to what you said to me the night Leroy was killed."

"What?"

"That he was looking into Rick's murder. What did he find, Justin?"

"I wish I knew."

"But you're fairly certain Leroy was killed because of his re-interest in Rick's murder?"

"Yes. The trouble is, I can't prove it one way or another. If St. John uncovered something new, he didn't share it with anybody. We've found no notes, no link between his trip here and Preston's murder. No link, that is, except you."

"The person he came all the way from Boston to see."

"The last person to speak with him. The woman who knew Rick Preston best."

Paige rose and began to pace. "He didn't tell me anything."

"St. John or Preston?"

"Neither."

"Preston's service record made him out to be some kind of superhuman."

"Superman," she said quietly. "Some days I think he believed it to be true."

"What happened eight months before his death?"

She stopped before him. "What do you mean?"

Justin stared into Paige's waiting face and considered telling her his growing suspicions about Rick Preston. That the absence of motive in the St. John homicide was not the only thing his late night had produced. In fact, his complete absorption in Preston's service record left him with more questions than answers and a growing feeling that Rick Preston was a cop gone bad.

He clenched his jaw. Would it solve anything? Help the case in any way? He didn't believe it would. "Are you aware of Preston having any problems?"

"What kind of problems? Problems at work?"

"There or in his personal life that might have affected his work."

Paige began to pace once more, down the length of the couch and back again. "Rick didn't

217

talk to me about work. Not ever. His job meant everything to him, yet remained something he never shared with me."

"That must have been difficult for you."

"I accepted it. I accepted a lot back then. He shaped me into the type of woman he wanted, one who didn't question when his cell phone would ring and he'd just stand up and leave. Who didn't wonder about the large areas of himself he didn't share with me or the increasing number of nights he wouldn't come home."

Anger tightened the knots in his side and sent a shaft of pain down his arm. He leaned back and swore under his breath. "Another woman?"

She stopped pacing and pressed the heel of her hand against her forehead. A minute passed before she replied, "I honestly don't know. Maybe." She closed her eyes for the space of a heartbeat. "Probably."

"When did this happen?"

"About six months before his murder." Her intense, unwavering gaze locked with his. "What did you find in his service record?"

He stared up at her. He knew nothing short of the truth would appease her. "Nothing definitive, just a feeling that something's missing. More questions than answers, really."

"I'm sorry I can't be more helpful."

He remained silent, studying the way the

morning sunlight danced like fire through her thick, dark hair. Absorbing the appealing lines of her profile, the elegant curve of her throat. After a moment, she raised her hand and tucked an errant curl behind her ear, looking frustrated and defeated.

He narrowed his gaze. The days of stress must be making him soft, for suddenly he wanted more than anything else, to chase the shadows from her green eyes, bring a warm, radiant smile to her lips and know it was all for him. To experience just once what it felt like to have a woman look at him the way Suzanne looked at Allan. The way his mother looked at Nicholas Parsons.

He couldn't. He didn't even know where to start.

"Justin, how old are you?"

Justin blinked, more bemused than stunned by her sudden and abrupt change of topic. "Where did that come from?"

She shrugged dismissively before tilting him farther off axis by settling herself on the coffee table directly before him, her knees sandwiched between, though not touching, his. "Here we are, digging through the ghosts of my past and I know very little about you. Tell me everything about you that I don't know."

"What do you want to know?"

"Have you been a cop long?"

"Going on thirteen years."

"Do you enjoy it?"

Her innocent question made him more uncomfortable than he liked. The job was all he had. It defined him. For thirteen years he'd lived it, breathed it and been happy. Only recently had he begun to wonder if it was enough. "I'm good at it."

"Thirteen years, huh? That would make you about thirty-four?"

"Thirty-five," he corrected.

"Have you ever been engaged?"

"No."

"Married?"

"No. And before you ask, no, I don't have any children." His mouth lifted into a wry curve. "However, I am about to become a godfather."

She gave him a bright smile. "Really?"

"Allan and his wife, Suzanne, are expecting their first. They've asked me to be the child's godfather."

Her smile grew. Her voice went soft and serious. "You and he are close."

"Allan's more than my partner, he's my family. He's like a brother to me."

"How long have you been partnered?"

"Ten years."

"You don't have any family?"

"My mother. A few aunts and uncles."

"But no siblings."

"No. Maybe that's part of what brought us so close."

She gave him an odd little grin. "Sort of an odd pair."

"Allan and I? Why do you say that?"

"You seem very outgoing and he's so quiet."

"He's got a lot on his mind right now." Like worrying about his partner's ability to do the job he'd only just returned to. "Our caseload is pretty hefty and Suzanne is having a problem with her blood pressure all of a sudden."

"Pre-eclampsia?"

"Pre-what?"

"Her blood pressure problems, do they think it's preeclampsia?"

"I have no idea. The point is, in another couple of weeks, Allan will be back to talking your ear off."

"Will I still be around in a few weeks?"

Paige watched as the warmth of his smile chilled by ten degrees. Justin dropped his stare and curled the fingers of his right hand around his left. "I don't do relationships, Paige."

"You mentioned that before."

"I told you I wasn't looking for a relationship. Now I'm telling you I'm never looking for a relationship. I don't do relationships."

Feigning indifference, she took a sip of coffee and studied him over the rim. "What's there to do? You enjoy someone's company, spend time with them. Talk."

Silence locked in.

Just when she thought they were at the end of their conversation, he spoke up. "My mother is getting married, again."

The slight emphasis he placed on the word 'again' spoke volumes.

"This will make husband number four. It's been a while for her. My father left us when I was five. By the time I turned sixteen she was going through her third divorce." He wore his cop face—a mask as cool and emotionless as his voice. "I thought she was through with it, her relentless pursuit of happily-ever-after. You'd think she'd have figured it out by now."

"What?"

He sighed and returned his gorgeous brown eyes to hers.

Paige set her mug aside. She grazed his knuckles in a light caress. "Figured what out, Justin?" A muscle in his jaw ticked. His throat began to work, but no explanation came. She didn't need one. "You don't believe in happily-ever-after."

He stared at her, his expression intense. "I don't believe in love."

Her heart knotted in her chest. Ignoring the alarm blaring in the back of her mind, she shifted closer. He didn't bother breaking the intimate contact, just closed his thighs around hers. Her skin heated beneath her jeans. Her mind clouded with desire at this smallest of contact.

Paige had lost count of the times she'd told herself to stay away from him. She couldn't stay away from him. Even as his words confirmed without a doubt they had no future together, the vulnerability in his eyes called out to her. She removed her fingers from his and slid her left hand up his chest to cup his jaw. His gaze warmed, the color of his eyes deepened as she dragged her fingers back and forth across the scruff of his beard stubble.

He would never love her.

She shifted her hand again, this time boldly smoothing her fingers across his lips. What should have been the catalyst that pushed her across the room drew her closer.

Justin reached up and curled his fingers around her wrist. "Be sure you want this," he warned in a low growl. "I can't make you any promises."

She didn't want any promises. She wasn't looking to the future or worrying about the intelligence of her decision. For once, she wanted to live in the moment. To let reason slip and need take its place. "I want this," she whispered, her thumb exploring his bottom lip. "I want you."

The hand he held curled around her wrist flexed once, otherwise he did not move. She pulled her bottom lip between her teeth and stood, straddled his legs and settled atop his lap, her knees hugging his hips. The hard press of his erection shot white hot desire through her body like lightning bolts and drove a little growl of pleasure from the back of her throat.

He pulled her even closer, plowed his fingers into her hair and arched her head back. They were inches apart, staring into each other's eyes, breathing the same air. His eyes weren't cool now, they simmered with life, with greed and desire. His mouth hovered over hers for what seemed like an eternity then settled.

He was gentle at first, then, as she surrendered, his mouth explored hers with greater intent. He kissed her almost roughly, completely on fire, sweeping his tongue possessively into her mouth. His hands settled on her hips, gliding upward beneath her shirt until his palms closed over her naked breasts. His moan of approval, so raw and husky, vibrated into her mouth and made her heart pound even harder. The sensation of bare flesh against bare flesh sent waves of heat spiraling from her head to her toes. Her nipples hardened. Her belly quivered.

Arching her back, she pressed herself firmly into his palms and invited his hands to explore her more fully. He did, rolling her straining nipples between his fingers then worrying them with the friction of his palms. Her body shuddered. Wet heat flooded her core.

"Paige," he breathed, as his mouth

plundered her throat, fastened on that incredibly sensitive spot beneath her ear, then continued down to fasten on one of her breasts. He drew in the rigid tip of her nipple and sucked.

Her lips parted on a quiet moan. She wrapped her arms around his neck and threaded her fingers into his hair as pleasure arrowed through her system. The hot wet feel of his mouth on her was almost more than she could handle. And yet, it wasn't enough. His hands smoothed down her sides to settle on her hips. His fingers curled into her flesh as he used his teeth, his tongue, his lips.

A gasp escaped her when he lifted her, sealing his torso to hers as he settled her along the length of the couch in one smooth motion. Bracing himself with his arms to keep his weight from crushing her, he came down on top of her, shifting his hips and pressing his erection more fully against her. His mouth returned to hers in a dizzying kiss.

She wanted to touch him. It took her breath away, the wanting. It made her shake. With trembling hands, she tugged the shirt from his waistband, desperate to explore the muscled planes of his chest. But then she froze.

"Justin!"

The sound of a woman's voice carried into the room from the kitchen along with the steady tap of shoes on the tiled floor. With his mouth pressed against the hollow of her throat, she heard Justin's mumbled curse clearly. She wiggled, attempting to shift his weight enough for her to slide out from under him, but he ignored her efforts.

"Shh, maybe she'll go away."

"Justin, are you home?" The voice moved closer. "Justin?"

Her shirt was snagged somewhere above her naked breasts. Paige disengaged her hands from Justin's body, pulling her shirt down and covering herself just as a woman's face appeared above them.

"Oh, my!"

One look at the stunned expression on the woman's face and Paige began to squirm. She pushed her palms firmly against Justin's chest, eager to untangle their bodies and assume a position a whole lot less compromising. He didn't budge. When she hazarded a quick glance toward him, her plea for release died before it passed her lips.

Pleasure darkened his eyes as he stared at her. He used the back of his fingers to ever so gently brush the hair away from her temples and out of her eyes.

"I'm sorry," the woman said. "I didn't realize."

Justin sat up slowly, draped his left arm over the back of the couch. "Hey, Mom. What brings you around today?"

Mom? Paige pushed herself into the opposite corner of the couch and blinked. She struggled to clear the fog from her mind and concentrate. No way had she heard him correctly. This stunning woman who stood before her couldn't be his mother. Tall and blonde, she was perfectly dressed, hair and makeup in place. Thanks to remarkable bone structure, she had the look of someone too young to have a son Justin's age.

"I can't believe it," his mother replied.

Neither could Paige. Quickly, she scanned her gaze over herself, making certain she was properly covered.

Justin smiled at his mother, totally unapologetic while Paige felt a heated blush warm her cheeks.

"You have a woman here." Her tone was more wonder than accusation. "To say I am surprised would be an understatement."

Before Paige had a split second to process his mom's words, Justin made introductions. "Yes, I do. This is Paige Conroy. Paige is...a friend of mine."

Her dark eyes, so like her son's, calmly took in the scene. "So I see." A knowing smile lit her face, brought out the dimple in her left cheek. "I certainly didn't mean to interrupt."

Justin cocked his head. "If I pointed out you did just that, would you leave?"

Smirking, she swatted his arm. "No.

227

Didn't your mother teach you any manners?"

"She tried. They didn't stick."

"Obviously." As she spoke, her gaze settled once again on Paige. She extended her hand. "Since my rude son isn't going to do this, I will. Thelma Kincaid."

"Nice to meet you," Paige said, returning Thelma's handshake.

"I didn't mean to interrupt," Thelma stated as she tugged at the crease on her slim navy slacks and slid a hip onto the back of the couch near Justin's outstretched arm. "I never stopped to think that I might be, for you see, Justin has never brought a woman into his home before."

Surely that couldn't be. Paige shifted her gaze to Justin, as his mother continued without pause.

"He has this idea that women start to think they have certain rights after spending time at his place. Though how he would know is beyond me."

An easy smile played the corners of Justin's mouth. "Wonderful, isn't she?"

His mother laughed in response. "I don't mean to give away all of your secrets."

"Of course you do."

"Not at all. Doing so was not in my plans when I stopped by this afternoon. I only wanted to drop off my shower gift for Allan and his wife." As she spoke, Thelma motioned through the swinging door Paige had left propped open, and toward the kitchen table where a large box sat, artfully wrapped in pale yellow and tied with varying shades of the same color. "Their baby shower is today, isn't it?"

"You're asking me?"

"Really Justin, the man is your best friend as well as your partner."

"Yes, he is."

"But you don't know whether Suzanne's shower is today?"

"Must have slipped my mind. Baby showers just aren't my thing."

Smiling, Paige watched the interplay between mother and son. Now that she looked closer, it was easy to see the two shared genetics. They both had the same dark brown eyes, the same smile, even the same dimple in their left cheek.

"You know, Justin, it might do you some good to pay attention to these things. Someday, you know—"

"Mom. Please don't start. It's been a busy week."

"Do tell." Thelma placed her hand on his forearm.

"You know I can't talk about work."

She sighed and turned her attention to Paige. "Paige, what a beautiful name. Were you named after someone?"

"Not that I was ever told, no."

229

"Interesting. Justin, he was named for my great-grandfather who was killed in The Great War."

"World War One, really?" Paige wondered whether Thelma Kincaid was always this friendly, or if the fact that she'd walked in on her son in a clinch with a woman had anything to do with it. She sent a questioning look at Justin.

"Yes," he said, answering her unspoken question. "She's always like this."

His mother ignored him. "Tell me, Paige, where did you meet my son?"

"Work," Justin replied before Paige could answer.

Thelma's eyes widened. One perfectly arched brow rose.

"A friend of mine was murdered," Paige explained.

"I'm so sorry, dear." All humor left her face. "Were you hurt, too? Is that what happened to your face?"

"Umm..."

"Yes," Justin said, saving her from a long explanation. "That's what happened to her face."

"That's terrible. It looks so painful."

Paige opened her mouth to reply but Thelma never gave her the chance.

"Did they catch whoever hurt you? What about your friend, did my son catch whoever killed your friend?"

"Mom."

Her gaze never left Paige. "It's all very interesting, isn't it?"

Maybe if it happened to someone else.

"Don't worry dear," Thelma continued, undaunted by Paige's lack of response. "My son will...Justin?"

The knife-sharp edge of concern in his mother's voice drew Paige's attention to Justin. His expression stilled and grew serious. He aimed a slight, almost imperceptible shake of his head to his mother, who continued without acknowledging.

"Are you all right?"

"Of course."

"Justin, your arm."

"I'm fine."

"But—"

"Mom," he countered instantly, his tone evoking no argument. "Let it go."

Thelma Kincaid nodded as she slid off the back of the couch. "Fine," she stated softly, worry wrinkling the fine lines about her eyes. It was not difficult to see that she wanted to say more. "I'll just be on my way. Make certain Allan gets that gift, will you? A pleasure meeting you, Ms. Conroy."

"Nice meeting you."

The room fell silent as Thelma made her way to the kitchen. When the door clicked shut behind her, Paige turned to Justin. "What's going on?"

The slow curving of his lips was meant to reassure. "Nothing."

She pushed her hand through her hair and told herself she should let it go. She couldn't. She reached out and closed her hand over his arm. "Justin, my God, you're trembling."

"It's nothing."

Before she could argue, he slid his arm out from under her hand and stood. He tucked the fingers of his left hand into his jeans pocket and rolled his shoulder three times, the entire time watching her with an 'I dare you to argue with me' gleam in his eyes.

She opened her mouth to do just that when the sudden ringing of a telephone stopped her. Justin crossed the room, retrieving his cell from atop the desk.

"Harrison." He listened for a minute, his mouth turning down into a frown. "I'm on my way." He replaced the phone before turning back to her. "I gotta go."

"Work?"

"Yes."

Meaning someone had died.

Shoulders squared, he disappeared into the bedroom. A few moments later he came back out, a chambray shirt tucked into his jeans, boots on his feet. Silently, he returned to the desk and pulled open the bottom drawer. She watched him as he strapped his shoulder holster into place. Watched, as he slid his back-up weapon into his boot and then clipped his gold shield to his belt before scooping up his cell phone.

As she watched, she waited for the fear that normally accompanied any reminder of his job to grab her by the throat. For her heart to begin thumping wildly against her sternum and her breath to back up.

It didn't.

She didn't know what to make of that.

The change in his eyes and stiffening of his stance told her he had already slipped into work mode. She waited for him to close her out, or forget her presence altogether. That didn't happen either.

"I don't know how long I'll be," he said, crossing to her. Justin slid his right arm around her waist and brought her to her feet. He drew her to him slowly, until their bodies met, and pressed his mouth to hers for a single, closed-lipped kiss. "Lock the door behind me."

Taken aback, Paige found herself unable to reply. He released her, headed through the kitchen and walked out the door.

Mechanically, she followed and did as he instructed.

* * *

With the orange glow of the setting sun

streaming through the clear glass, Justin stood before his living room window, his unfocused gaze aimed at the cool, spring night. Dressed in jeans and a gaping chambray shirt, he raked his fingers through his hair and waited for the absolute silence of the house to soothe his jagged nerves.

In his years as a homicide detective, today's was not the first murder/suicide he'd worked. Not the first time he'd felt the sadness wash over him as he studied the outcome of domestic violence, the frustration of being too late to save the life of the innocent child caught in the middle.

It was, however, the first time he couldn't seem to let it go. He'd remained away from his house for as long as he felt he dared. Yet even now, hours after leaving the scene, his emotions ran too close to the surface. His hands fisted at his sides and his blood churned over the senseless destruction of human life.

Unbidden, the images returned. The tricycle in the driveway, wedged beneath the front bumper of the family sedan. The blood trail that led through the living room, into the baby's room—to the young mother sprawled on the floor in front of the crib. Gut shot and bleeding to death, her only thought had been to protect her child from the monster unleashed in their home.

The child's father.

Her husband.

Ruthlessly pushing the memory away, Justin could only be thankful that Paige had turned in early and wasn't around to witness his state of mind. She wouldn't want to be with him now, when he had nothing to share with her but this driving need to purge his mind of the images burned into the backs of his eyelids. To forget, just for a moment, the horror one human being could inflict upon another. And did, with what lately seemed to be increased frequency.

He dragged in a slow breath, acknowledging it wasn't just the homicide he'd worked that had his stomach churning with anxiety and frustration, but the ache in his side and the numbness in his left hand. Since his return to active duty and the murder of a Boston narcotics officer, his pain had become progressively worse. Twice this week his side had gone into spasms severe enough he'd sought solace in his brown bottle of pills. He wanted those pills now, their sweet oblivion. Especially after turning to his physical therapist for help, only to be told that he pushed himself too hard.

Pushed too hard? Damn his pain and his fragility. He had no other choice but to keep pushing himself. Not if he meant to keep the woman, who at this very moment lay asleep in his bed, safe. And he would. No matter what it took, no matter how long, he would keep her safe.

He had to, for over the past week she had become very important to him. He'd never wanted a woman so much in his life. Not the way he wanted Paige. What he wanted from her was on a far different level than what he'd wanted from any other woman before her. Frankly, that scared the hell out of him. He knew nothing of relationships past the pain of being left behind when someone walked away from one.

Suddenly weary, Justin pressed his fingers against his closed eyelids. What had she said about relationships?

"You enjoy someone's company—spend time with them. Talk."

He could do that. Right now, he wanted to talk to Paige almost as much as he wanted to catch the sweet scent of her skin as he slid inside her warmth and lost himself in mind-numbing sex. Only, faced with the choice, he was fairly certain he would opt for the sex. And with anger still coursing through his veins, boiling his stomach acid, he couldn't take the risk. If he hurt her, in his race to escape the images still tickling his retinas, he would never forgive himself.

No, he couldn't turn to her now, when he wasn't one hundred percent. When the stench of death still clung to him, a testament to the violent end of one young family's future. He couldn't turn to Paige, or move to his desk and swallow one of those damnable pills.

A vicious case of frustration had him balling his hands into fists. When an answering stab of pain shot down his left side, Justin cursed under his breath.

He was in for a long night.

Alone.

With nothing more than his thoughts to keep him company.

None of them pleasant.

CHAPTER ELEVEN

Paige hadn't known sorrow had a scent. That it could pulse off a person like perfume and emanate throughout a room. Be drawn into her lungs and set off an answering ache inside her. She hadn't known, until she stepped into the living room and discovered Justin before his front window.

He stood with his back to her, his spine rigid, body held perfectly still as if he had a board strapped between his shoulder blades, making it impossible for him to relax his stance. Like so many times in the past few days, he had his left hand securely tucked in his pocket, while his right clenched and unclenched against his thigh.

She wrapped her arms around her middle, wishing she had grabbed something more substantial to put on than one of his T-shirts when she heard his key in the door. She was suddenly cold all over, the fine hairs on the back of her neck standing up.

As one hour alone shifted into two, then two into three, she'd begun to suspect the worst about what had called him out on a Saturday afternoon. His stiff, unyielding posture and troubled expression as he stood across the room and watched the night confirmed her suspicions. It had been bad, the scene he worked today. Bad enough to follow him home, to haunt him all these hours later.

The need to staunch his pain grabbed her by the throat. How could she have ever mistaken this man for the hardened, unaffected cop Rick Preston had been? Both men might define themselves the same, by their job, but that's where all similarities came to an end.

Drawn by the iron set to his shoulders, she walked toward him, laying her hands upon the tensed muscles of his back. "Justin?"

"Go back to bed, Paige." His gaze locked with hers in the window's reflection. "You don't want to be around me right now."

"Are you okay?"

He stepped away from her touch and turned to face her. "Fine."

But he wasn't. His words were clipped, his stance even more severe and in his eyes, she could clearly see both pain and burning anger.

"You can talk to me, you know."

"No."

That hurt. More than she wanted to admit. "You don't think I would understand?"

He shook his head. His eyes closed and then opened quickly as if something he didn't wish to remember remained behind his lids.

239

"There are some things you are better off not knowing about."

She reached up and cupped her hand to his face, smoothing the fingers of her left hand to his cheek. His pain was tangible. Her heart bled for him. "You have to let it go. There's nothing more you can do tonight."

"It's not that simple."

"Justin—"

"I've seen things that would make you sick. I know, because they make me sick. But it's what I do, Paige, what I am. I'm a cop."

A tiny shiver ran down her spine. She moved marginally closer to him. "Is it me you feel the need to remind? Or yourself?"

"I know what I am."

"So do I. You're a man, with feelings that are eating you up inside. Tell me how I can help you."

Anything, she'd do anything to help him.

"Go back to bed."

Except that.

"If you want to rage, I'll rage with you. If you need to break down, I'll hold you. Whatever it is, I can take it. I'm here for you."

His nostrils flared. The intensity in his brown eyes shifted. Sorrow vanished like a wisp of smoke, leaving behind fire and devastating need.

"Whatever I need?"

No one had ever looked at her quite like

that before. A burst of heat snapped along her nerves. She leaned into him, breathed in his spicy scent and placed a soft kiss against his throat. "Whatever you need."

His hand came up then fell back to his side without touching her. "I don't want to hurt you."

"You won't." A tiny shiver rippled through her as she splayed her palms against his shoulders and pushed his shirt down his arms to fall to the floor at his feet. "You won't hurt me, Justin."

Her fingertips grazed the skin along his collarbone before sliding lower to circle his nipples. She turned her hands over, used the back of her fingers to follow the trail of hair down to the quivering muscles of his stomach, memorizing his body inch by inch. She skimmed her lips slowly across his shoulder, to the curve of his throat, pressed them against the steady beat of his heart. Her fingers splayed, slipped up his sides.

She stood too closely to see, but she could feel. The tight knot of muscle. The tic in his left side, just below the raised flesh of a long, jagged scar. Her fingers traversed the length of the scar once, twice and then again. Beneath them, his body tightened like a bow.

"This is a bad idea," he said, his voice low and rough.

Later she would ask him about his injury,

how he got it, how bad it had been—still was, by the way his arm twitched ever so slightly. Now, she had other things to focus her thoughts on—the need to feel his hands upon her body, the heady male taste of him on her tongue.

God! Just the thought had her turning her body and pressing her chest against his until no space separated them. A soft grunt of arousal escaped him yet he kept his hands at his sides as if he didn't trust himself to do anything with them. Beneath her palms, his body vibrated from the effort of holding himself back.

She didn't want restraint. She wanted the fierce, mindless passion his eyes promised. Heat emanated off him in waves, chased away her chill. Greed began to grow inside her, set off a soft, wet pulse between her legs.

Her mouth skimmed across his chest, while the warm, salty taste of him seeped through her system. His breathing grew shallow, and still he didn't touch her. In desperation she used her teeth to nip his flesh and was rewarded when her name passed his lips on a throaty moan.

"Touch me." Her words were a hoarse whisper against his chest. "I want your hands on me."

His arms came around her suddenly, crushing her against his hard chest. His hands trailed down her back, cupping her bottom, lifting her off her feet. Cursing, he staggered a few steps until the cool, glass-covered desk pressed against the back of her thighs. He settled her there, his hand shifting to cup her nape as he laid her atop the desk.

His mouth took hers in a hard, angry kiss. She drank in the flavor of him as she wrapped her legs around his hips, tilting her pelvis, seeking. The coarse scrape of his denim-covered erection nudged at her. Pleasure arrowed through her system.

His impatient hands tugged at the hem of her shirt, then pulled it swiftly over her head to expose all of her. His hard gaze swept over her bare breasts, lingered on her tightly puckered nipples. Anticipation tightened her stomach. Panting, eager to feel more of him, all of him, she reached for the top button of his jeans.

To her surprise, his hands swung down, gripping both her wrists. "Not yet."

Desperate, she pulled against her manacled wrists, only to have him tighten his grip and stretch her arms over her head. "Keep them there."

The dangerous edge in his voice heightened her excitement. Her gaze skimmed downward, over the broad expanse of his chest covered with softly curling dark hair that veed down, drawing her eyes to where his button-fly jeans lovingly cupped his crotch. At the sight of her pubic curls pressed so intimately against that part of his anatomy, she shuddered.

His name tumbled from her lips.

He bent his dark head and settled his mouth on her breast, drew in her nipple and pressed it against the roof of his mouth. Her breathing grew shallow, irregular. Electricity arced through her, connecting her breasts to her loins as he used his teeth, his tongue, his lips.

Her heartbeat quickened. Her body trembled when he slid his hand down her side, across her hip before slipping it between her legs. Her vision grayed as he slid his fingers, one at first, then two, inside her. He filled her, pushing deep, deeper before withdrawing with her next breath, the pleasure so intense it was almost painful as he stroked her with those skilled fingers. The tremors vibrated from her center out, expanding and multiplying until she exploded. She arched and bucked beneath him as sensation after sensation tore through her, causing her inner muscles to contract and peak, then slowly begin to ebb.

His hoarse whisper broke the silence. "Do that again."

Limp with satisfaction, she lay boneless beneath his weight, her heartbeat throbbing in her ears. "I'm not certain I can."

"You can."

His knuckles brushed between her legs as he hurriedly unfastened his jeans and stepped out of them. Her heart tripped against her ribs at the sight of his magnificent male body. The glorious lassitude began to fade, letting her know he may be right, she could do that again. Only this time, she wanted him along for the ride.

She dug her nails into his hips and caught her breath. With no barrier between them, skin brushed skin, heat pressed against heat. He swore softly, under his breath, and grasping her behind her knees, dragged her to the edge of the desk and positioned himself between her thighs. She barely had time to catch her breath before he pushed inside her in one deep, welcoming stroke.

He held her legs wide, a growl of raw, animal pleasure vibrating in his throat as he thrust deeply and repeatedly inside her, all control gone. The longing inside her grew, became hunger. She met each stroke eagerly, every cell in her body focused on the feel of his flesh against hers.

The sensation was electric. Every stroke of his body inside hers pushed her closer to the edge. He hitched her legs higher, increased the depth of his penetration and she cried out with the pleasure of it. An answering growl rumbled in his throat again. He flexed his hips, pressed his face into her neck and came in a series of hard, fast, deep thrusts that completely undid her, catapulting her over the edge with him.

Eyes closed, Justin lay unmoving while their bodies cooled. He didn't speak, couldn't, past the rush of emotion flooding him. Had he ever felt like this? So satisfied, so perfectly matched?

"Hmm," Paige murmured, her breath tickling his neck. "I guess I could."

He laughed softly, amazed he could find humor while their bodies remained so intimately linked. With some effort, he extracted his hand where it remained tangled in her hair.

Her eyes drifted partially open and focused on the ceiling. Her mouth curved into a contented smile. "Only, maybe we could make it to the bed before the next time."

"I'm sorry," he said quietly, gently brushing her hair away from her temple. He wanted to say more, but he didn't know how to put to words what he was feeling. His chest ached, his eyes burned, and for the first time in his life he felt complete.

She arched up, caught his lower lip between her teeth. "I'm not," she murmured against his mouth.

Inside him, need flared back to life. He sealed his mouth with hers, lifted her off the desk and would have gathered her to him and carried her to his bed had a white blaze of pain not sliced down his side. Justin bit back a groan before it could slip past his lips. He ground his molars together and drew in a shallow breath. The last thing he wanted just then was for Paige to discover his discomfort.

Wordlessly, she locked her fingers with his and led him into his bedroom to stand at the side of his bed. He blinked, momentarily blinded, as the lamp atop the nightstand flared to life beneath her touch. Slowly, his eyes adjusted. Then, he got his first good look at her.

She was beautiful—small, firm breasts, slender waist and endlessly long legs. He stroked his knuckles along the swell of her breast, admired its dusky pink nipple. She was pale and smooth everywhere he touched. He hadn't taken the time for a slow, thorough exploration of her body. He wanted to now.

He shifted his hand, cupped it at the front of her throat. His thumb caressed the soft underside of her jaw. Justin angled his head and kissed her once, twice, a light touching of the lips. Beneath his fingers, her pulse tripped.

"Justin." Her lips met his in a lingering kiss. Her fingers, cool against his skin, ran the length of his arms, across his shoulders and down his bare back. "Lie down on the bed, Justin."

Silently, he lowered his frame to the mattress and stretched out on his side, propping himself up with his elbow. He'd been too rough with her, careless. This time he'd show her tenderness. Reaching out he stroked his palm

247

down the curve of her hip and urged her closer to the side of the bed. As she shifted, he caught sight of a square, flesh-toned patch attached to her lower abdomen. Intrigued, he ran his fingers over it. "Are you trying to quit smoking?"

"It's not a nicotine patch, it's birth control."

Birth control.

"Oh, hell." He'd forgotten to use a condom. "Paige."

"On your back."

He opened his mouth, but her gaze cut him off. Her eyes were bright and inscrutable in the shaft of light. He rolled onto his back.

A minute later, he felt his first inkling of uncertainty as her fingers circled the round puckered mark near his shoulder before moving on to the larger, angrier red gash at his side. He tensed when she knelt at his hip and with gentle strokes, began to work the knot of muscle under his arm.

"Paige, I need to tell you something."

"Relax," she coaxed. "You can tell me later."

She was right. The deed was already done. "What are you doing?"

"You're hurting."

He didn't argue with her. How could he when beneath her fingers his side continued to twitch? Instinctively, she seemed to know not to apply direct pressure to the hyper-sensitized flesh of his scars. Choosing instead to work her way around them, firmly pushing and prodding the tightened muscles, forcing them to loosen.

Unable to resist, he lifted his arm over his head, granting her better access to the source of his discomfort. Her cool hands quickly warmed as they moved over his skin, easing away the tension. He sighed with satisfaction as her thumbs moved deeply along his side, easing away the worst of his pain. His eyes drifted shut.

"Tell me what happened," she said softly.

"I caught a bullet."

Damn. He hadn't meant for it to fall out quite so bluntly.

Her fingers paused as a shiver worked through her body. "Line of duty?"

"No. I was on my way home after a particularly bad day on the job. Out of smokes, I stopped at a convenience store. Just my luck I picked one that had just been robbed. I'd just slipped out of my car when it happened. Guy came out the front of the store, caught sight of my shield and started shooting."

Her voice remained deceptively mild even as he reminded her why she hadn't wanted to get involved with him in the first place. "How bad was it?"

"Broken ribs. Punctured lung. Some nerve damage. It happened so fast, I never really knew what hit me until I came to in the hospital. Even then, it was some time before I was with it enough to process the facts as they were given to me. I almost didn't make it."

"That day at the precinct, the officer mentioned something about two days back."

"I've been back on active duty for a week now."

"Back working with Allan."

"Yes."

Her hands never stopped moving, moving over his skin in long, sensual strokes. "After how much time off?"

"Just over six months." Justin swallowed tightly. He braced for the questions and the arguments. For the censure he was certain to hear in her voice. He braced for her withdrawal, surely the reality of his having been shot would be the final wedge that pushed her from his arms.

The press of her lips against the scar at his side snapped his eyes open. His gaze settled on the ceiling above his bed as his breath backed up in his throat. She moved higher, acknowledged the scar on his shoulder with her lips and he was lost.

Alone. He'd been alone for so long. Never knew just how alone until just then. He cupped the back of her head and buried his face in her hair, drowning in its intoxicating scent as her mouth pressed against the mark of a bullet.

Suddenly, everything changed. The pain

and doubt that plagued him since that day he woke up alone in the hospital remained, yet somehow seemed less daunting.

Because he was no longer alone.

"Allan doesn't think I'm ready to come back just yet. He thinks I need more time," he admitted quietly against her hair.

"What do you think?"

His mouth opened, then closed. His body shuddered at the gentle scrape of her teeth across his shoulder. "I think if I hadn't returned to work, I might never have met you."

Her face tipped. The smile upon her lips stole his breath. "I can do my job, Paige," he promised her, determined to make his words truth. "I *will* do my job. I'll find this guy before he hurts you."

"I know you will."

He held his breath as a whole new set of doubts assaulted him. His chest tightened—the feelings so new to him that he couldn't put a name to them. The trembling started again, only this time it didn't stem from the pain of his injury.

Justin brought her mouth to his, kissing her softly, passionately. Invading her mouth with his tongue, stroking hers, teasing sensitive places. She responded eagerly and his arousal pulsed. He slid his hands along the sides of her ribcage until they reached her hips. His fingers curled around the warm, smooth flesh of her

251

thighs as he urged her astride him.

She straddled his hips without much persuasion. With her knees tucked against his sides, she pressed herself intimately against him and began to move back and forth, sliding along the length of him. She was already hot and wet and he groaned with the need to be inside her. His fingers tightened against her thighs in anticipation.

Reason surfaced. Damn it, he'd nearly forgotten the condom again. "Paige, wait."

Her eyes were wide and smoky with desire as she stared down at him. "What's the matter?"

"I don't have any condoms."

Her hand slid up her right thigh, her long slender fingers flitting over the patch affixed to her abdomen. "I've got it covered."

"I've never had sex without a condom before," he admitted softly. "Not before you."

The slow, sensuous curving of her mouth went straight to his brain. "Then I don't see the problem."

She leaned forward, used her teeth to nip at his lips, before pressing her mouth against his in undeniable invitation. He deepened the kiss, drinking greedily of her taste before urging her back a few inches. "Sit up," he encouraged breathlessly. "Let me look at you."

She did, staring down at him with focused intent as she lifted her hips slightly and positioned him at her entrance. She let her weight down slowly, as she sank fully onto him. Momentarily paralyzed by the shaft of pleasure that arced through him, he grasped her hips and held her in place.

"Justin," she whispered, her voice throaty with desire.

"Tell me what you like," he growled, the sound strangled even to his own ears. "Tell me how to touch you."

Silently, she guided his hands up the front of her body and placed them atop her breasts. She pressed her hands against the back of his, closing his palms over her. Their hands moved together as one unit, gently kneading her breasts, squeezing and releasing. His thumbs circled her nipples, rasped back and forth over the top of them.

A moan rose from deep in her chest and she tilted her head back, her long hair brushing the top of his thighs. Her internal muscles tightened around him, squeezed him as she rose to her knees until only the tip of him remained inside her before easing down. Rising. Falling. Her hand centered on his chest to steady herself, she rode him. Lifting herself almost off him then sinking down. Eyes closed, breath panting, drawing out the pleasure she gave to him so freely. He'd never seen anything so erotic in his life. A ragged groan slipped from between his teeth. Every muscle in his body contracted.

He sat up, caught her face in his hands and kissed her. The move changed the angle of his penetration and drove him deeper into her. She cried out, still she moved against him, shifting her hips back and forth. He felt the rising pressure, knew he was moving swiftly toward climax. He wanted her there with him.

"My God, you're beautiful," he murmured against her mouth. Clamping both hands on her hips, he pulled her harder against him even as he thrust up until he was as deep inside her as he could get. "Come for me, Paige. I want to watch you."

Her hands moved up his arms, her fingers curled around his biceps. Her body began to tremble and her breath came in short, sharp gasps. He watched her pupils dilate just before she closed her eyes and gave herself to him completely.

"Justin..."

"Yes."

She cried out his name, shuddering wildly as her body milked his. Heat and sensation crashed down on him, the first shock wave hit him with enough force to drive the air from his lungs. One hot, shuddering spasm after another battered his senses. Holding her tightly he pushed deep, deeper, and was rewarded with a climax so powerful, his chest ached.

* * *

Justin automatically reached for his Glock atop the bedside table and sat up slowly, blinking residual sleep from his eyes as he tried to pinpoint what had awakened him. The first faint glimmer of light streaked the sky outside his bedroom window revealing Paige as she lay sprawled half across his body, her arm draped across his waist. Her breathing was even, relaxed as she continued her exhausted slumber, their legs tangled, his thigh snugly between hers.

His blood heated as he looked down at her, her hair a wild tangle over his sheets. In the dim light her skin glowed. Reaching out, he stroked his free hand down the length of her, savoring the feel of her, the scent of her. Her body arched, her lips parted on a sigh. The desire to roll her over and lose himself in her warmth was strong. Instead, he eased out from beneath her and slid his legs over the edge of the bed.

When the sound came to him again, like someone moving around in his kitchen, his gaze drifted to the doorway. His fingers tightened around the grip of his automatic as the fuzz cleared from his mind.

Tossed across the seat of the ladder-back chair near his bed lay a pair of jeans, which he quickly donned. Taking time to fasten just enough buttons to keep them on his hips, he slipped soundlessly into the living room, pulling the bedroom door closed behind him. Back to the wall, one foot at a time, he crept. His gaze shifting from the empty room around him to the shaft of light showing beneath the swinging door that led to his kitchen.

There was definitely someone in his kitchen. A gurgling hiss sounded through the door, the sound familiar enough that he shook his head. Adrenaline pumping, he edged toward the kitchen door, straining to hear something else, something that would clue him in to the position of the intruder. No further noise came.

He stopped to the right of the door, took a deep breath and prepared himself mentally. Using his knuckles, he swung the door open and slipped through, conducting a quick visual sweep of the room before leveling his Glock on the man sitting at his kitchen table.

"Allan?" Sucking in a breath, Justin aimed the automatic at the floor. "What are you doing here?"

Allan lifted the empty coffee mug in his hand. "Making coffee."

Justin glanced toward the gurgling coffee pot on the counter, at once recognizing the sound he'd heard through the door. Sure enough, Allan was making coffee. He scrubbed his hand over his face and shook his head. "I could have shot you."

"You aren't the type to shoot first and ask questions later," Allan replied glibly as he crossed the room and filled the mug in his hand as well as a second mug he removed from the cupboard. "Put that gun away and join me."

Justin stood rooted in the doorway, considering his partner. How he'd gotten in wasn't the question since he'd given Allan a key years ago. The question was *why* he'd come. Something was going on here—it didn't take a detective to figure that out.

Allan returned to the table, placed the second mug of coffee before the empty chair across from him. "It's about time you woke up. I've been banging around this kitchen for the past ten minutes. I was just about to go shake you awake myself."

Seconds ticked by while Justin pictured the scene Allan would have stumbled upon. The image of Paige as she'd been just a few moments ago, all lithe limbs and soft flesh as he held her possessively against his chest, swam through his mind. Their bodies twined intimately together without the cover of the sheet, which lay tangled across the end of the bed.

The awareness in his partner's eyes told him Allan knew exactly what he would have walked in on. "Yeah, that's what I thought." He lifted his coffee, took a cautionary sip. "Just so you know, Lieutenant Taylor has asked whether I believe you to be too close to this to do your job."

"What did you tell him?"

"I assured him you wouldn't let it compromise the case."

Justin expelled a slow breath of relief. "Thank you."

"It might not do any good. You know how Taylor is when he gets something stuck in his mind."

"I know."

"So what are you going to do?"

"Find our shooter. Keep him from getting to Paige."

"And Taylor?"

Justin raised his shoulder. "I'll deal with him when the time comes."

Allan leaned back in his chair and crossed his legs at the ankles. "This one is different, isn't she?"

"Yes."

"You care for her."

"I do."

"You've changed, Justin."

When Allan said those exact words barely a week before, every cell in Justin's body had cried out in denial. Today, he felt no compulsion to argue. He had changed and Paige had played a large role in that change.

Still, it wasn't a topic he felt comfortable discussing. He glanced at the digital clock on the microwave. "You going to tell me what brings you to my kitchen at such an ungodly hour?"

Allan sat for a moment, not responding. Justin didn't have to look at him to feel his intense scrutiny. He shifted his weight.

"I wasn't ready to go home yet," Allan at last admitted. "I've been up all night. At the hospital with Suzanne."

Justin's gaze returned to the table and for the first time since stepping through the kitchen door, he noted the dark stubble covering Allan's cheeks, the smudges of fatigue beneath his eyes. Concern for his partner, his best friend, filled him. "What's wrong? Is something wrong with the baby?"

"He's fine," Allan stated, and Justin remembered to breathe. "Two weeks early, but fine."

"Good. That's good..." His words trailed off as what his partner had just said registered. "Suzanne had the baby?"

"Red faced and wailing, he decided to make his grand entrance at exactly three fifty-six this morning."

"Congratulations. How's Suzanne?"

"Suzanne is beautiful," Allan replied, damn near glowing with pride. He rubbed at the five o'clock shadow along his jaw and spoke, his voice full of stunned bewilderment. "Alexander's amazing, Justin. Two arms, two legs, ten fingers and toes."

Justin smiled, amused by his friend's awe. "That is the preferred package. Wait, did you say Alexander?"

A lopsided grin overtook Allan's features. "About halfway through labor Suzanne informed me that we were doing our baby's godfather a disservice by not naming the baby after him. I'll tell you something, you don't argue with a woman in transition. That meant Alexander if the baby was a boy, Alexandra for a girl."

Alexander—Justin's middle name. Justin Alexander Harrison. Allan and Suzanne had given him a most precious gift. They named their son after him.

Justin dropped into the chair across from Allan and placed his Glock on the table next to his untouched mug of coffee. "I don't know what to say," he managed in a voice that had gone strangely hoarse.

"I love you like a brother, Justin. You know that."

He did know and he felt the same. Still, he felt completely unprepared for the affect this conversation had on him. He breathed deeply to steady himself. "Allan."

"Just be careful these next few weeks," Allan responded, his voice choked. "Suzanne would never forgive me if something happened to you while I wasn't there to watch your back."

Allan's family leave would start today— had probably started the moment his son drew his first breath. "Don't worry about me, I can take care of myself."

But he was going to miss his partner's grounding presence at the precinct. As well as his cool, analytical mind.

In a flash of intuition, Justin knew that no matter how difficult it had already been keeping up the pretense that he was back in top form, it was only going to get harder. His days would stretch longer. His stress would increase tenfold.

For the first time in his career, he didn't look forward to doing his job.

"I'm sorry, Justin. I know this couldn't have come at a worse time. Maybe you should approach Taylor yourself, ask him for help. Admit you're struggling."

"I'm not struggling," Justin insisted, trying to ignore the bad taste in his mouth brought on by his denial.

"No?" Allan gazed pointedly to where Justin unconsciously manipulated the ache in his side.

Justin's hand stilled. He shifted it away from his side and rested it atop the table. "It's not what you think."

"Then tell me what it is."

"I've just overdone it recently. Therapy wise."

"Let me guess, you decided if once a week was good, twice was even better?"

He opened his mouth, shut it. Sometimes it really rankled that Allan knew him so well.

"Justin, there's more to life than being a cop."

"I *am* a cop."

"A damn good one, if not a very intelligent one. You didn't see yourself in that hospital bed, Justin. I didn't know if you would pull through. Then, when it became obvious you would, all you could talk about was getting back to the job."

"What's your point?"

"You're back. But at what cost to yourself? A few more weeks—"

"I can't do that, Allan. I need to help Paige."

"You are helping her. She's safe here, with you."

"For how long? She won't hide here forever."

Allan sat forward, curled his hands around his mug. "You want her to? Stay here with you?"

"I want her safe."

Allan's left eyebrow rose a fraction. He gave Justin a pointed look. "Does she know how you feel?"

"She knows I'll do everything to keep her safe."

"Of course you will." But that wasn't what Allan had asked and they both knew it.

Justin pushed to his feet and shoved his hands deep into his pockets. He looked away from his partner's knowing gaze and focused on the wall instead.

"Do you want to talk about it?" Allan asked.

"No," he replied with a shake of his head. He rubbed his hand over his face and mumbled under his breath. "I don't know how I feel about her."

"Choosing not to risk can be lonely, Justin," Allan said, his tone full of understanding.

"This from the man who, only a few days ago, told me to stay away from her."

"You've been known to ignore my advice in the past. I never really expected you to listen to me." He lifted the mug to his lips and gave Justin a level-eyed look over the rim. "I really wish you'd listen this time. Talk to Taylor, Justin."

"I can do the job."

"Are you certain of that? What if you're too close to this? We both know from experience that emotion clouds judgment."

"You said you believed in me."

"I do, damn it!" Allan set his mug down with enough force to send coffee sloshing over the lip and onto the back of his hand. He swore under his breath. "At least ask Taylor to reassign someone to help you with this. Face it, you're running out of time. You have his attention now. He'll be watching you like a hawk."

Justin wanted to be angry. He didn't need Allan reminding him of his limitations, his own traitorous body did that on a daily basis. But then he looked at the man who'd been his partner these past ten years, his best friend. In his eyes he found compassion and concern.

Justin ran his palm over the knotted muscles in his neck. Allan was right—he was running out of time. Hell, if he were honest with himself he'd admit to already being out of time. With Lieutenant Taylor already looking so closely at him, come Monday, he would inevitably be pulled from the case.

Unless he did as Allan suggested and went to Taylor before Taylor could come to him.

The muscles in his neck and back tightened as a strange sense of foreboding stole over him. He locked his eyes with Allan's and wished, not for the first time, things had worked out differently. Why now, when he needed his help the most, did Allan's leave have to begin? If only his godson had waited a few more weeks to arrive, Justin could back off, leaving the case in the hands of the man he trusted above all others.

"What is it?" Allan asked, reading his discomfort.

Swiping a hand over his gritty eyes, Justin sank back into his chair. "I can't shake loose the feeling that I'm not the only one running on borrowed time."

"You're talking about Paige. What haven't you told me?"

"He searched her house. Not just her studio, but her living quarters as well. He took enough time doing it that she didn't immediately notice anything out of place."

"Any idea what he wanted?"

"No."

"So he might have found it."

"Or he might be back to have another look."

Pushing his mug aside, Allan leaned forward and rested his elbows on the table. His forehead furrowed. "You think he will be back, that he's not done with her yet."

"I don't think he's done with her, no. He left something for her, to let her know he'd been there."

"Besides the pictures you mean. Another scare tactic? What did he leave her?"

"Her engagement ring, the one Preston gave her." He'd bagged the ring on the off chance that he could get a viable print off it, but Justin would bet his career there'd be none.

"Didn't Paige mention that the picture left in St. John's hotel room was taken at her engagement party? Do you think it's a message?"

"I think it's a ploy to bring back painful memories. She took Preston's murder hard—

265

very hard. She ran away from the pain of Preston's death, ran clear across the country. If he can bring that pain back…"

"Maybe she'll run again. He certainly seems to know which buttons to push."

"He'll keep pushing them until he gets what he wants. The only problem is, Paige won't run."

Because she wasn't the same person as she had been then. Whether she saw it in herself or not, Paige was strong, she was tough. Where a few years before she had settled for an unsatisfactory relationship, had allowed pain to push her from her home, today she stood her ground and threatened to face her fears head on.

"Eventually, he's going to figure that out."

"Yeah," Justin muttered as unease crept up his spine. "That's what I'm afraid of."

CHAPTER TWELVE

The day was warm. The sun shone brightly through the living room window, casting a shaft of light across the computer screen that made it impossible to read. Paige adjusted the angle of the monitor and glanced at the bottom right corner of the display. The clock read quarter to twelve.

She groaned as she realized that she had been sitting there for over an hour, staring sightlessly at the monitor. She'd turned it on to check her e-mails, to keep her mind focused on something other than Justin's absence. Obviously, her plan for distraction failed.

She'd drifted awake that morning in the center of Justin's bed, surrounded by a tangle of sheets and the scent of him. Filled with contentment, she'd reached for him, but instead of warm flesh, her hand met with cold, empty space. Barely awake, she wrapped the sheet around her middle and stumbled into the living room, expecting to find him sitting on the couch, buried in his files. But the couch was empty and the files gone.

It wasn't hard for her to figure out where

he'd gone or what he was doing. Still, that didn't stop the seed of disappointment that filled her. More than anything, she had wanted to wake up in his arms, the warm press of his body against hers. Wanted to make love with him again, look into his dark chocolate eyes and see her longings reflected back at her.

Instead, she'd been alone. Left to wonder if he regretted a single moment of their night of lovemaking—regretted that he'd opened up to her.

Justin had done more than claim her body last night—he'd claimed her heart. He'd told her of his injury, his struggle to recover, and his partner's concerns about his ability. As a result, she felt his pain, heard his own unspoken fears, and quietly slipped the rest of the way in love with him.

Leaning back in the executive chair, she stared at her web provider's home page and waited for the realization to stop her cold. But like the previous day, as she'd watched him prepare to go to work, it didn't. She loved Justin. No matter his job or the chance that he might never return her love, she loved him.

It was that simple.

It was that complicated.

Raising her hand to her forehead, she carefully fingered the stitches that bisected her left eyebrow. Odd, how things could change so drastically in less than a week's time. The swelling around her eye had lessened so she could once again see out of it, the bruising shifted from vibrant purple to an unfortunate combination of purple and green. Still, it wasn't the signs of violence that she saw the most change in, but herself.

She accepted that Justin might never return her feelings. Knew that falling in love with a man who didn't want a relationship wasn't her smartest move. Yet she'd done it. She loved him and that left her future even more up in the air than ever.

The phone on the desk rang, snapping her out of her thoughts. Since it was Justin's home line, Paige didn't answer it. Instead, she squared her shoulders and entered her password.

She held her breath as the page loaded, breathed a sigh of relief when she discovered no more threats awaited her in cyber-space. After deleting the spam emails promising her a better sex life or wealth beyond her wildest dreams, only one new message remained. A message from her father. She positioned the cursor over the command to open the message then stopped as a deep, male voice sounded from the answering machine.

"Sergeant Harrison, this is Detective Jon Brennan."

Brennan. Didn't Justin tell her that Leroy's partner was named Brennan?

"I'm trying to reach you regarding the murder of Detective St. John. I'm in San Diego, staying at the..."

Paige lifted the phone from its cradle, cutting off the recording mid-sentence. Normally, she would not have answered Justin's telephone. But nothing about the past week could be called normal. Besides, she figured he would want to talk to this man as soon as possible.

"Detective Brennan?" She waited while the detective realized he was no longer speaking to a machine.

"Hello, yes?"

"Justin's not here right now. You might try the station where he works."

"I've left multiple voice messages there for him already," he said briskly. "He has yet to return any of them."

She glanced at the coffee table, to the spot where the files had sat all day yesterday. No files sat there now. "I'm reasonably certain that's where he is right now. I can give you directions from your hotel."

"I know where it is. I'll head over there right now. Thank you."

"You're welcome."

She hung up the phone and turned back to the computer. The subject line attached to the message from her father drew her attention.

Second honeymoon.

She stared at the two words for a few minutes before their meaning clicked. With everything that had happened to her recently, she had forgotten her parents' anniversary.

A warm smile curved her lips. Her parents had been married for thirty years. In love with each other, even longer than that. Her mother always dreamed of a trip to Europe and this year, her father surprised her with one.

He'd spoken of nothing else, the last time Paige had talked with him. His mood giddy, his excitement contagious. In great detail, he'd told her of the trip he'd planned, about each stop they would make, and the sights they would see. He'd been so pleased that he'd managed to keep the trip a secret from her mother, not an easy feat, Paige knew. Elizabeth Conroy had the uncanny ability to uncover any and all secrets. None were safe around her. Yet somehow, her husband had managed to keep her from finding out about a major trip overseas, a second honeymoon, he planned for her.

She looked at the subject line again and opened the message. Read with delight the words on the screen before her, telling of the good time they were having and some of the adventures they'd taken. Her smiled broadened at the attached photo—her parents, arm in arm before the Eiffel Tower.

As the cell phone near her elbow went into its own unique rendition of Beethoven's fifth symphony, Paige reached out and snapped it up. She'd forwarded all calls coming in to her business phone to her cell two days ago, before leaving with Justin to come here.

"Conroy Photography," she replied automatically.

Silence.

"Hello?" No one spoke. Only light static, the kind that told her the line was open. "Hello?"

Nothing.

Pressing the 'end' button, she replaced the cell atop the desk and decided that while she was on the internet, she would begin her search for a new car. She entered the web address, classiccars4sale.com, and waited while the web page loaded.

Her cell phone began its dance again.

Believing the person was calling her back after getting a bad connection the last time she answered, "Conroy Photography."

Silence.

Her mouth went very dry. A flicker of apprehension coursed through her. Unsettled, Paige pulled her cell phone away from her ear and looked at the display.

What she saw there caused the hair on her arms to stand on end as a chill snaked up her spine.

* * *

Justin set aside Rick Preston's autopsy report and rubbed at the ache in his neck. He'd been at this for hours. Poring over what information they had on Preston and St. John, searching for that one piece of information that made everything slide into place. It was here, somewhere, it had to be. The niggling in his gut told him so.

For days now, something had been bothering him, something he couldn't quite put his finger on. He felt it again now, the sense that there was something he should be seeing. Some clue, hidden amongst the reports he had read uncountable times. He needed sleep, he told himself, blowing out a breath. Everything he looked at seemed to be clouded in fog because he hadn't been sleeping well all week. His concentration suffered as well, no matter how hard he fought against it, his mind kept drifting back to Paige.

She looked good in his bed, her dark hair spilled out across his pale sheets, arm wrapped tightly around his pillow. He'd stood by the edge of the bed and watched her as she slept, all the while fighting the need that rose inside him. More than anything he wanted to shuck his jeans and slide back into her arms. He wanted to forget she was in danger and that it was his job to help her. For once, he wanted something more than his job.

Because he wanted it so badly, Justin

273

gathered the notes he could have reviewed at home and headed into the office. He needed time, space to get used to the unfamiliar emotion. He knew that if he wasn't careful *he* would be the one to get ideas. Like coming home to her on a regular basis. Waking up with her in his arms on a regular basis. Her caring enough to stay with him after he closed the investigation.

What had he been thinking? He'd believed he could take her to bed and work her out of his system. But what he'd expected just to be good sex was much, much more.

So what was he supposed to do now? Damn it, he didn't know how to handle this. He had no idea how to act the morning after the most amazing night of his life.

Rubbing at his gritty eyes, he had to wonder if Allan was right. Could he be falling in love with Paige? Had he already fallen?

No. No way. Just because Paige was the first woman to slip under his skin, the first he needed as much as he needed his next lungful of air. The first to make him imagine there could be more to life than work.

Justin tightened his jaw against the very idea. He slid his fingers into his shirt pocket then mumbled under his breath when he found the pocket empty. Love equaled pain. Loving Paige—a woman who told him she couldn't handle his being a cop—was suicide. Eventually she would leave him. Better now than later, after getting used to her in his life.

Ignoring the tightening in his chest at the thought of letting her go, he refocused his mind on the information spread across his desk. He shifted the items found in a locked drawer of St. John's desk before him and shuffled their order the same as he'd done on the morning St. John's partner had finally showed up.

The telephone on his desk rang. Thinking it was Sunday and therefore no one should be expecting him to be here, he listened to its insistent ring for a few seconds before answering it. "Harrison."

"Justin. I hoped I'd find you there."

"Paige? What is it, is something wrong?"

"My cell phone rang. I didn't think anything of it, I just answered it."

"And?" he asked, knowing there had to be more in order for her to be as upset as she sounded.

"No one was there so I hung up. When it rang again right away, I figured because of the bad connection the person called back. But there was no one on the line, just silence."

Games. More games. "He's trying to scare you."

"He's doing a good job. The calls are coming from my house. I always program my home telephone number into my cell's phone book in case I lose the phone. Then, when it's found, the person who found it has a number to contact me." She drew in a steadying breath that he heard through the phone. "The two calls just now, they appear on my caller ID as 'home'. He's in my house."

"How long ago did you get the calls?"

"Ten, maybe fifteen minutes ago. I told myself not to panic. That there is no way for him to know where I am, and that I'm safe here. I told myself not to give him the satisfaction of letting it get to me but...I needed to hear your voice."

He propped his elbows on his desk and absorbed the hot spike of emotion that her words caused. "I'm sorry I'm not there with you."

"You don't have to apologize for doing your job, Justin."

Except that it wasn't his job that drove him from his home this morning, but his growing feelings for her. He sighed, rubbed at the knot of tension in his neck. "I'll swing by your place and check it out."

"No! I mean, you don't have to do it, do you? Can't you send a patrol unit instead?"

Warmth spread through him at the concern that colored her words. Concern for him. "It's okay, really. He's just trying to scare you. He'll most likely be gone by the time I get there."

Unless he'd come back to finish his

search.

On the off chance that he just might be able to catch the guy at Paige's home, bring an end to this once and for all, Justin rose. He pulled his leather jacket off the back of his chair.

"You'll call me?" she asked. "Once you check it out?"

He shifted the phone to his other ear in order to push his arm into his jacket sleeve. "If you'd like."

"I would."

Justin hung up the phone and began collecting the information that littered the top of his desk. As he did, he debated taking a few uniforms with him to check out Paige's house. With the chance of the caller still being in her house when he got there so slim, back up could either be necessary, or a waste of manpower. There was no way to be sure.

"Sergeant Harrison?"

He cast a glance over his shoulder to find a tall, wiry man with straight black hair and dark eyes standing behind him and to his right. Although he had a healthy dose of gray at his temples, Justin guessed the man's age to be somewhere close to his own thirty-five years. The man stood with his hands behind his back in an almost military stance and surveyed him openly.

"I don't have time right now," Justin said,

turning his attention back to the files on his desk.

"That seems to be your prevailing attitude," the man replied flatly. "However, in the interest of professional courtesy, I think you could give me a few minutes of your time."

Professional courtesy? The muscles in Justin's side tightened one by one.

He gave his full attention to the man behind him. "Who are you?"

The man slipped his hand into the inside pocket of his navy sport coat and withdrew a leather case. He flipped it open in a move smooth from long practice and replied, "Detective Jon Brennan, Boston PD."

*　*　*

Paige shut off the tap with a flick of her wrist, frowning as the water continued to spill over the side of the pitcher and down her hand. Distracted, lost in thought, she hadn't noticed the level of the water until it was too late. So much for making herself some lemonade.

She dumped the contents of the pitcher down the drain and reached for a towel to dry it. She'd been like this ever since talking to Justin about her two telephone calls. Unsettled and edgy; unable to keep her mind off thoughts of him as she waited impatiently for his call back. Something had to happen and soon. She didn't know how much more of this she could take.

Setting aside the pitcher along with her chance for a tall, cool drink of lemonade, she removed a glass from the cupboard and crossed to the refrigerator for a bottle of water. Why hadn't he called her back yet? Surely enough time had passed for him to get from the precinct to her warehouse.

Pressing her free hand into her stomach, she told herself to get a grip. She breathed deeply, slowly, doing her best to restore her calm. But calm would not come. No matter how hard she tried, she couldn't shake the feeling that everything was coming to a head.

Today.

Her stomach tightened painfully. As soon as the thought presented itself, she knew it to be true. Before this day ended, she would know the identity of the man who'd killed Leroy, the man who'd been getting his thrills keeping her on edge.

The man who wanted her dead.

High-pitched, melodious notes sounded throughout the house sending Paige's heart into her throat. She jumped at the abrupt sound, barely biting back a scream. The glass slipped from her hand. She fumbled it and the water bottle a few times before they both landed on the tiles at her feet. Glass shattered, scattering tiny shards in all directions.

"Hello?" a voice called from the other side of the front door. The doorbell sounded a second time. "Sergeant Harrison, it's Jon Brennan."

The doorbell, it was only the doorbell. It took a few seconds for her heart to return to her chest.

Mindful of the broken glass, she pushed through the swinging kitchen door. She'd progressed halfway across the living room before her mind caught up with her feet and her steps halted. Why would Jon Brennan come here, to Justin's house? She'd just spoken with him not forty-five minutes ago and informed him Justin was not home today.

Unease settled in. Every instinct she possessed screamed at her to get out of there. She took a deep breath. Where could she go? Even if she slipped through the kitchen and out the side door, whoever waited for her outside could catch her before she got away. Perhaps if she remained silent, the man would think no one was home and leave.

"Sergeant? I heard glass breaking, is everything all right in there?"

Paige pressed her lips together to keep her gasp of alarm from breaking free. She had to think. She needed to figure out how to get out of there.

Edging around the couch, she moved as quietly as possible toward the desk and her cell phone. She could go back into the kitchen and use the telephone in there, but she didn't have Justin's mobile number memorized. She needed her cell phone and the information programmed into its memory.

"Ms. Conroy?"

She froze, her hand in mid-air as she reached for her phone. *He knew her name? How did he know her name?*

The feeling of being watched had her glancing to the window. She couldn't hold back the squeal of alarm when a face suddenly appeared in the front window. The man—brown hair, her mind catalogued, bleached tips spiked above dark sunglasses—looked right at her. His mouth curved into a smile that under different circumstances she might have described as charming. Today, right now, she found it supremely unnerving.

"Ms. Conroy," he repeated, his smile firmly in place. "Could you open the door please, I need to speak with Sergeant Harrison."

She couldn't take her eyes off his face. Reaching out blindly, she stretched, brushed her hand across the desk a few times but couldn't locate her phone.

Suddenly, his head turned, his attention locked on her searching hand. His smile dimmed.

She weighed her need to keep the man in her sights against her need to get hold of her cell phone. Accepting the risk, Paige turned her gaze to the desk and snatched up the phone.

She looked away for only a moment, still,

281

he no longer stood at the window when her gaze returned. Precious moments where wasted as she wondered where he had gone, what his next move would be. Moments she should have spent calling for help.

A sudden thump sounded against the door, then a second time, louder than the first. She jumped, her pulse skipping as the sound came again and again, until with a resounding crack, the front door swung in and slammed against the inside wall.

The man stood, framed in the doorway, one arm raised and holding the door against the wall to keep it from swinging back at him. His glasses were gone now and the sight of those eyes looking at her, staring at her from a stranger's face, actually made her feel faint.

Her breath clogged in her lungs. Her body began to tremble even harder. She'd seen those eyes before, staring down at her as she slept. She'd thought she'd dreamed them, but here they were. Eyes so blue that had she not known better, she would have believed they were colored contacts.

"It can't be," Paige whispered, clutching her cell phone so tightly her fingers went numb. "You're dead."

"Put down the phone, P.C."

* * *

"I don't like not being kept abreast of your

investigation," the man claiming to be Detective Jon Brennan stated. "I've called, left numerous messages. I think you could give me the consideration of returning my calls."

The department's voicemail had been down for days now. Every time someone attempted to retrieve their messages, the system would play their outgoing message back at them. A technician had been brought in and the system was supposed to be repaired. However, Justin hadn't checked his messages yet today. He'd been too busy worrying over his growing feelings for Paige. Busy shuffling through reports, searching for answers.

He glanced at the telephone now, as he struggled with what the man before him was saying. "There's just one problem. Jon Brennan arrived on Friday."

The man straightened his stance ever so slightly. "I assure you, Sergeant," he stated quietly, "I am Detective Jon Brennan."

Justin's gaze shifted between the man standing before him and the identification he held. He went very still inside as his mind fought against the truth. He couldn't allow himself to believe it because if he did, the man he'd been searching for all week had been right under his nose. He'd sat in nearly the exact spot the real Jon Brennan now stood and garnered every bit of information they had on the St. John homicide.

283

"Let me get this straight. You're telling me a man came to this department, claiming to be me?"

Justin couldn't wrap his mind around it either. "That's what I'm telling you."

"How?"

A damn good question.

"I flew in yesterday," Brennan announced, tucking his identification back into his pocket. "Half our department is down with the flu and I couldn't make it out here until then. I left all of this information on your voice mail."

"The system's been down most of the week. Apparently it takes messages just fine, it just won't allow us to retrieve them."

Justin's gaze returned to his desk, to the items he'd begun to clear off the top of it. That something niggled his mind again, but still remained just out of reach. "You were St. John's partner for the last three years?" he asked the man at his side.

"Yes?"

"Tell me something, did you know your partner well?"

"Of course. He was my partner."

Justin pushed aside anger at himself. He'd known, deep inside he'd known something was wrong when the other man who'd called himself Brennan claimed not to know his partner. His heart started to beat faster. Dread spread throughout his body, painfully tightening the muscles in his side.

He needed to get a handle on what was going on. "Then can you tell me why St. John came to San Diego?"

"He came looking for a woman by the name of Paige Conroy. He wanted to interview her again. To see if she saw what she thought she saw."

What she thought she saw?

"He had a picture," Brennan continued. "It haunted him."

Justin shuffled aside the items on his desk searching for the photo found in St. John's hotel room. He showed it to Brennan. "This picture?"

"No. A picture of a man."

"You saw it? Describe him to me."

"Medium build, early thirties I'd guess, brown hair, blue eyes."

It could be the first Jon Brennan. Of course with such a vague description it could be anybody. "Did you notice any scars or tattoos? Anything to help identify the man."

"Not that I saw. It wasn't much of a picture, just a snapshot of a guy, but it haunted Leroy. He said it was the man's eyes. 'Dead eyes,' he called them."

Eyes.

What had been bothering him for days clicked in that instant.

Paige had mentioned Preston's eyes. The morning of St. John's death, as she'd told them of Rick Preston's shooting, she mentioned his eyes and how she'd never forget the look of his eyes after he'd been shot.

Justin fisted his left hand, gritting his teeth against the pain that knifed down his side. He stared at the autopsy report atop his desk. The report that described the body of Rick Preston, and how the injury to the man's face was so extensive, he was unrecognizable. If he believed the body the coroner autopsied was that of Rick Preston, there was no way Paige would remember his eyes.

"Brennan." He could barely catch his breath. It was all so unbelievable. Almost too unbelievable, yet it would make sense. "What are you saying?"

"My partner didn't believe Rick Preston died that night outside that restaurant, Sergeant. Leroy believed Preston is still alive."

It would explain the man's ability to get where he shouldn't have been able to get, to fool an entire precinct into believing he was Detective Brennan. It would explain his ability to duplicate crime scene photos because he would know, from his own experience as a detective, what angles would be taken. Most importantly, it would explain why Paige remained alive. Why he'd chosen to use fear in order to force her to run instead of killing her outright, as he'd done with St. John.

"I think your partner was right. Rick Preston is alive. I met him a few days ago when he presented himself as you."

"When he..." Brennan's words trailed off. Justin watched the man absorb what he'd just heard. It didn't take him long. "Damn," he said quietly. "He needed to know what you knew. Just how much Leroy managed to pass on before he died."

"Exactly." Justin continued to talk out loud, bouncing his thoughts off Brennan the same way he would have bounced them off Allan. "The thing is, once he discovered we had nothing, no physical evidence, no motive, why didn't he leave town? Why not just disappear again?"

"How do you know he didn't? Have you seen the man since then?"

"No, but he's made his presence known," Justin replied, thinking of Paige's late night visitor. The thought brought him full circle, back to where he'd been heading before Brennan approached him. "Why'd he call her?"

"Who?"

"Unless...unless he doesn't know I'm not with her."

"Sergeant, what are you talking about?"

"He called Paige from her home, knowing I'd go investigate. He didn't know I wasn't with her."

287

"Paige? You're talking about Paige Conroy?"

Justin nodded, fear rising as everything seemed to slip into place. "That means he knows where she is. How can he know where she is?"

The moment Justin gave voice to his question the answer came to him. With perfect clarity, he recalled the events of the morning Preston sat at the apex of his and Allan's desk, pretending to be a Boston detective. How their conversation had been cut short by Paige's arrival and Preston's hurried departure. A departure that came on the heels of Allan's statement that Paige was there to see Justin.

Paige had described Rick Preston as charming, slick and incredibly smart. The type of man who could ease into new situations, make everyone believe in him, and walk away unscathed. It wouldn't take long for the man she described to figure out where she'd run off to, once he made the connection between Paige and Justin. And it wouldn't take much for a man like that, to charm Justin's home address out of someone.

"Jesus." Fear tightened his gut, mixed with the dread already swirling there. Bile crawled up the back of his throat. "Jesus, he's going after Paige."

He needed to warn her. He had to find Preston before Preston could get to Paige. Before he could kill her.

Paige. Instantly he imagined his life without her. In that moment, he realized the truth. He loved her. He hadn't meant to do it. Hadn't even realized it was in him to do. He'd told her he didn't believe in love, but that was before he felt its power, the reality of the emotion pulsing through his body like blood.

If only he'd realized it sooner. He wanted what Allan had—a life outside the job. A family. Love. He wanted these things with Paige.

Justin just had to keep her alive so he could convince her she wanted the same from him.

With shaking hands, he pulled his cell phone from his pocket and punched in his home telephone number. He waited until the machine picked up. "Paige, honey, pick up the phone. Paige? Listen to me. Get out of there. He knows where you are."

He disconnected, shoved his phone back into his pocket and was nearly to the archway before realizing Jon Brennan remained hot on his heels. He stopped, leveled his gaze on the man.

"I'm with you on this," Brennan stated boldly.

Justin hesitated.

"You'll need another set of eyes. Someone to watch your back."

The man wasn't going to back down, that much was obvious. There was a fierce gleam

289

visible in Detective Jon Brennan's eyes. A thirst for justice.

"The bastard killed my partner," Brennan reminded Justin unnecessarily. "I can help you keep him from getting the woman."

"All right," Justin acquiesced, his voice unsteady. He forced back panic, refusing to even consider that he might be too late. He'd made Paige a promise and he was damn well going to come through for her. "Did you bring your sidearm?"

"No. Too much hassle to fly with it."

Justin reached down and removed the .38 from the holster he'd had custom made for his boot. He handed it to Detective Brennan. "Then you're going to need this."

CHAPTER THIRTEEN

Paige couldn't move. She couldn't seem to draw a deep breath. In some sick way, everything made sense. It was all suddenly so clear to her. Because Justin was right, her stalker knew her. He knew her intimately.

"Put down the phone, P.C.," Rick Preston repeated as he stepped further into the room and swung the door closed behind him.

He'd been shot in the face, in the forehead, near his left temple. He'd been down. Bleeding. Dying. She'd watched it all transpire. Saw, with her own eyes, the ambulance's arrival, the paramedic's hurried attempts to stabilize him. The mad rush to load him into the waiting ambulance and speed him to the hospital.

Where he'd been pronounced dead.

Rick.

Her heart hammered so hard it hurt. She swallowed, a bit hard to do since all her saliva seemed to have dried up. "How? I saw you..."

"What? Die? You saw a man shoot me," he replied, leveling an automatic at her chest.

His old service weapon, the one she'd kept

in a drawer all these years. He'd done more than just call her while in her house. He'd armed himself.

Rick's gaze followed hers to the Beretta. The coolness of his smile sent a shiver down her spine. "You know, when I swapped your wireless security remote for an identical one, while you lay there on the sidewalk, I wasn't sure I would even use it. I'm glad I did. I can't tell you how pleased I was to discover you'd held on to my service pistol all these years. I didn't know you cared, P.C."

"I don't. And stop calling me P.C. You know I hate that nickname."

His smile faded. "Drop the phone. Now!"

She dropped the phone. It clattered off the edge of the desk and landed at her feet.

"Good. Now move away from the desk." He gestured with the Beretta. "Have a seat. On the couch."

There had to be some mistake, she kept telling herself as her legs moved mechanically. This couldn't be Rick standing before her, holding a gun on her. Rick, the man she'd once planned to marry. The man she believed had loved her.

He couldn't be alive.

Yet even as part of her denied the plausibility of it, another part of her recognized it as truth.

He'd changed dramatically over the past

three years, more than could be explained by the passing of time. Obviously, he'd undergone reconstructive or cosmetic surgery to alter his features. His cheeks were sharper than they'd once been, his chin broader.

But his eyes, they were the same.

Paige blinked, struggling with the harsh reality of it all. "Why?"

"We'll get to that." Piercing blue eyes tracked her progress across the room until she stopped alongside the couch. "Sit down."

She obeyed, settling onto the very front of the cushion, prepared to spring to her feet and run for the door should the chance for escape arise. It stood open a good three inches, its latch damaged when he'd kicked the door in.

Seconds ticked by, turned to minutes. Paige stared at him. He stared at her.

"Now what?" she asked when she couldn't take it any longer.

"Now we wait."

"What are we waiting for?"

He moved closer, the automatic centered on her chest. "Are you trying to piss me off?"

"No, I—"

"You want to have a nice little chit-chat for old time's sake, is that it? We can do that. We're waiting for your cop lover to arrive."

Icy fear twisted around her heart. "Who says we're lovers?"

"Don't insult me. I know what the two of

293

you have been up to."

"Justin won't come here."

Rick smiled.

"He won't, he's—"

The ringing of the telephone cut short Paige's denial. Her pulse jumped. Her fingers curled around the edge of the couch cushions. She watched Rick, waiting to see what he would do.

On the third ring, the answering machine clicked on.

Justin's voice sounded from the machine.

"Paige, honey, pick up the phone."

"Let me, Rick. Let me tell him I'm fine. He won't come then."

"I want him here."

"Paige?"

The sharp edge of fear tinged his voice. It tore into her, cut her insides like glass. Her fingernails punctured the fabric of the couch as she gripped the cushion harder.

"Listen to me. Get out of there. He knows where you are."

The machine clicked off.

"Excellent! Let the game begin."

"Game? This isn't a game, Rick."

"Yes, my dear P.C., it is."

She shook her head. But as she stared into his eyes, the only part of his face that resembled the man she once knew, she saw the truth. Rick Preston might not have died that night outside the restaurant, but whatever humanity he'd ever possessed did.

A new kind of fear froze her blood in her veins. "Why, Rick?" She still didn't understand. If she was going to die, she needed to understand. "Why are you doing this?"

The cold fury in his face made her stomach roll. "Leroy just couldn't let it go. As far as everyone was concerned, I was dead. I died that night outside of the restaurant. He should have let it go."

"You killed him."

"He knew I was alive. I had to stop him before you found out, too." He moved another step closer to her. "You should have run away, P.C."

There was something in his voice, a change. He no longer sounded cold and disconnected, but... "You almost sound as if you care."

"All you had to do was run—away from San Diego, away from Harrison."

"Which bothers you more, Rick, the fact that you have to kill me? Or that I'm involved with Justin?"

His eyes darkened. His hand tightened around the grip of the Beretta until his knuckles went white. "You should have stayed away from him."

"He's a better cop than you. A better man."

295

In the blink of an eye he had her by the throat, jerked her to her feet. Paige choked and gagged. She staggered, her shins making painful contact with the coffee table before he pulled her away from the couch and against the front of his body.

"I know what you're trying to do," he said, his face so close to hers his breath brushed across her lips. His fingers tightened. Her vision blurred. "But you won't push me into ending this before he gets here."

Desperate for air, she tugged on his arm, raked her fingernails across the back of his hand. As abruptly as he'd taken her by the throat, he released her. She gasped, then began to greedily suck oxygen into her lungs.

He produced a long, thin strip of plastic from his back pocket. If the item had a name, she didn't know it, but she knew what it was used for. Securing a suspect's hands in place of handcuffs.

"Turn around."

In order to free up both of his hands, he tucked the automatic into his waistband at the small of his back. When she didn't immediately do as he'd ordered, he clamped onto her wrist and twisted her arm until she had no choice but to offer him her back. Forcing both arms behind her, he tightened the plastic strip and bound her hands together.

Immediately, she began to struggle

against the restraint. It tightened around her wrists, biting painfully into her skin. "This is suicide, Rick."

"I survived a shot to the head, remember? No one can take me down."

She faced him, noted the Beretta once again aimed at her chest. "You got lucky. You're not really Superman, you know."

"Damn but you've changed, P.C. Where's that malleable young thing that used to believe everything I told her?"

Gone. She was no longer that woman. Hardly recognized herself in the person he continued to describe.

"I liked that girl so much. I liked coming home to her knowing she had no idea the things I did, the man I really was."

"You mean that you're a liar and a manipulator? I figured it out."

"Not soon enough though, right?"

Fire burned through her wrists as she continued to twist and tug in an effort to pull her hands free.

"You might as well give up. You can't break free. Your efforts will result in nothing but further pain."

Paige clenched her jaw and ignored him. She feared he was right, her struggles would get her nowhere, but she couldn't give up. She wouldn't give up.

"You do know that's what attracted me to

you in the first place, don't you? Your innocence? Well, that and your mouth. Baby, you've got a mouth on you just made for wrapping around a man's co—"

"I get the point."

Rick laughed. "I forgot how much of a prude you are. Is it any wonder I had to go elsewhere for fun?"

"If you found me so disappointing, why did you stay? Why the act the night you were shot?"

"I told you, I got off on the fact that you were so clueless."

"I didn't remain clueless for long."

"Long enough for me to get what I wanted."

"What did you want?"

"I got tired of busting my ass on a case just to watch it fall apart. Tired of witnessing just how much money could buy. It taught me money is power. I wanted some of the power so I approached Alex Trubane with a deal. The entire time I was with you, I worked for Trubane. Did you know that, P.C.? Was that one of the things you figured out about me?"

"Who?"

"Ah, there's a glimpse of that naïve young girl I know and love," he said with derision. "Alex Trubane, the largest drug trafficker in Boston. He runs a very profitable operation under cover of his three nightclubs."

The pain in her wrists increased. A warm trickle of blood ran down her hand. "Why would he even consider letting you in? What did you have that he wanted?"

"I'm Superman," he stated baldly, his mouth curved into an arrogant smile. "I held the highest closure rate in the department. They needed me either out of the picture, or on their side. It's cheaper to buy a cop than it is to kill one."

"So you switched sides and then what happened? Trubane turned against you?"

"I worked both sides, until Internal Affairs began looking at me. Hard. Seems they got a tip about me."

"From Leroy," Paige guessed.

"My very own partner tipped them off. Can you believe that?"

A measure of satisfaction crept through her fear. Leroy St. John was everything Rick wasn't. He was honest and loyal. He never would have stood idly by while Rick abused the system Lee believed in.

"I had to disappear. I decided the best way for that to happen was for me to die. I had it all arranged, the hospital switch, my new identity, everything down to the last detail. I'd even paid off the coroner to falsify records identifying the body delivered to them as mine. It wasn't very difficult. The man had a nasty drug habit."

"You took a bullet to the head just to get out of facing an indictment?"

He rubbed his temple. The move brought to her attention a thin, pale scar at his hairline. "The bastard wasn't supposed to go for my face."

"You went through the trouble of faking your own death. You took a bullet in order to keep it real, and for what? Just to die today?"

"It's not me who's going to die today."

"If you're going to kill me, do it. What are you waiting for? Do it, Rick!"

"I told you," he said, his tone as flat as his eyes. "We're waiting for your cop lover. He won't let this go. He'll keep digging and I can't let that happen."

The realization that Rick could in fact kill Justin came hard and fast. Rick had the upper hand. He had the leverage. He was armed with both a Beretta and a hostage. With her standing between them, Justin would hesitate to take a shot.

Rick wouldn't.

A skitter of panic crept up her spine. Desperate, she began to beg. Not for her life, but for Justin's. "Please, Rick, please don't do this."

His head came up. His blue eyes glinted as he smiled at her.

"Please, Rick, just shoot me now. You still have a chance to get away."

"You're in love with him. This will be even better than I planned."

Frenzied, Paige lashed out at him. She brought her heel down atop his foot as she rammed her shoulder into him. The move pushed him back but failed to knock him off his feet.

His eyes darkened. "Bad move," he growled just before the back of his hand smashed against her cheek.

Light splintered. Pain exploded in her head and she dropped to her knees. Tears filled her eyes. She blinked them away, forced her eyes to focus as his gun hand pulled back to swing at her again.

"Let her go," a hushed voice demanded.

Paige's gaze shifted toward the voice, locked on the man who'd entered the house unnoticed and now stood near the front door, his Glock aimed in both hands.

"Justin," she whispered as her panic ratcheted up another notch. "No!"

Instantly, the man Justin now knew was Rick Preston grabbed Paige by her bound wrists and forcefully yanked her to her feet. Using her body as a shield, he pressed the muzzle of his automatic against her ribcage, just under her right arm. "We've been waiting for you, Sergeant Harrison."

"Here I am," Justin countered, doing his best to keep his expression carefully schooled as a mix of rage and fear tore through him. "Now let Paige go."

"That's not gonna happen. Drop the gun."

"That's not gonna happen."

"I'll kill her," Preston said, his voice calm. Viciously calm.

Justin kept his finger firm on the trigger of his Glock. "The way I figure it, if you wanted her dead she would be by now."

"Are you willing to risk her life on that?"

Justin's throat tightened at the possibility that he was wrong. He pushed back the panic as best he could. He needed to believe Preston wouldn't shoot her. He'd had too many chances before this if her death was all he wanted. Silently praying he was right, Justin held his ground. "You made a mistake. You should have left after you learned how much we knew. You never should have threatened Paige. Now it's over."

Preston pulled her closer to his body and pressed the Beretta more forcefully into her ribs. He made himself as small a target as possible. "Is it?"

No way could Justin take a shot with her body so effectively shielding his. "Let her go, Preston. It's me you want."

"Justin," Paige cried softly.

He didn't look at her. He couldn't risk it, couldn't allow himself the distraction. One turn of his head and he just might lose it all. A split second of lost concentration and Preston just might follow through with his threat. He might kill Paige.

Justin couldn't let that happen. Everything he never knew he needed was there, in the grip of a killer. Now that he'd found her, he couldn't lose her. He kept his attention focused on Rick Preston.

"So, Harrison, you figured it out. I've got to give you credit on that one. I didn't think you had it in you."

"What about your partner, did you think he had it in him? What made St. John go to IA about you? He catch you skimming from a bust?" His words were pure speculation but as Preston's gaze narrowed, he knew he'd guessed correctly. "Money or dope? Man like you, it had to be the money."

"Money *is* power."

Out of the corner of his eye, Justin caught a glimpse of movement as the kitchen door shifted minutely. The action assured him Brennan had gained access to the house undetected and even now stood with the .38 aimed at Rick Preston's back.

"I bet that stung," he said, his tone full of forced calm. "Having your partner rat you out like that. Damn!" If he could just talk Preston into shifting that gun away from Paige, then maybe Brennan could move in. "But you got him back though, right? You paid him back with a bullet."

For the space of a heartbeat Justin

thought his taunting was going to have the desired affect on Preston. His grip on Paige loosened, the automatic he held pressed into her side shifted. Then, suddenly, he snaked his arm around her middle and pressed the hand with the Beretta into her stomach.

"Enough!" Preston leaned in and pressed his cheek against hers, cruelly yanking her head back and holding it in place with his free hand when she tried to move her face away from his. "Look at him, P.C."

"Don't do this, Rick. Please don't do this."

The anguish in Paige's voice damn near broke him. "It's over, Preston. You can still get out of here with your life if you release her."

Rick Preston laughed.

Justin's left arm went numb. Panic reared up inside him.

"It's time, P.C."

"No! Oh, God, no."

"Tell him you love him so we can end this." He lowered the pitch of his voice, but Justin heard him just the same. "Tell him, P.C. Don't you want him to know before he dies?"

Justin readied his grip on his Glock, careful to keep his gaze off Paige's ashen face.

"Please, Rick. Don't do this."

With a tug on her hair hard enough to cause Paige to cry out, Preston snarled, "Tell him! Say it, P.C.!"

"I love him."

Three words. Three little words were all it took for him to forget himself and shift his attention to Paige. He looked at her, directly at her, and his heart stopped. The cut above her eye had been reopened. A slow trickle of blood ran down her temple to the bruise forming on her left cheek. Fear and resignation swam in her eyes.

Justin caught a glimpse of his future as she softly repeated, "I love him."

His heart pounded hard. His lungs couldn't take in enough oxygen.

It was in that moment of distraction, while lost in her eyes, that Preston did what Justin had been trying to get him to do all along. He turned the Beretta away from Paige and aimed it directly at Justin's chest.

"No!"

Paige screamed. She lurched in his direction, her sudden movement pulling Preston off balance.

Justin barely registered the shock of pain that coincided with the echo of a gunshot. Seeing his chance, he squeezed the trigger.

From behind the kitchen door, Brennan lunged, catching Preston in the side and sending them both to the floor. Caught together in a violent tangle they rolled out of sight behind the couch.

A cold sweat of fear misted Justin's skin while on the floor Paige struggled to get to her

305

feet. Fighting against the restraint securing her hands tightly behind her back, her legs nearly went out from under her once before she regained her footing.

He catalogued each of her injuries in turn. She was all right. Hurt, but alive. A rush of weakness swept over him. White-hot fire seared his chest. Confused, he reached up and fingered the hole in his shirt.

"Justin?"

Pain and exhaustion destroyed his ability to stay upright and he sagged against the wall and sank to the floor.

"No!" Paige cried out. She skirted the couch, moved past the steady stream of cursing and the wet sound of fists making contact with flesh. "Justin!"

He grunted in pain when she dropped to her knees at his side and promptly lost her balance, falling against his chest. Mind numbing agony washed over him. He blinked to bring her into focus. Her face was pale, her cheeks wet with a mixture of tears and blood.

"Did he hit you?"

Coldness slammed in from all sides.

"Answer me, Justin. Are you hurt?" She glanced down at him then yelled over her shoulder. "Help me!" Tears ran down her face. Sobs tore from the back of her throat as she struggled to free herself. "Help me! Somebody, help me."

Brennan suddenly appeared behind her. "Cut me loose! He needs help. Justin needs help."

"Ambulance is on the way," Brennan supplied, producing a jackknife from his pocket and using it to saw the binding that secured her wrists.

"Preston?" Justin managed to ask as pain grabbed him by the throat.

"Out cold and immobilized. He's got an entry wound in his shoulder that will need tending."

"Don't do this," Paige pleaded. "Damn you, Justin, don't do this to me." Tears continued to course down her face. She tore at his shirt. Pleading and mumbling words he didn't catch.

"Paige." Her wrists were bleeding, her cheek already turning purple. He'd promised to stop Preston before he hurt her. He'd failed.

"Are you shot? Where are you shot?" Her hands continued to move over him, struggling against the buttons of his shirt.

Justin couldn't catch his breath. Darkness pulled at him. Through the haze of pain, he managed to lift his hand to Paige's uninjured cheek. "I'm sorry."

CHAPTER FOURTEEN

Paige paced the hospital corridor. Two hours had passed since Justin was shot. Two hours, and her body had yet to cease trembling.

She knew it would be a long time before she forgot the sound of Rick's Beretta. Before she shook off the terror of watching Justin stagger, jerk as the bullets struck. Of struggling against fear and his shirt as she searched for an entrance wound and instead uncovered a bulletproof vest.

She didn't even want to think about what would have happened to him had he not been wearing that vest.

Her stomach abruptly knotted. Tears filled her eyes. She closed them and concentrated on calming her nerves. Rick's bullet had struck Justin's chest high on the left side, disturbingly close to the scar he bore on his shoulder. The force of the impact re-broke his ribs, but the Kevlar had done its job and stopped the slug from penetrating his skin. With time, ribs healed, bruises faded.

Because of his own foresight, Justin had that time.

It's over, she assured herself as she opened her eyes and stared at the closed door before her. It's over, and with time, Justin would be fine.

Yet her body continued to tremble, her hands to shake. A hard knot remained firmly in her stomach.

The waiting room down the hall was occupied by about a dozen people just like her. Friends and family anxious to see Justin with their own eyes, to hear him say, with his own lips, that he was okay. Paige had stayed in that room, surrounded by his friends and co-workers for as long as she could stand it, but the drone of conversation eventually drove her out into the corridor. Where she waited, chest aching as if it were splitting open.

His close call with death this afternoon made her realize life was too short to fear tomorrow. She'd wasted too much time already, worrying about repeating the mistakes of her past. Afraid of the intensity of her feelings for Justin.

She loved him. The relatively short period of time they'd known each other didn't matter. Paige was in love with Justin. And even if he never returned her love, she planned to tell him. He deserved to know how she felt, that he was loved by her. She needed to tell him, without force or coercion.

Without the hard press of a Beretta

against her midsection.

She shivered. Mindful of her throbbing cheek, she pressed her fingers to her eyes and leaned against the wall. If she didn't get into that room soon...

As she struggled to pull herself under control, the door swung open and a dour-faced nurse slipped into the corridor. She passed without so much as a glance, her rubber-soled shoes silent on the linoleum.

Unable to wait any longer, Paige barreled down the hall, pushed through the door and stepped into the room. She stopped short.

For just a moment she stood there, heart in her throat, reeling. Unable to do more than stare as Justin stood at the side of the examination table and struggled to wrestle his arms into his shirt.

Her body ached all over. Her head throbbed. Her wrists burned. But she couldn't possibly feel as bad as he must feel. Lines of pain creased his forehead and fanned out from his eyes. A soft sound of dismay slipped free at the colors of the bruise peeking out the top of the bandage wrapped around his ribs.

His head came up. "Paige."

He spoke her name as if he'd been as anxious to see her as she'd been to see him. He locked his gaze on her as she crossed to stand beside him.

"Need some help?" Without waiting for

his answer, she reached out and took hold of the shirt. He dropped his hands to his sides and allowed her to take over the task.

Paige moved behind him, holding the button front shirt open so he could slip his arms into the sleeves with as little discomfort as possible. She eased the material up his arms, circled to his front and began working the buttons through their corresponding holes.

"Are you all right?" Justin asked quietly as he lifted his right hand and trailed his fingers lightly across the gauze covering her wrists.

"I'm fine," she answered, her voice not as strong as she would have liked. "However, I think that is a question I should be asking you."

His warm, gentle hand cupped the side of her face where the purplish bruise had formed. His eyes darkened. "I'm sorry, Paige."

The lump in her throat tightened. She stiffened her spine and struggled to hang onto control. "That's the second time today you've apologized to me. Why are you sorry, Justin?"

"He hurt you." The fingers against her cheek trembled. "I promised I wouldn't let him hurt you."

"Yes, he did," she agreed and he flinched. "Not you, Justin, Rick. *Rick* hurt me."

She listened to his carefully indrawn breaths. Noticed he'd already stuffed his left hand into his pocket against the ache in his side. Her gaze trailed over the dark bruise peeking out the top of his wrappings and tears welled in her eyes. "He hurt you, too."

"Paige...God, Paige, don't cry." He slid his free hand to the back of her head and urged her closer. She went willingly, gingerly into his arms. "Please don't cry."

"When I saw you slide down that wall..." Her throat closed hard. "I've never been so scared. I thought you were going to die. I couldn't stand it."

Carefully, she slid her hand up his back and settled against him. Closed her eyes and sighed when his arm slipped around her and he pressed a kiss to her temple before burying his face in her hair.

"It's over now."

"I knew he planned to kill you and I was helpless to stop him. I believe he meant to kill me, too, but only after I watched you die." After he'd caused her as much pain as possible by forcing her to say good-bye to the man she loved.

Rick's insistence that she proclaim her love for Justin had not been a final act of decency, but a move made to make what he perceived as the last few moments of their lives excruciating. Maybe it was some twisted form of jealousy, there'd been something in his voice when he told her she should have stayed away from Justin, or perhaps it was just ego. That she would dare get over him and move on.

Something made even more insulting by the fact that she'd moved on with another cop.

Who knew? Paige figured she never would.

Justin held her away from him, brushed his thumb down her unblemished cheek. "Brennan waited in the kitchen. Even if Preston had taken me out, he would have been stopped before he could shoot you, too."

"The man who cut me loose? He's the real Detective Brennan?"

"You don't sound surprised. Did you know Preston was going around claiming to be Brennan?"

"Yes." She smoothed her hand down his chest. Beneath her palm, his heart beat steady and sure. "When Rick came by, supposedly to find you, that's how he identified himself."

"By doing so, he thought you might open the door to him."

"I think so. He didn't know I'd already spoken with the real Detective Brennan and told him where he could find you." Her eyes drifted shut when he smoothed his palm down her hair. "What happens next, Justin?"

She was almost afraid to ask.

"I've got the next week off. I guess after that I'll be riding a desk. At least for a while."

"Are you in trouble?"

"A few days off with pay is standard after an officer-involved shooting. I have a few more because of the ribs. This time I'll take my time getting back. Take things slowly."

"Actually, I meant what happens next for us," she admitted quietly. "I won't walk away from you. That might not be what you want to hear, but I'm going to be hanging around." She was stronger now, no longer afraid of his job. And Justin, he was nothing like...

Paige pushed the thought aside. She wouldn't think of Rick now. Of the pain of living with him, losing him, and then finding out it had all been a lie. All of it. To do so wouldn't be fair to Justin, because Justin was real. He didn't lie. Even when the truth was painful to hear, he'd given it to her.

"I'm not walking away from you," she repeated.

"If you did," he said fiercely. "I would follow you."

Surprise rendered her mute.

"Paige." His hand moved to her chin, tipped her face up. "There's something I need to know if you can deal with."

She didn't know how she remained standing. Her body trembled, her heart pounded so hard she thought it would dance right out of her chest. "What is it?"

"I'm in love with you."

The simple statement hit her hard. Everything inside her went still. The chill left her body, chased away by the warmth of his gaze, the warm emotion behind his words.

"I love you, Paige. I didn't think it was possible, never believed I would find it. Then I met you."

She closed her eyes briefly. "But you said—"

"I was a fool. I made a huge mistake telling you I didn't want a relationship with you. I do."

"You do?"

"Yes. Before you came into my life, being a cop meant everything to me. It's who I was, all that I was. You showed me I could be more than that. You showed me I have worth other than the job."

"Of course you do," she argued, angry that he could think otherwise.

"Before you I was half alive. Too afraid to risk, too afraid of getting hurt." His voice dropped an octave. "If you take me, I'll do everything in my power to make you happy. There will always be things I can't share with you, things that have to remain confidential. But I promise you, no secrets or deception."

"Are you saying what I think you're saying?"

"I'm saying I don't want to spend the rest of my life wondering what could have been."

He winced a bit as he slid his left hand out of his pocket and raised it, gently framing her face between both hands. "I'm saying I love

315

you. More than I believed possible." He pressed a kiss to her forehead, just to the side of her stitches. "You said you loved me. Tell me again, Paige. Tell me you love me."

"I love you, Justin."

He gave her a broad, heart-stopping smile just before his mouth took hers in a slow, deep kiss. "Enough to spend your life with me?"

"Are you asking me to marry you? We barely know each other."

"I know I love you, the rest is just pillow talk." He pulled her tighter against him, until she could no longer tell where he ended and she began. "Marriage, a family, I want it all."

"That's good," she said, looking deeply into his dark brown eyes and seeing her future shining back. "Because I'm an all or nothing kind of woman."

A Note from Sarah

Thank you so much for reading **Not Without Risk**. I do hope that if you liked the story, that you would please leave a review. Not only does a review help spread the word to other readers, it allows authors to learn whether you'd like to see more stories like this from us. I love hearing from readers and talking to them whenever I can. You can always drop me an email at sarah@sarahgrimm.com

If you'd like to stay up to date with me and what's coming next you can sign up for my newsletter at www.sarahgrimm.com where you can also find links to my Facebook Page, my Black Phoenix Reader Group, and my Street Team.

Thanks again for reading my book. You are the reason I get to do what I do.

About the Author

As a young girl Sarah Grimm always had a story to tell. At times they were funny, other times scary, but they always ended with a happily-ever-after. Sarah spent years scribbling in notebooks, filling the pages with partial chapters and the margins with titles and story ideas. She told friends the characters spoke to her, and that she was compelled to get their stories on paper. Eventually, she sat down at a computer and wrote her first tale of dangerously sexy suspense.

Sarah lives in West Michigan with her husband, two sons, and three rescue dogs. Between mom's taxi service, her day job, and keeping the books for the family marine repair business, Sarah can be found curled in her favorite chair, crafting her next novel. Visit her online at http://www.sarahgrimm.com

Other Books by Sarah Grimm